Hook, Line, & Sinker
A Sylvia Avery Mystery
BOOK FOUR

Jan Bono

Sandridge Publications
Long Beach, Washington

HOOK, LINE, & SINKER

This is a work of fiction. Names, characters, places, and incidents are either the product of the author's imagination or are used fictitiously, and any resemblance to actual persons, living or dead, business establishments, events, or locales is entirely coincidental.

Copyright © 2019 by Jan Bono

All rights reserved. No part of the contents of this book may be reproduced, transmitted, or performed in any form, by any means, including recording or by any information storage and retrieval system, except for brief quotations embodied in critical articles or reviews, without written permission from the author.

First Printing, Spring, 2019

Printed in the United States of America
Gorham Printing, Centralia, WA 98531

Sandridge Publications
P.O. Box 278
Long Beach, WA   98631

http://www.JanBonoBooks.com

ISBN: 978-0-9906148-8-3

DEDICATED

to those of any age, race, nationality, or sexual orientation
looking for love, online or otherwise.
Yes, there are still plenty of fish out there, and I hope you
find your perfect match, and you fall for each other,
Hook, Line, and Sinker.

OTHER BOOKS BY JAN BONO

Sylvia Avery Mystery Series:
  Book 1, *Bottom Feeders*
  Book 2, *Starfish*
  Book 3, *Crab Bait*

Health and Fitness:
  Back from Obesity:
    My 252-pound Weight-loss Journey

Collections of humorous personal experience:
  Through My Looking Glass: View from the Beach
  Through My Looking Glass: Volume II
  It's Christmas!
    Forty-three stories and three one-act plays
  Just Joshin'
    A Year in the Life of a Not-so-ordinary 4th Grade Kid

Fiction:
  Romance 101:
    Forty-two Sweet, Light, Delicious, G-Rated Short Stories

Poetry Chapbooks:
  Bar Talk and *Chasing Rainbows*

A number of Jan's books are now available as eBooks at Smashwords.com. Find them at:

http://www.smashwords.com/profile/view/JanBonoBooks

NORTH BEACH PENINSULA

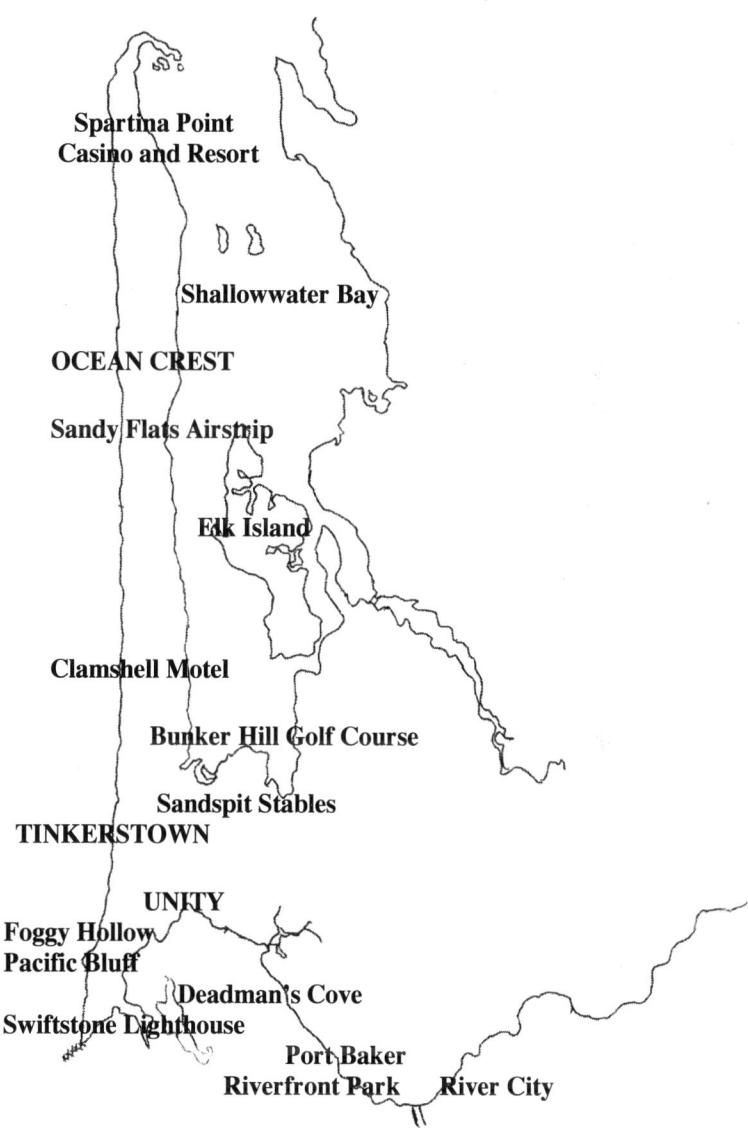

HOOK, LINE, & SINKER

HOOK, LINE, & SINKER

CHAPTER 1

"Ladies! Ladies!" I intentionally used my outside voice and clapped my hands sharply three times for extra emphasis.

"I beg your pardon?" asked Jimmy, standing at the sink, refilling the carafe with water for a second—or maybe third—pot of coffee.

"Ladies—and *gentleman*." I looked pointedly at Jimmy as I corrected myself. "Could you all please take a seat over here in the kitchen?"

"That's more like it," said Jimmy. He pushed his glasses up with his middle finger, a gesture I'm sure he does just to annoy me. "As the only guy in the room, I have a duty to make sure it's all PC around here."

When I didn't say anything, he continued, "PC stands for politically correct."

"I *know* what it means, Jimmy." I sighed, but steadfastly refused to roll my eyes. Instead, I lowered my voice and spoke only to him. "Thanks for hosting us, Jimmy. I hope it's not too much of an imposition."

As the manager of the Clamshell Motel, spikey-haired, bleached-blonde, 40-year-old Jimmy Noble often found himself in the position of providing Sheriff Donaldson,

Deputy Morgan, and me a place to compile our investigation notes at a location roughly midway up the peninsula. The aged cinderblock motel office doubling as his personal residence wasn't the Ritz, but his WIFI was top-notch, even if his coffee left a lot to be desired.

I'm quite sure Jimmy encouraged us to meet here to work because he thoroughly enjoyed being "in the know." Yet this time the purpose of our gathering was purely social, and did not include the sheriff or his number one deputy, Freddy Morgan, my sometimes boyfriend.

Felicity, Orpha, Nadine, Goodie, Nova and Meredith left their individual conversations in the living room half of the common area and quickly pulled chairs around the table in the kitchen side of the room. Hands folded on the tabletop or in their laps, they sat at rapt attention, like a group of eager young students.

"Jimmy! You darling!" gushed Meredith. "You got some extra folding chairs for us!"

Jimmy beamed. "You noticed!"

Thank goodness Merri had noticed, because the magical appearance of several more places to sit at the yellow Formica table had totally escaped me. Still standing, I leaned down to whisper in her ear. "Thanks, Mom." I was still getting used to calling Meredith Avery my mother, but she seemed to like it when I did.

"No secrets!" crowed Orpha, loudly pounding on the table in front of her. "If you can't say it to the whole group, it needn't be said!"

As the eldest of the women, little 85-year-old Orpha Starr made it her sacred responsibility to make sure we were all included in the inside scoop.

"You're absolutely right," I apologized. "I was just telling Merri that I was pleased everyone got here on time, and that several of you brought along your personal electronic tablets or laptops to work on."

Orpha nodded enthusiastically, making even her tight Brillo-pad gray curls bob up and down. "That's what I thought," she said. "Don't know why you couldn't just have said it for everyone to hear in the first place."

I smiled fondly at the entire group, now quietly chatting among themselves. All five members of The Veiled Rainbow, a geriatric belly dancing troupe my mother created to help them stay fit and flexible, were present, along with Felicity Michaels, an early 40-something high school history teacher, and a darn good friend. Six women, five of them widows and one never-married, had come together this bright Saturday morning in early October for one common goal: To explore the world of online dating.

Good grief and gravy, what had I gotten myself into when I agreed to help them navigate the ins and outs of staying safe while meeting men online?

On second thought, of course it came down to me. Who but me had both the ear, or ears, of the North Beach Sheriff's Office and the respect of the—let's call them "mature" ladies—looking for love? My mother and her friends were certainly not without their quirks and challenges, but when push came to shove, I knew we'd always have each others' backs.

"Ladies? *And Jimmy?*" I spoke softly and their attention refocused. "Who's ready to meet Mr. Wonderful?"

They all enthusiastically cheered, either raising their coffee cups, or pounding their hands on the table to add to the convivial cacophony.

"Back in the day, I'd have settled for Mr. Will Do, rather than Mr. Wonderful," said Orpha, "but I've decided against signing up. I'm just too long in the tooth to break in and train a new man in my life. After all, I'd only spend my days cleaning up after him. So I'm just here for moral support."

Nova Johanssen ran her hand through her close-cropped gray hair and cleared her throat. "Uh… As long as it's okay with all of you, I'm also opting out. I've only been widowed a few months, and there's so much work to do on the *Estrella Nueva* before crabbing season starts up again, I just don't think I have the time to—"

Meredith interrupted her by waving her hand energetically in the air like she was erasing everything that was coming out of Nova's mouth. "Excuse me, but this wouldn't have anything to do with a certain handsome charter boat fisherman named Richard Morgan, would it?"

Nova flushed scarlet, then stammered like a kid caught with her hand in the cookie jar as she tried to explain herself. "It's no secret that Rich and I are good friends. You all know that. He's been a big help to me since Mateo died. Of course, we see each other at the port all the time, but it's really no big deal." She shrugged as if she could pull off an air of nonchalance.

Everyone in the room smiled a knowing smile that deepened Nova's blush.

"No big deal, huh?" said Meredith. "Well, if you insist…"

"Yes," said Nova, not meeting anyone's eyes, "I insist."

"That's fine, Nova." I reached over and gave her hand a squeeze. "You just follow your heart, honey, and don't let them tease you into denying your attraction to Rich."

"My what?" Nova's mouth opened and closed like a guppy. Then she shrugged. "I guess there's no getting anything past this group, is there?"

Collectively, we all shook our heads.

"Is there anyone else who's opting out?" I asked.

"Well, now that you mention it," said Jimmy, moving around the table refilling coffee cups, "I might have, sort of, uh, recently happened to meet someone."

Seven heads snapped in his direction and everyone spoke at once.

"Spill it!" said Nadine.

"Do tell!" said Goodie.

"Well, I'll be," said Merri.

"Will wonders never cease?" said Nova.

"Details!" said Orpha, pounding the table again. "We want all the juicy details!

Felicity and I wisely kept our mouths shut. Whatever Jimmy chose to share, or not share, about his love life should be strictly up to him.

"Well, uh, you see…" Jimmy set down the coffee pot and pulled up a chair. "You know the guys who own the Cinco Amigos Chinese Cuisine?"

"Juan, José, Fernando, Julio, and Luis," recited Nova. "They've all been especially good to me since Mateo died. I'm very grateful for their friendship."

Jimmy eyed Nova suspiciously. "So you're good friends with all five of these guys, and you never thought to tell me that one of them might be my age—*and gay?*"

Bless her heart, Nova stood her ground with Jimmy. "What did you want me to do? Take out an ad in the newspaper? It really isn't any of my business."

"That never would have stopped me," Orpha piped up.

At Orpha's honest interjection, the tension was broken, and we all laughed.

"Sorry, Nova," said Jimmy. "I know I'm kind of sensitive about these things. Women are always setting women up with guys they know, but not very many give any thought to introducing their gay friends."

"I'm sorry too, Jimmy," said Nova. "I do know that Juan, José, and Fernando are all married, and Luis is divorced, and has custody of his three kids. And yes, I knew Julio was gay, but I don't know him well enough to introduce him to anyone." She lifted both hands, palms up, and shrugged again. "But apparently that's a moot point now."

Jimmy nodded. "We met a couple months ago when there was a mix-up in my take-out order. Usually, Julio is back in the kitchen, but he came out to personally apologize to me, and… well… there was definitely some chemistry, and he called the motel phone number the next day to ask if I wanted to go see a movie with him on his day off."

"If you'd like some help with your Spanish, I'd be happy to tutor you," said Felicity. She was the only one of us fluent enough to offer this help.

Nadine, who hadn't had much to contribute until now, suddenly raised her hand, as if she were in school, and waited for me to call on her.

"It seems to me," she began, peering at us through her thick glasses with faux tortoise shell frames, "that of the eight of us here, four are already spoken for, and the rest of us are getting older by the moment without a single man in sight."

Meredith chuckled. "Not a single man in sight. Good one, Nadine."

Nadine Larsen looked from face to face, confused. "What? What did I say?"

At 80, Nadine was far from senile, but she'd smoked enough pot in her lifetime to have disconnected a few synapses. She'd worked for Greenpeace for most of her adult life, and was still a strong champion of environmental issues.

Goodie Godwin, Nadine's best friend, despite the fact that they squabbled more than most married couples, jumped in to clarify Nadine's concerns.

"I think what Nadine's saying is that half of us are here today, eager to find dates and/or mates, and so far, we haven't even decided which online dating site we're going to use."

"Excellent point!" I said, glad to be getting our mission back on track. "So let's start there. Which site shall the four of you choose?"

Merri, Goodie, Nadine and Felicity all just looked at each other and either shrugged or did the "palms up" universal body language sign for clueless, which Nova had already demonstrated.

"Okay, well, I wouldn't want to tell you all what to do, but given your ages and location, I've narrowed the options down to five." I ticked them off on my fingers. "Connections, Hook-up, eMeet, Sole Mates or Swinging Seniors."

"I think," said Felicity, tentatively, "we can eliminate Hook-up and Swinging Seniors. Those two sites sound like we're all out on the make or something, and I believe we're here to find a true connection and relationship that will last. Am I right, ladies?"

Merri, Goodie, and Nadine nodded in silent agreement.

"Good! Now we're making progress," I said. "That leaves us with Connections, eMeet, and Sole Mates."

"In my opinion," said Nadine, "eMeet asks an awful lot of irrelevant questions."

"That's how they narrow down the matches," said Merri. "The more questions you answer, even on the trivial things like 'Do you usually eat breakfast?' the better they can match your personality with the perfect guy."

"But isn't that site kind of expensive to join?" asked Goodie.

I considered asking, once again, how the wealthy widows of The Veiled Rainbow were spending all the life insurance money they'd collected on their dearly departed husbands, but now didn't seem like a good time to throw us into another detour.

"Well, if cost is an issue," said Felix, "then we should go with Sole Mates. It's free."

"Free is a good price," said Jimmy.

"Hush," said Nova to Jimmy. "Now that we've opted out of signing up, you know they aren't going to let us vote."

"Well, Sole Mates is more geared to people along the coast—or at least west of the Cascades," said Merri. "That's why they spell 'Sole' like the fish, S-O-L-E, instead of like the spiritual part of a human being, S-O-U-L."

"Sole Mates," said Goodie, reading from the screen in front of her, "where we guarantee there are still plenty of good fish left in the sea, just swimming around out there waiting for you to reel them in."

"Even for old stinky fish like us," said Orpha.

Felix snorted some coffee up her nose and Jimmy handed her a paper towel. "Hey, watch who you're calling old and stinky, will you?"

Poor Felicity. We all knew her biological clock was ticking, but once again, the school district had failed to hire even one eligible male to pique her interest. It's not that she wanted children—she'd had plenty already in her 20 years in classrooms. But now knocking hard on the door of middle-age, she figured she'd have to find a good guy online to import to the community, or just give up and adopt a few more cats to keep her company.

"Well, you know what they say," offered Nova, the only bona fide fisherperson among us. "If you don't put your line in the water, how are you going to catch anything?"

Goodie couldn't help giggling. "Is catching anything still a worry at our age?"

"I guess we'd all better go out and buy some condoms," said Nadine, matter-of-factly.

I don't know why my face was turning so red while none of theirs were. I guess I just figured that for these grandmother-types, sex wasn't an option for any of them, and here they were talking in such a way that I was sure they had never stopped thinking about it!

"Well, heck," said Meredith, "if I find a guy my age who can still get it up, I'll be ecstatic!"

"Mother!"

Raucous laughter emitted from everyone in the room but me. Thinking of Merri—or any of these women for that matter—having sex, was more than I could, or wanted to, wrap my mind around. It was an image I never wanted to visualize, because then I'd never be able to unsee it.

At that moment, the Clamshell Motel's only long-term tenant, Kanjirappally Kumera, along with his Golden Retriever puppy Elvis, came knocking on the inner door of the motel office.

Jimmy, still laughing at my expense, swung the door open wide. "Welcome to the loony bin, Kanji, where the only thing crazier than the idea of these women finding true love on the internet is thinking about them having sex with their yet-to-be-determined mates!"

The look on Kanji's face was priceless. I'd bet anything that about now he was second-guessing his recent decision to retire on the North Beach Peninsula!

"Please do excuse me, I do not mean to interrupt your gathering this morning," he began. Still aghast, he stood in the doorway and bowed slightly. "I recognized so many of your vehicles in the parking lot when I took Elvis out for a walk in the dunes that I impulsively decided to knock and employ the social graces of expressing my greetings to all you lovely ladies."

"Please, please, come on in," said Meredith, motioning with a rolling gesture of her hand for him to step inside the room. "We're just starting to embark on this online dating adventure, and we could use a man's opinion."

Jimmy cleared his throat and pointedly glared at me. Under his breath he said, "Once again, I'm left holding the coffee pot and feeling like chopped liver."

Meanwhile, Elvis had helped himself to the crumbs left in the bottom of Jimmy's cat Priscilla's bowl, then zeroed in on Goodie. He gently put his head in her lap, looking up adoringly into her face as she stroked his head.

"I think he remembers me," gushed Goodie, a frequent volunteer at the Humane Society where Kanji had adopted the pup several months ago. "He's getting so big!"

"And his coat's so shiny," said Nadine, running her hand along his back.

Elvis's tail swished back and forth so hard we could have used it for a fan.

"It's certainly easy to tell he's well cared for," said Goodie. "No need for anyone to come out to do a welfare check on this beautiful boy!" she cooed.

"So why are you still living out in Unit 6?" asked Nova.

"Oh, that is because I am what you ladies would call, shall we say, very picky," explained Kanji. "I have yet to come upon the ultimate home in which Elvis and I will happily reside." He sighed. "It is my good fortune that Jimmy has been most helpful in allowing us to stay here, renting by the week, until we at last find a perfect place to call our own."

"It's good that you're waiting for the right house to come along," said Merri. "That way you'll never be disappointed, and you'll never have to move again."

"That, my dear lady," replied Kanji, "is precisely why I

have not rushed into purchasing anything that is lacking in our requirements. I steadfastly refuse to be hurried into a poor decision."

"Well, I swear," said Orpha, "you're getting more handsome every time I see you, and I can't imagine why one of the single women your age around here hasn't snapped you right up!" She looked pointedly in my direction.

Kanji looked at the iPad on the table in front of me. "Miss Sylvia?" he asked softly. "Are you also entertaining the thought of finding love online?"

It was an honest question, but for some reason it made me squirm. "No, Kanji, I am merely the I.T. girl: Information Technology, if you can believe that!"

Kanji bowed slightly once again. "I can believe that you are as smart as you are beautiful, and that you are able to do anything you set your mind to."

Jimmy might as well use my flaming face to heat the room.

Kanji turned to Meredith. "And may I ask what it was that you were suggesting would benefit by my opinion when I came in?"

"Well," said Merri, "do you think there are still single men—single *gentlemen*—who are about our age, give or take a few years, who are still interested in dating?"

Holy Criminitly! For a second there, I thought for sure Meredith was going to ask Kanji if he still liked the idea of sex!

Kanji smiled politely, but I wondered just how much he had heard before we knew he had entered the outer motel office.

"I have it on good authority, Miss Meredith, that there are plenty of single gentlemen who would be more than proud to have you accompany them to dinner or a movie."

"Thank you, Kanji. That is most helpful." Meredith either had something in her eye, or was purposely batting her eyelashes to beat the band.

"Now that we have that settled," I said quickly, "it's time for you to leave, Kanji. No offense, but we need to get down to the business at hand."

Kanji dipped his head again. "No offense was taken, dear Sylvia. But I am most relieved that you are not among those who will be trolling for any new fish."

So he *had* heard more than he let on before he came inside the kitchen! I gently turned him around by the shoulders and guided him to the door. "Good to see you, Kanji."

"Very good to see you as well, Miss Syl." He whistled once for Elvis, who immediately left the women who were lavishly fawning over him, to follow his master home.

"Well, that was certainly interesting," said Merri, as I closed the door.

When I turned to look at her, she was fluffing up her hair. "If you hadn't thrown him out when you did, I'm certain he would have asked me out."

"Oh no you don't! No! No! No! No! No! and hell no! You just keep your hands to yourself and leave Kanji alone. I don't want to think of him following in Walter's footsteps!"

The moment the words were out of my mouth, I wanted to rip my tongue out. The room got suddenly very, very, quiet, as I'm sure we were all thinking of our dearly departed friend Walter Winston, who had unfortunately died in bed with Meredith a few months ago.

"Relax dear," said Merri after several painful moments of uncomfortable silence. "I was merely thinking it would be fun to have a gentleman companion who liked to attend movies and things." Her lower lip stuck out and she looked for all the world like she was going to pout because I'd told her Kanji was off limits. "You could come with us, if you want."

I didn't know which was worse: Thinking about my 75-year-old mother dating 60-year-old Kanji, or believing she thought I'd enjoy the three of us going to the movies together. Did she think we'd be one big happy family, or was she merely being polite, knowing I'd never choose to tag along to be an unwelcome third wheel?

Fortunately, Nadine saved me from replying to Meredith when she asked if they were supposed to use their real names for the online dating profile.

"No way," Jimmy answered before I could. "Your screen name is supposed to reflect who you really are as a person, so the guy gets some idea of your personality."

"Oh!" said Merri, perking right up. "You mean like 'Red Hot Mama'?"

CHAPTER 2

I glared at Meredith. I could almost feel the steam coming out of my ears. "No, Merri, Jimmy certainly did *NOT* mean using a name like 'Red Hot Mama'! Good grief and gravy, you have no clue what kind of mistaken ideas that might give some screw-loose nut-job of a guy trolling the website looking for an easy mark."

"Now you look here, Syl, I think you shot down that name a little too quickly," said Merri. "For one, I have red hair. For two, I drive a red Saturn. For three, four, and five, my belly dancing costume color is red, I'm always complaining that I'm too hot, and I'm your mama. The name, my dear daughter, is absolutely perfect!"

"You're not using that name," I said quietly. "And that's final."

Now Meredith was officially in pout mode. "Well, who died and elected you Chief Killjoy?"

"Listen up—" My voice sounded louder and harsher than necessary, and I toned it down just a smidgeon before continuing. "You all asked me to help you navigate online dating. Therefore, I have veto power over all names, all headlines on your ads, and everything else you write about yourselves, got it?"

Felix nodded. "Yes, we did ask for your help, Syl, and I, for one, am very happy for your wisdom in this endeavor. I'm very serious about finding someone. Someone kind and decent and good-hearted and educated and— and quite frankly, this may be my last shot. I have complete faith in you, Sylvia. So if anyone here feels otherwise, well… Well… they don't have to stay. No one is twisting their arm or keeping them here against their will." She blew out a big breath. "Now please, let's get back to work!"

It was quite a long speech for the usually quiet and demure Felicity, and the other women duly noted that fact. While this was mostly entertainment for them, Felix was the only one actually wanting to find potential marriage material.

"Why don't you all take a few minutes and brainstorm your own list of potential screen names and headlines?" I suggested as calmly as I could. Then I stood up and took two steps away from the table and opened Jimmy's fridge, allegedly in search of a diet soda.

What I really wanted was to distance myself from the group for a moment and use the open fridge to both put a barrier between me and the would-be daters. I also knew I had to cool down a little. I stood there and took a couple deep breaths before I returned to my chair empty-handed.

"Would you like me to start a pot of decaf?" Jimmy asked softly.

I shook my head. "It's not noon yet. I think I could have another full-powered cup of real coffee without the world coming to an end."

He put his hand on my shoulder as he poured me a half a cup. "You can do this," he whispered. "You're really good at people wrangling."

I silently wondered if that were true.

"This is kind of hard," said Felicity. "I don't want to use 'Teacher' as my screen name, or even in my headline, because I'm afraid that would immediately cause some men to scroll right on by without giving me a second look."

"Only if they are intimidated by intelligence," said Nova.

"I think you're both right," I replied. "You've got to grab their attention first. But you could certainly share your occupation in the body of your profile if you choose."

Felicity nodded and chewed thoughtfully on her lower lip. "Uh-huh. I need to pique their interest, before I reel them in."

Jimmy laughed. "I love extended metaphors. Reeling them in on Sole Mates. Good one, Felix!"

The expression on Felicity's face told me she hadn't intended to make a joke, but bless her heart, she accepted the compliment gracefully.

"So…" I drew the word out so that it sounded several syllables long. "What has everybody come up with?" No one said a word, so I was forced to prompt. "Nadine? How about you?"

"Well, since my belly dancing costume is green, and I worked for Greenpeace, I was thinking about using the name 'Green Bean' and the headline 'Environment and 420-friendly.'"

I hope she didn't see me cringe. "Perhaps you could save your acceptance of recreational pot for a little further down in the profile. You wouldn't want to scare anyone away, like if they thought you were a drug addict or something."

That inspired a hearty laugh from the group. Nadine is definitely the group's loveable little pothead, but it was something the rest of them politely didn't talk about.

"And," I continued, "you know I love you, but I'm not sure referring to yourself as a skinny green vegetable is quite the image you're going for, either. Kind of makes you sound like Popeye's girlfriend Olive Oyl."

"Oh, right," said Nadine. "I'll try again."

"Do we have to mention our costume colors in our names?" asked Goodie. "The only thing I can think of for yellow is lemons, and that might put a sour spin on any potential dates."

"Another good one," said Jimmy, but no one was paying him any attention.

"What about sunshine?" said Nova. "You've always got a sunny outlook."

"Well, maybe…" said Goodie, but she sounded doubtful.

"Bananas are yellow," said Orpha.

"No!" shouted everyone in the room.

"Just trying to be helpful," said Orpha. "You don't need to get so loud while you're shooting my ideas down."

"Goodness!" said Felicity. "I hope you don't expect me to compare my personality to a certain color for my profile name." She chuckled. "I'm not in the dance troupe, so I don't have a color."

"You could be Violet!" crowed Orpha. "We still need a Violet!"

"Now's not the time for recruiting new dancers," I said, shaking my head at Orpha. "If you really want to help, you can help Goodie brainstorm some serious name suggestions."

"Fine," said Orpha. "Then how about 'Oldie but Goodie'?"

Goodie looked mildly miffed. "Just remember, I'm not nearly as old as you are, Orpha."

"That's right," said Nadine, "but I don't think any of us know just exactly how old Orpha is."

Meredith was wisely keeping her mouth shut. She publicly admitted to a young 70-something, but I'm probably the only one who knows she's already beyond the midpoint of that particular decade.

"Does anyone—anyone signing up or not—have any name suggestions for the ones who are willing to put their best selves out there?"

"Well, we already call her Goodie-two-shoes," said Orpha.

"You do?" asked Goodie.

"Well, not to your face, of course," said Nadine.

"How about 'DMV Approved'?" asked Orpha. "There's probably a bunch of men out there our ages who've had to surrender their driver's licenses, and it could be a good selling point."

"Speaking of driver's licenses," said Merri. "Hasn't yours already expired?"

"I'm not signing up," replied Orpha, "so it doesn't matter."

Before those two got any further into the illegalities of driving without a license, even if they never left the peninsula, Nova spoke up. "What about using the NATO phonetic alphabet?"

"The what?" asked Merri.

Jimmy piped right up. "The NATO phonetic alphabet, officially denoted as the International Radiotelephony Spelling Alphabet, and also commonly known as the ICAO phonetic alphabet, and in a variation is also known officially as the ITU phonetic alphabet and figure code, is the most widely used radiotelephone spelling alphabet."

Everyone in the room except Nova, who had spent a short time of her youth in the military, erupted with some form of the phrase "Say what?" to Jimmy's lengthy explanation that actually explained nothing. They were all used to him possessing a virtual encyclopedic mind, but what he had just said made very little sense to any of us.

"Each letter of the alphabet, when said over the radio, might get misheard or confused," said Nova. "So each letter has a word that is used on the airways instead. Like instead of saying the letter 'C,' which could be garbled by static to sound like B or D or E or G or P or even T, the NATO alphabet says 'Charlie.'"

The majority of the group still stared blankly at Nova.

"Ok, so my initials are N.J." Nova continued. "So I would be November Juliet."

"Ohhh..." murmured the group.

The light had suddenly dawned, and Felicity, Merri, Goodie and Nadine all quickly accessed the NATO alphabet on their tablets and laptops.

Nadine was the first to speak. "November Lima? Is that pronounced Lima like in Peru, or Lima as in the bean? If it's the bean," she sighed, "then I might as well go back to being Green Bean. At least it's an American vegetable."

"I think it's the bean," said Nova. "This code was created for the English alphabet."

I shot a look at Jimmy, expecting him to launch into the lima bean also being called the butter bean, but thankfully, he didn't open his mouth.

"Oh fiddlesticks!" said Goodie, exasperated. "Goodie Godwin would be Golf Golf, and I don't even play the game!"

Felicity snorted. "Foxtrot Mike? It sounds like I'm a guy who's hot to trot!"

"Well, aren't you?" asked Orpha Then she added, "The hot to trot part, not the guy part.

Felix glared at her. "Even if I were hot to trot, I wouldn't want to advertise it!"

"Hmmm," said Meredith. "I'd be Mike Alpha. Not only is that a guy's name, but it also suggests I'm an Alpha personality! How wrong is that?"

Merri's pout returned when we all laughed uproariously.

Nova exhaled a huge sigh. "Well, it was just a thought."

"It's interesting," I said as I tried to cheer Nova, "and thanks for the suggestion. But I don't think the NATO Alphabet was meant to be used to determine appropriate aliases for anyone."

Jimmy chose this moment to offer up a few suggestions. "How about 'Coastal Creature' or 'Beach Babe,' or 'Sexy Seashore Gal,' or—

"No!" I stopped him before he could annoy, insult, or offend any of the four. "I'm just going to jump in here and assign you temporary screen names so we can continue with this process. Nadine, yours is Deenie. Goodie, yours is GiGi. Merri, yours is…"

"Mad Max?" she interjected. "Marvelous Mom?"

I held up my hand to shush her and finished my sentence "Mermaid."

"*Mermaid?*" Meredith looked at me first in shock and then in awe. "Mermaid?" She said it slowly, softly, like she was testing it out for sound. "Mermaid? Hey, honey, I really like that! I mean I really, really like that!" She beamed. "Mer is the Latin word for "sea," and also the first syllable of my name, and maid, like a young unmarried woman."

Before any of us could object to her claim to being a young unmarried woman, especially since we all knew she'd buried three husbands, Jimmy spoke up again.

"A Mermaid is also really appropriate for this Sole Mates dating site," he added. "I like it."

"What about me?" asked Felicity. "What screen name are you giving me?"

"Well, I'm using Nadine's and Goodie's nicknames, so I thought maybe you'd use Felix," I began.

"But again, it sounds like I'm a guy," said Felix, grimacing.

"Yes, it sounds like a guy, but you know we use it as a term of endearment."

"I know, and I don't mind, but you already know me," said Felix. "This is a name that's supposed to attract a guy who's never met me."

"So how about using the name Lexi?" I held my breath while she tossed the name around in her head.

"It's definitely a girl's name," I prompted.

"Sexy Lexi," said Orpha, as if we all weren't secretly hoping no one would say that out loud.

"AND," said Jimmy, again interrupting at exactly the right time, "it hints of her having a good vocabulary and good education and having a solid command of the language, as it's the root of lexicon! Great name choice! Good job, Sylvia!"

Felicity beamed. "I hadn't thought of it that way, Jimmy." She turned to me. "Lexi will be just fine, Syl. Thank you."

"Great!" I breathed a sigh of relief. "Now we've got that settled, Deenie, GiGi, Mermaid and Lexi, let's move on!"

But before there was time to do any moving on, 6-foot 4-inch Sheriff Carter Donaldson, more like 6'8" if you counted his ever-present Stetson, strode boldly into the room—without even bothering to knock.

"Carter!" I exclaimed. "What are you doing here?"

"Is that any way to greet me?" he asked.

"Would you like some coffee?" asked Jimmy.

Sheriff D grinned. "Now, that's more like it! Yes, Jimmy, I'd love a cup of joe."

A large man in full uniform, especially a police uniform, often draws a lot of immediate attention, and although we all knew the sheriff on a more personal level, he still commanded the respect of his elected office. Always a gentleman, Sheriff D took off his Stetson and set it on the kitchen counter as Jimmy handed him his coffee.

"So what brings you here?" I asked again, in a slightly less annoyed tone as the sheriff took his first sip of the hot, freshly brewed beverage.

"Mercedes said you'd all be meeting here today, and she said to tell you thanks for the invite, but she won't be joining you. She's quite happy with her current boyfriend."

Carter and Mercedes, the sequin-sporting lounge singer at the casino, and one of my dearest friends, had been dating for several months, despite the fact that his wife of over 40 years was still alive. It was complicated, but since Mary Ann was in the Alzheimer's care ward at the nursing home and hadn't recognized Carter in a very long time, we were all comfortable with the fact that he and Mercedes were finding a little happiness together.

"Oh," continued Sheriff D, "and Freddy says hello, Sylvia." He paused, waiting for my reaction, but I think I disappointed him when I didn't immediately say anything.

Freddy, also known as Deputy Frederick Morgan, also known as the owner of the Spartina Point Casino and Resort by recent inheritance, was my maybe part-time boyfriend, although it didn't set quite right with me to say the word "boyfriend" out loud. Freddy is nearly 15 years my junior, and I can't imagine him pushing around my wheelchair when I'm 80 and he's only 65. Most of my women friends say I should get over that. Mercedes says I should be happy to have a young one so I can raise him right!

I came back from my reverie with the knowledge that Sheriff D had asked me a question, but I didn't know what it was.

"Freddy hopes you're not signing up on the dating site." He paused. "So are you?"

I squinted my eyes. How dare Freddy send the sheriff to get that information out of me. "Well, I might be…"

"She's not!" Orpha blurted out. "She's got her hands full trying to decide between Kanji and Freddy."

Good old Orpha, always coming straight to the point.

Sheriff D smiled. "Well, I'm sure Freddy will be more than happy to hear you're not planning to bring any other men into the mix."

"Is that the reason you're here, Carter?" I glared at him through narrowed eyes. I knew I couldn't intimidate him, but perhaps I could make him take a step back.

Sheriff Donaldson shook his head, and set his coffee cup on the counter. "Ladies," he began, "I think very highly of all of you, and I'm glad Sylvia is here helping you to try to stay safe on the Internet. The world of dating is not what it used to be, and there are plenty of online predators out there who are just waiting for some naïve woman to succumb to his made-up charms and false profile and willingly send him a boatload of money and—"

"Carter! Get to the point!"

Meredith stood up and put her hands on her hips. "Naïve? Did you just call us naïve?"

"Well, not you, personally, Meredith," said Sheriff D, backpedaling like crazy.

"Then me?" asked Nova, standing.

"Or me? said Nadine, also getting to her feet.

Goodie just sat and shrugged her shoulders. "I can't complain. I *am* naïve, and I'm scared to death of dating for the first time in 50 years!"

"Ladies, ladies, please. Everyone sit back down. I meant no offense." Sheriff D, who towered over us all, suddenly looked rather small next to the mighty female outcry of indignance. He knew better than to push the envelope about their collective naiveté just now, so he took another route to make his point.

"How many of you have a concealed carry permit?" he asked.

"Carter," I said, with just a tinge of exasperation in my voice, "I'm the only one here who owns a gun, which you know if you've checked the county records, as I'm sure you have."

Sheriff D nodded. "Ok, so how are you all going to protect yourselves in the case of an actual emergency?"

"Condoms!" exclaimed Orpha without hesitation.

Sheriff Donaldson tried again. "Say you're out on a date and the guy gets fresh and tries to force you to do something you don't want to do."

It was a serious question and needed a serious answer.

"Wh— What do you think we should do, Sheriff?" Goodie timidly asked.

Sheriff D made meaningful eye contact with everyone in the room, then turned to me. "So there's seven of you signing up?"

"Actually, there's only four," I replied. "Meredith, Nadine, Goodie and Felicity." I unnecessarily pointed to them as I said their names. "Jimmy, Nova and Orpha have opted out for personal reasons." No need to open the door for him to hear about Nova and Rich dating so soon after her husband Mateo's untimely death. The death had been ruled an accident, but the sheriff had been none too happy to see Nova so chummy with Rich during the investigation.

"Four," repeated the sheriff, nodding thoughtfully. "Four is manageable."

"What do you mean by 'manageable'?" asked Meredith.

"I mean it will be far easier to keep track of just four of you, and it won't take as long to run reports on their dates through NICS."

"Are you dyslexic, Sheriff?" asked Orpha. "Don't you mean NCIS?"

"NICS is the National Instant Criminal Background Check System," interjected Jimmy. "It's a specific file division of NCIC, the National Crime Information Center. The NCIC consists of 21 files, 7 of which are property files, and 14 are persons' files."

"Thank you, Jiminy Cricket," said Sheriff D. "I couldn't have said it better myself."

Nobody blinked when the sheriff called Jimmy 'Jiminy Cricket.' By now we were all used to Jimmy's encyclopedic mind, and the sheriff's reference to Pinocchio's smart sidekick didn't faze any of us in the least—including Jimmy.

"You want to run criminal background checks on our dates?" asked Merri.

"Isn't that what I just said?" asked the sheriff.

"Uh... Carter? There's a flaw in your thinking," I said.

"Don't you go arguing, Sylvia. As sheriff of this county, it's my duty to do what I can to keep its citizens safe. Background checks are just a little extra information that could save a lot of heartache, or worse, later on. Do you know how many people—men and women— fall victim to Identity Theft each day?"

"The flaw," I continued, "is that nobody knows a person's real name, at least not their full name, until after they've met. The initial anonymity protects them from stalkers and bad guys like that. Nobody gives out their full name right away, not the men and not the women, and later... Well, later it probably wouldn't do any good."

Sheriff D rocked back and forth on his heels, smoothing

his mustache out from the center to the ends with his right index finger and thumb several times. I'd learned early on that it was a mannerism that meant he was thinking something through, and I kept quiet.

Finally, he said, "Just hold on tight here a minute." Then he set his coffee down, picked his Stetson back up, plopped it on his head, and abruptly left the building.

"He's got a lot of nerve," said Merri, drumming her fingers on the table. "Does he think we're complete idiots who can't take care of ourselves?"

"I'm sure he has our best interests at heart," said Felicity, not wanting conflict, but not wanting to stay silent as if she were agreeing with Meredith.

"What he's telling us is scaring me," said Goodie. "And he's right. There are a lot of men out there who would like to take advantage of women like us."

"It's information I suppose we need to have," admitted Nadine.

"I think we'd all do well to hear him out," said Nova, "whether we think we're in a safe situation or not."

"I don't think we have a choice," said Jimmy, over his shoulder to Nova. He was looking out the kitchen window. "The sheriff's on his way back in."

"Good deal," said Orpha, "cause I could look at that man all day long. He's real easy on the eyes, a real hottie, add the uniform, and he's quite the fantasy."

CHAPTER 3

But before any of us could comment on Orpha's fantasy life, Sheriff Donaldson came back through the door carrying a small, crumpled-up paper bag sporting the name of our local hardware store on it. This time he did not bother to remove his hat, and I hoped that was a sign he wouldn't be staying long. He walked briskly around the table, handing each of the four participating women a pocket-sized container of pepper spray.

"I can't stand the thought of you all being out there without some form of protection," said Sheriff D. "Maybe I should have brought condoms," he added under his breath as he walked around the back of my chair.

"Now a good shot of this pepper spray won't kill anybody, but it will certainly slow them down." The sheriff completed his table circuit and stood back by the door. "It's got a little loop on the end so you can clip it to your keyring."

The women silently examined their unsolicited gifts, turning them over in their hands, and flipping the safety switch on and off. Thankfully, no one pressed the spray button to test it out.

"It's really small," said Nadine. "It's no bigger than one of those little LED flashlights."

"It's not *that* small," said Meredith, scowling. "What if I'm not wearing anything that has pockets? It's too big to tuck into my bra."

"Can I use this on dogs when I'm out walking?" asked Felicity.

Goodie, our faithful Humane Society volunteer, gasped. "You wouldn't want to hurt a sweet little innocent dog, would you?"

Felicity backtracked in a hurry. "I only meant it might protect me from *vicious* dogs," she said. "Dogs that aren't on a leash. The ones that growl and nip at me, and act like they are going to attack. There are times, Goodie, that I'm sincerely afraid for my health and safety."

Goodie nodded. "But you promise you'll only use it as a last resort?"

Felix crossed her heart with her right index finger. "I promise."

"Hey! How come we all don't get one?" Jimmy asked Sheriff D. "Don't you want to keep the rest of us safe? Is this some kind of dating discrimination?"

The sheriff pushed the brim of his Stetson up an inch or two on his forehead, which I instantly equated to one of my trademark eyerolls. "Now Jimmy, the county budget can't be supplying these to everyone. The rest of you can get your own at the hardware store. I just happened to have a few in the car for emergencies, and decided to share them with these women, since they seem to be intent on putting themselves at personal risk."

"At personal risk?" echoed Goodie, looking at the faces of the women around her before meeting the sheriff's eyes. "You really think it's that dangerous to meet a man online?"

But before Sheriff D could open his mouth, Meredith reached over, put her hand on Goodie's, and gave it a squeeze. "Now honey, don't you worry. That's why we asked Sylvia to help us with our profiles. She'll make sure we are all perfectly safe."

I looked up at Carter. "No pressure, huh?"

Sheriff D smiled. "I'm sure you'll do the best you can, but horses don't change color, and I know some of these women are downright stubborn."

"We're right here, you know," said Meredith, glaring at him. "We can all hear you."

"Good!" said the sheriff. "Then hear this, loud and clear: Scam artists present themselves as ordinary, everyday people. They might say they are looking for a traveling companion, because paying for "single occupancy" is too expensive or they just hate to travel alone. They might be looking for a woman who can teach them to dance. Or maybe they need a 'classy lady' to attend their niece's wedding with them so their nosy relatives won't try to set them up."

"But wouldn't a nice guy write any of those things?" asked Goodie. She fussed at the fuzz on the sleeve of her sweater, and looked around at the rest of us for reassurance.

"I know plenty of women who met the man of their dreams online, got married, and are living happily ever after," said Felicity. "Otherwise I wouldn't be here."

"Yes," admitted the sheriff, "there are certainly some success stories, but the bad guys outnumber the good guys about three to one."

"Three to one?" asked Nadine. "Those aren't very good odds."

"Pish-posh!" said Meredith, waving her hand in dismissal. "You're just trying to scare us, Carter!"

"Well, he's doing a pretty good job of that," said Goodie. "I'm not sure I want to go through with this after all."

Meredith reached out and extended her pinky finger to Goodie on one side, and Nadine on the other. "All for one and one for all."

Goodie linked her pinky finger to Meredith's, and with the other hand, reached over to include Felicity in their vow. Felicity, in turn, linked with Nadine to complete the circle.

"All for one, and one for all," they said together.

The sheriff smiled. "Ok, then. Since you're all determined to do this, and you promise to have each other's backs, I'll relax a little. But I gotta say one more thing—"

"Of course you do," said Merri, under her breath, but loud enough for all of us to hear.

"I sure as holy hell hope that—" he began, then stopped and corrected his language. "For gosh darn and golly sakes, DO NOT tell any of these men that you're a wealthy widow!"

Felicity cleared her throat. "I beg your pardon, Sheriff Donaldson, but I am neither wealthy, nor a widow."

Sheriff D touched two fingers to the brim of his Stetson, not to push it up, but to make the universal sign of saluting, or tipping his hat. "I beg your pardon, Miss Felicity."

Although Felicity had inherited her teaching colleague Walter's life insurance, she had already put the lion's share of the money to good use, providing college scholarships and donating to many local charities. As for the rest of The Veiled Rainbow, their lips were sealed tight, and I had no idea what they'd done with their windfalls after the deaths of their husbands. For all I knew, they had it stuck in their sock drawer, not even collecting interest.

In the moment of silence that followed, I complimented Carter on his personal editing. "Mercedes must be a good influence on you," I began.

"How's that?" he asked.

"In all the time I've known her, I've never heard Merc use a single cuss word. Now it seems her attention to polite language is rubbing off on you. You can't deny that you just cleaned up what you started to say." I laughed. "Gosh darn and golly sakes? Really, Carter?"

Sheriff D's face, which was naturally ruddy and always had a pink tinge to it, turned a shade darker. "In polite company, I *am* trying a little harder not to swear. Thanks for noticing."

I stood up, and took his elbow. "If you've said all you've come here to say, it's time for you to leave." I guided him the three steps to the inner door, and opened it for him.

He was surprised by my insistence, but not unwilling to depart.

"We'll be sure to call you if or when any of us need further assistance. Thank you for the pepper sprays."

With one foot out the door, Sheriff D turned for a parting shot. "Please don't give out your social security numbers for any reason. Hang tight to your credit cards. And for heaven's sake, don't use your PIN where it can be observed!"

"Out, Carter! Out! Out! Out!" It was déjà vu all over again, and not all that long since I'd escorted Kanji out that very same door and in the very same manner. Jimmy's place had turned into Grand Central Station once again!

I waited for Sheriff D to exit the tiny motel office to make sure he wouldn't think of another reason to hang around, then closed the inner door. Returning to the group, I saw that Nova was also getting ready to leave.

"You don't need me here," she explained, "and I've got plenty of work to do on the boat."

"Sure you do…" said Orpha, drawing out the words suggestively and grinning from ear to ear. "Lots and lots of work to do, uh-huh."

"Orpha?" asked Nova. "Would you like a ride back down to Unity? I'll be driving right past your apartment on the way to the docks."

"I know very well what town my apartment's in, thank you," said Orpha, looking perturbed. "I'm not the senile old woman everybody thinks I am!"

"Orpha, you know I meant no offense," said Nova, slightly taken aback. "But since you're not signing up on the dating site, I thought you might not want to stick around any longer."

"I came with Felicity, and I'll go home with Felicity," said Orpha, her gray curls bouncing as she made her point. "I wouldn't dream of leaving yet. For my money, this whole online dating adventure looks like it's going to be a hoot, and a lot more entertaining than any reality TV show I'd be watching at home."

"Just thought I'd ask," said Nova. She zipped up her blue plaid flannel jacket. Then to the rest of us she added, "And I sincerely wish you all the very best!"

We chorused our good-byes, and as the door closed again, I held up my hands. "No gossiping about Nova and Rich! None! We have plenty of work left to do here today without taking time out to speculate on the status of their relationship!"

"Yes, about the work left to do…" said Meredith. "We've been here over two hours and all we've gotten done is chosen the dating site and filled in our nicknames."

"If I'd known this was going to take all day, I'd have packed a lunch," said Nadine.

"Lunch sounds like a great idea," said Jimmy. "Would anyone like me to go pick up an order at the Cinco Amigos Chinese Cuisine?"

"You anxious to go see your hottie?" asked Orpha. "I'm not sure exactly which one he is, but I think all Mexican men are exotic! I'll bet he's just adorbs!" She beamed. "With his skin so caramel colored, and yours so lily white, I'll bet the two of you make the cutest couple!"

Jimmy flushed three ways to Sunday, as the saying goes.

"No food until we get the profile headlines written!" I admonished them.

"You're holding our lunch hostage?" asked Nadine.

"If we settle down and focus, we can get this part done in no time," I said. I didn't really believe it, but I said it anyway. "Now let's remember the sheriff's cautions. Nobody put down anything that screams desperate, vulnerable, rich—"

"Or ripe for the picking!" exclaimed Orpha.

"Jimmy," I said, ignoring Orpha's comment, "you can pass around the take-out menu while the gals work on their headlines and they can initial their choices. Perhaps it will encourage and inspire them to finish this step so we can all eat."

Felicity grinned. "You'd have made a great teacher, Sylvia."

I shook my head. "I honestly don't know how you do it. I can't even wrangle a couple of eld— I mean *mature* women, and you've got five full classes of around 30 students every 50 minutes. You're my hero."

Felicity grinned again, obviously pleased with the praise.

In short order, all four women had come up with what they considered an interest-catching, but not too revealing headline, and it was time to share the results.

"Who wants to go first?" I asked.

When no one volunteered, I looked pointedly at Felix and waited.

"See?" she said. "You'd be a natural in the classroom."

I laughed. "Ms. Michaels, would you please read your proposed headline?"

"I wrote several," said Felix. "I was trying to hone in on

getting my point across in just a couple words. It's not as easy as you think."

I nodded, but said nothing.

Felicity took a breath. "Okay, here goes: 'Educator seeks sapiophile.'"

The room erupted, they all talked at once, and I couldn't tell who was saying what. For a few minutes I thought I might need a coach's whistle to restore order.

"Ladies! Ladies!"

Jimmy glared at me.

"Ladies *and gentleman!*" This day really was beginning to feel like I was stuck in a continuous loop. Somehow I'd gotten enmeshed in something similar to the movie plot in Groundhog's Day, and I wondered how I'd ever get out. "Okay, people! Let's try this again."

And again, the room erupted with everyone talking at the same time.

Felicity, sitting next to me, leaned closer and said, "Maybe you should have us raise our hands if we want to speak."

"Not funny," I replied.

"Hey, if it works for high school kids, it might work here," she said.

"Might is the operative word."

I've never been able to muster up a good whistle, so I decided clapping my hands again might be the most effective way to get them to stop talking. I clapped my hands sharply in a rhythmical pattern this time, one loud, two quick and softer, one loud: ONE-two-three-FOUR. ONE-two-three-FOUR. Thankfully, the noise subsided.

"I'm telling you," said Felix. "You'd be amazing in the classroom."

"So...," I said, totally ignoring her. "Can someone please

raise their hand and tell me what they think of Felix's headline attempt?

Meredith went first. "If she puts 'educator' in the headline, it's the same as putting 'teacher.'"
She will eliminate the men who didn't like school, or who have a preset idea of a bossy teacher, maybe even a nun, cracking their knuckles with a ruler." Merri took a quick breath. "And... And it could also have an effect on the men who have a fetish about Catholic school girls."

Felicity's eyes opened wide, but she said nothing.

"If she puts 'educator'," said Nadine, "the guy will already know exactly where to find her, and could stalk her at school."

"You're starting to sound like Sheriff D," said Meredith.

"But it's true," Nadine insisted.

"Let's get Goodie's opinion of the headline," I said before the conversation could get any more derailed.

Goodie sighed. "I didn't catch the educator part," she said. "I hate to admit it, but I don't know what a sap... sap... You know, what that other word means, and I have a feeling most of the men won't know either."

"Sapiophile," said Jimmy, speaking as if he were a contestant in a spelling bee. "S-a-p-i-o-p-h-i-l-e. A sapiophile is someone who is attracted to intelligence or intelligent people."

"Thank you, Jimmy," I said, trying not to sound annoyed. Jimmy was as close as anyone I knew to fitting the sapiophile definition, or maybe the word I was thinking of was savant, but I didn't want to start any more side conversations at the moment. "Does anyone else have input for Felicity?"

After a short pause, Felix said, "Wow! You guys are tough. I just thought I wouldn't want anyone to respond who disliked teachers, so I used the word educator. And I don't think I want anyone who doesn't know what a sapiophile means—no offense, Goodie. I never thought for a second about stalkers or guys with schoolgirl fetishes."

"Apparently, it takes a village to write a dating profile these days," said Orpha. "I'm doubly glad I didn't sign up now, cause I wouldn't want all of you critiquing what I wrote!" She cleared her throat. "I thought Felicity did just fine!"

"Thank you, Orpha," said Felix.

Nadine looked at Orpha. "It's how we plan to stay safe, remember?"

"Well, then, Miss Smarty Pants," said Orpha, "let's hear what you wrote."

Nadine immediately complied. "Beach lover, 420-friendly."

"Four-twenty friendly?" said Goodie. "Are you sure you want that in there?"

"What?" said Nadine. "It's legal now, so I might as well say it upfront. I don't want any self-righteous prudes applying. I want a guy who likes to smoke a bowl from time to time."

"And beach lover?" asked Meredith. "Is that a soft reference to your Greenpeace background?"

"Right you are!" said Nadine. She re-read her headline: "Beach lover, 420-friendly." Then she looked at me. "What do you think, coach?"

"I think... I think it's pretty well done," I said, and I meant it.

"Hooray!" said Jimmy, waving the take-out menu in the air. "I'm already salivating!"

We ignored Jimmy; he wasn't the only one with a growling stomach.

Meredith read her headline next. "Emigrate to the coast!"

"Emigrate to the coast?" asked Nadine.

"Yessiree, Nadine. I want someone who's willing to move here. We need some fresh meat on the North Beach Peninsula!" said Merri. "Sylvia? What do you think?"

"I think it suits you," I said, somehow managing to keep a straight face.

"Two down and two to go!" said Jimmy.

"Mine's kind of religious," Goodie began.

"You didn't say he has to be a Catholic altar boy, did you?" asked Orpha.

"No," said Goodie. "I wrote 'Christian Woman Desires Companion.'"

"Companion?" said Nadine.

"Well, I don't think I want to get married again, and the word 'partner' sounds like I'm either gay, or want a partner in crime, or a partner to play Bridge, or something not as emotionally connected as the word 'companion.'" Goodie looked around for support.

"It's perfect," I said sincerely. "I think the essence of what you're looking for is very well stated."

Goodie beamed. "Thank you, Sylvia. I tried really hard."

"Three and one!" said Jimmy, apparently unaware that we could all keep score for ourselves.

Felicity sighed. "Any suggestions?" she asked the group.

"Intelligence is sexy!" said Orpha.

Everyone turned to look at her.

"What?" she asked, all innocent like. "I just used different words to say what she'd already written."

"And it still doesn't work," said Nadine, sparing me having to say it.

"How about, 'Smart woman wants smart man'?" asked

Meredith.

There was total silence as we pondered Merri's suggestion. Smart woman wants smart man. Simple. Direct. Honest.

"What do you think?" I asked Felicity, not wanting to push her into something she wasn't totally comfortable with.

Felix smiled and nodded. "I can live with that."

"Yippee!" yelled everyone in the group.

"Then it's settled," I said. "Who's ready to have Jimmy call in our lunch order?"

Jimmy already had the phone in his hand. "Hi Juan, this is Jimmy…. Fine, thank you… Yes, we're all here helping Meredith, Nadine, Goodie and Felicity get signed up for online dating… Uh-huh, just the four of them… Right!" Jimmy laughed at something Juan had said, and that we were not privy to. "We'd like four Number 4s and three Number 3s, please… Yes, and two sets of chopsticks; everyone but Sylvia and Felicity will be using forks.

"Or a shovel," said Orpha. "I'm starved."

"Uh-huh," continued Jimmy. "And maybe some extra fortune cookies in case someone gets a fortune they don't like." He laughed. "Yes Juan, as a matter of fact, they do add 'in bed' after they read them aloud." He laughed again. "Nope, I'm not telling them that." His eyes darted around the group as Juan continued speaking. "Fifteen minutes? Great! I've already got the car keys in my hand. See you soon."

With that, Jimmy hung up, waved goodbye, and went on out the door before we could try to pry what Juan had said about us out of him.

"Easy-peasy," said Orpha. "Even Goodie ordered right off the menu this time and didn't ask for all kinds of special treatment!"

Goodie glowered at Orpha, but it was Nadine who

answered. "Goodie is new to this. She just started liking Chinese food a few months ago, remember?"

How could any of us have forgotten? We were all at the restaurant after Mateo's funeral, and all but Felicity and I had gotten snockered on baijiu, the equivalent of Chinese vodka.

"Yes, of course I remember!" said Orpha. "Why do you all think I can't recall anything any more? First Goodie tried some egg flower soup, then some fried rice, and before you know it, she was enjoying the whole family style meal with the rest of us."

"It wasn't my fault," said Goodie. "Larry had never taken me out for Chinese food, and he convinced me I wouldn't like it."

"Men!" said Orpha.

"Men, indeed!" said Merri, lifting her coffee cup high into the air. "Don't you just love them?" She smiled. "That's why we're all here, right? Because we love men?"

The way Meredith got all dramatic and flamboyant as she said it earned her a chuckle from all of us.

"And all the meals are the same price, too," Goodie informed us. "So it will be easy to split the bill."

"Speaking of splitting the bill," said Orpha. "When my husband Bill died—"

No way did I want Orpha to start talking about her deceased husband Bill, so I quickly interrupted her. "Let's stay on track while Jimmy's gone, and see how much else we can get done. Did everyone bring a nice electronic picture to put on their profile?"

CHAPTER 4

Apparently my idea of a 'nice picture' came nowhere close to the ideas Merri, Nadine, and Goodie had for their profile photos, and Felicity's wasn't much better, but for an entirely different reason.

I don't normally consider myself a prude, and I'm rather proud of The Veiled Rainbow gals using belly dancing to stay in good shape. Nevertheless, I thought a photo of their beaded and bangled half-clothed body might just be a little too much for any serious-minded potential boyfriends.

On the other hand, if they were just looking for a good time, or a one-night stand— No! I couldn't bring myself to go there. That image I'd never be able to erase from my overactive imagination, so I stopped the thought right in its tracks before I could visualize any such thing!

I observed the photos they wanted to upload for all the world to see as I quietly took a lap around the table, looking over their shoulders. Now I returned to my chair and sat down.

"Um, Mom?" I began.

"Don't you love it?" Meredith exclaimed. She was fairly bouncing in her chair. "Raven took it last spring the night we did our dancing debut at the casino. I think it really captures the essence of my personality, don't you?"

Raven, the young woman who had interned as a reporter at the North Beach Tribune for a few months, had caused more grief than joy for the entire troupe when she'd jumped to conclusions about what she saw through her camera lens and wrote stories for the newspaper before getting all the facts straight. She was off pursuing a career as a physical therapist now, but obviously the influence of her photography skills lived on.

"It's very nice, Mother," I said, overemphasizing the word 'mother,' "but I think in these circumstances it sends the wrong message."

Meredith's lower lip came out just a fraction, but enough to know she was on the verge of pouting again. "You don't really like it do you?"

Her photo showed her doing some kind of a hip flip, her arms extended over her head, her back arched, her chest thrust forward, her coin belt and hair caught in mid-swirl. She was looking back at the camera, over her shoulder, with a gleam in her eye and what I would call a rather lewd and lascivious smile.

"It's not that I don't like it," I said carefully, "I just think that your first impression might attract what you're really looking for if it were a bit more, uh, demure."

Meredith laughed with her whole body. "Demure?" She looked around incredulously at each of her friends, her mouth agape, purposefully exaggerating her surprise. "Has anyone ever—I mean *ever*—used the word *demure* to describe *my* personality?" She didn't wait for an answer. She raised her arms above her head and did a chair shimmy. "What you see is what you get, baby cakes, and I'll not apologize for being a sensuous woman!"

Oh boy. For the fifth or sixth time today, I was second-guessing my volunteer role as their online profile navigator.

"So you don't like mine, or Goodie's photos either?" asked Nadine.

"Ladies! It's not that I don't like your pictures. You're all very unique and beautiful and lovely and charming and—"

"That's enough, dear," said Merri, reaching over and patting my hand. "We get it. You don't think we're putting our best foot forward by showing these men what we do for exercise."

Well, that was one way to put it.

"What about my picture?" asked Felicity.

Felicity had chosen a photo taken in her classroom, where she's sitting behind her desk, correcting a stack of papers. She has a red pen in her hand, and she's wearing the glasses she calls her "cheaters," looking out over the top of them at the school yearbook photographer who had been assigned to take "candid" pictures of the staff.

I cleared my throat. "For starters, your last name is visible on the placard on your desk."

"Oh!" said Felix. "I never even noticed that! This will never do."

Good. I wouldn't be forced to tell her what all else I didn't like about the picture, which struck me as the quickest way to keep any guy from ever, ever, and I mean *ever*, contacting her!

Fortunately, I had my phone handy, and I quickly took a photo of each of them that they all agreed was good enough for their profiles. Another bullet dodged! In short order, Meredith, Nadine, Goodie and Felix all had their photos uploaded and we could move on to the next hurdle, which theoretically would be the easiest.

"Next up is pretty simple," I began. "There are pull-down menus for each blank on the profile form, so you just have to choose from the list of responses available."

The blanks to fill in included city, ethnicity, astrological sign, education, profession, height, and age. The age was calculated automatically when you filled in your birthdate, which was not shared publicly.

The trouble started when I caught Meredith counting on her fingers. I leaned down and whispered in her ear. "Mom? What are you doing?"

"I have to figure out what year to put down as my birthdate so that my age corresponds."

I choked. "Are you ever planning on meeting any of these guys?"

She looked up at me and nodded.

"Then don't you think any relationship should start with honesty in all things?"

Merri glowered, but her lower lip stayed tucked in. "Do I have to?"

I shrugged. "Not really my business if you want to lie about your age."

"You know I act so much younger than anyone my age—"

"I know from my research that every other guy or gal on this site says exactly the same thing," I countered. "Everybody thinks they act young for their age, but really they don't."

"They don't?" asked Nadine.

"If you want to know what 80 looks like, Nadine, just look in the mirror." I didn't mean to be mean, but it was well past time for some brutal honesty.

Meredith pointedly sighed through her nose. "It's only a number, you know."

Goodie looked up from her keyboard. "If you're not admitting your true age, Merri, then Nadine and I will have to change ours, too, cause we're all born within a couple years of each other."

"So how much are we shaving off?" asked Nadine,

hopefully.

Orpha snorted. "And here's another reason I'm glad I'm not signing up for all this folderol. I could do better just sitting on a barstool and waiting for some drunk to buy me a drink!"

Naturally, we all laughed, but there was some truth to what Orpha had said.

"So do you all agree to be honest here, or are you all going to reinvent yourselves, as if the guys will never find out you lied?" I asked the group.

Felicity shook her head. "There's no way my age could ever stay a secret," she said. "Eventually, my deceit would be discovered. Driver's license, birthdays, eventual AARP membership, getting Social Security, etc. etc. Maybe you elder ladies could pull it off, but not me, and I don't think I'd want to begin any relationship based on falsehoods."

Orpha laughed. "How many years do you think I've gotten away with being 85?"

No one said a word. We'd long suspected Orpha had trimmed a few years off, but no one had ever really called her on it. When she claimed she would be in her 'mid-80s' until the day she died, we had all politely gone along with her.

"So how old are you, Orpha?" said Meredith.

"None of your damn business!" exclaimed Orpha, folding her arms across her chest as if to protect her secrets. "I'm not the one looking for online love!"

Fortunately for all concerned, Jimmy arrived with lunch, and the subject of age was dropped as we cleared off the table and helped him unload the big box of food.

Apparently, we had all worked up quite an appetite, and nobody said much of anything until we wolfed down a goodly portion of our Chinese meals, and it was Jimmy who finally broke the silence.

"So how far did you get?" he asked me. "Does everyone have their profiles up and running?"

"Nobody is 'going live' until I read and edit what they've written, and as of right now, they haven't started writing their bios," I replied.

"It's not all our fault," said Goodie. "Sylvia is just being overly cautious in the hopes we don't attract any online trolls or perverts."

I couldn't disagree.

"I think we can use this time to maybe talk about what kind of guys you do want to attract," I said. "What are you looking for, and what do you want to share about yourselves to eliminate men who aren't a good match?"

"Hmmm…" said Goodie. "Smart, funny, devout, financially secure…"

"And handsome," added Merri.

Our heads all snapped in her direction, but Goodie was the first to find her voice.

"Isn't that just a little shallow, Mermaid?"

"Shallow?" asked Meredith. "No, I don't think so. I just don't want to have to put a paper bag over his head when we're in bed."

I was extremely grateful none of us had a mouthful of food when she said that.

"I don't see anything wrong with wanting a partner to be easy on the eyes," said Orpha. "I think I'd be inclined to put 'sexually able and interested' if I were signing up."

Since it was Orpha who said that, we all took her words in stride. With old age comes some privileges, and getting away with saying such things was high on the privilege list.

"You can leave 'devout' off my list," said Nadine. "I don't much care what he believes in as long as he supports environmental issues and votes liberal. And of course, he has to either enjoy smoking pot, or be tolerant that I do."

Conversation, focusing on the 'relationship wish list' of the four women seeking companionship, continued until we finished lunch, and Jimmy passed out the fortune cookies.

"Remember!" piped up Orpha. "You have to add 'in bed' to the end of whatever your fortune cookie says."

Apparently, this was a game that went back generations, and I sat quietly while they all shared and laughed uproariously at their predicted futures in the bedroom.

"But what about your fortune?" asked Felicity.

"I think it's time you ladies all got back to writing your profiles." I hoped I sounded officious enough that they'd settle in to work right away, but it was only wishful thinking.

"Oh no you don't!" said Merri. She reached over and snatched my fortune out of my hand. Then she cleared her throat, and loudly read, "You will soon have to decide between two men."

"In bed!" yelled the rest of the group in unison. Then they laughed uproariously.

"That's *NOT* what it says!" I tried to grab the fortune from Meredith, but she clenched her fist around the slip of paper and smiled mischievously. How was I going to be able to restore some semblance of order, when they were all hooting and hollering? "That is most certainly *NOT* what my fortune cookie said! Merri made that up!"

"So who are you going to choose?" asked Orpha. "Freddy or Kanji?"

"Yes," said Merri, all sweet and innocent-like, "which one of them is better in bed?"

My face flaming, I tried to get my fortune back again by poking her with my chopstick.

"Assault!" yelled Merri. "You all saw it! My daughter just assaulted me with her chopstick! Oh my goodness!

Where's a cop when you need one?"

That got her desired laugh, but it still didn't solve my problem. That was NOT what my fortune cookie said, and I wanted to prove it. I looked to Jimmy for help, but he was just sitting there, smirking.

"Yes, Syl, please tell us," he said. "Which one? We're all wondering."

"You can forget me ever doing you another favor for the rest of your miserable little life," I hissed at him.

"Tell us! Tell us! Tell us!" Everyone in the group except Felicity started chanting.

Felix was apparently my last hope, but she, too, refused to come to my aid, so I held up both my hands and yelled, "Okay! Fine! You win!"

The room was instantly silent.

I took a deep breath and let it back out. "I honestly don't know."

"You don't know which one you're going to choose, or you don't know which one is better in bed?" asked Orpha.

"Orpha! That's personal!" said Merri.

At last, someone on my side. I admit I was surprised Merri would come to my aid, since she's the one who instigated this entire brouhaha, but I'll take any port in a storm.

But then she turned to me. "If you tell us which one you're choosing, we'll automatically know which one is better in bed!"

"Mom!" I looked from face to face as they all waited expectantly. "Fine." I sighed. "What you really want to know is if I've slept with both of them, isn't it?"

Not a word from the group. Not a giggle, not a squeak, not a sound. It was as if they were all collectively holding their breath.

I smiled. "A lady would never kiss and tell, and I suggest you could all do yourselves a favor and take a page from that handbook yourselves!"

I was being borderline rude, and I knew it, but what I'd said was all taken in good faith.

Meredith shrugged. "You win!" she said. "We'll mind our own business—for now—but if you don't stake a claim pretty soon, one of us might just swoop in and steal Kanji's heart while you're not paying attention."

I wasn't sure if she meant that as a blatant threat, or if it were just a mother's encouragement to make up my mind, already. And since it came from Meredith, who knew?

Fortunately, that interlude of food and laughter actually served to settle them all back down, and it didn't take nearly as long as I feared to get all four of them up and running with a fairly decent profile that shouldn't invite too many weirdos.

Merri, of course, was the only one I had to rein in. "Seriously?" I said reading over her shoulder. "You want to introduce yourself that way?"

My lowered voice got everyone's attention.

"Spill it," said Orpha. "What did you write that got Sylvia all up in arms?

Merri, our newly-named Mermaid, dramatically cleared her throat again. "Hair the color of sunlight dancing in the forest, eyes like warm milk chocolate, and a smile that heats up the coldest winter night."

Orpha and Nadine clapped enthusiastically.

"You're so poetic," said Goodie, admiringly.

Felix looked at me and shrugged. "She could have done worse."

"See?" said Merri, looking up at me hopefully. "Felicity said it was ok."

"Fine," I said, not wanting to argue further. "Whatever."

Jimmy caught my eye, smiled, nodded, and pushed his glasses up with his middle finger. "What comes next?"

"Now comes the fun part," I said. "Now you all get to see who's out there in the ether world, just waiting to meet you!"

Orpha scooted her chair in closer, so she could look over Nadine's shoulder, Jimmy was poised between Goodie and Felicity, and I figured I'd have my hands full just keeping an eye on what trouble Meredith might be able to stir up.

After a few minutes of silence, Felicity spoke first. "I think some of these guys aren't really trying," she said. "Have you noticed how empty their profiles are?"

"Uh-huh," said Merri. "A lot of them simply write 'I'll fill this in later.'"

"Or they put 'Ask me anything you want to know'," said Nadine.

"Quite a few just write 'I don't like talking about myself'," added Goodie.

Meredith lifted her head from peering at her laptop screen and looked around the table. "Are we all looking at the same bunch of guys?"

"Did you all set your preferred distance at less than 25 miles?" I asked.

All four heads bobbed up and down.

"And what did you set for preferred age range?" I asked.

Naturally, they all spoke at once, and I couldn't make heads or tails out of what they were saying. "Let's go around the table, starting with Lexi here."

"Well," said Felix, after she took a moment to realize I was speaking to her, "I decided to set the range from 7 years younger to 7 years older than I am. Do you think that's okay, or is it too broad?"

"I think it's perfect. Thank you." I gave her a supportive grin, then turned to Goodie. "How about you, GiGi?"

Goodie frowned thoughtfully. "Well, I'm 77, so I put 67-82, that's 10 years younger, but only five years older. I'm thinking if he's 82, he better be able to keep up with me! I'm not signing up to be a 24/7 caregiver."

Nadine and Meredith nodded their approval.

"Already been there and done that," said Merri. "I was a nurse both at home and at work."

"Now you're a nurse with a purse!" said Orpha. "That insurance money ought to come in right handy when you're trying to woo a new beau, Mermaid. You ought to have to beat them off with a stick! They'll be lining up for a gal like you!"

I didn't want to rain on anyone's parade, but from the guys I'd checked out during my stint as advance researcher, they'd all be lucky to find even one decent guy to date who resided anywhere within the immediate area.

"Deenie?" I said. "You're up."

"Well, since Goodie and I are closest in age," said Nadine, "I've put down the same range that she put. Is that a problem?"

"Not necessarily," I began, "but let's hear from our Mermaid before we do any tweaking to our preferred age settings."

"Simple," said Merri, "45 to 95."

Her surprising proclamation was met with silence. Dead silence. The kind of silence in which you're hoping it's not up to you to say something, but you're afraid it is.

"Um… Mom?... That's a 50-year age span."

"Yeah? So? What of it?" said Merri, sitting up taller in her chair and putting her hands on her hips, as if she were daring me to tell her she had to change it.

"You'll need to adjust that," I said quietly.

"Why?" she asked, knowing perfectly well she was

pushing most of my buttons.

"Get 'em young, so you can raise them right!" piped up Orpha, sounding a lot like Mercedes telling me to do that with Freddy.

"Because..." I began. "Because you're encroaching on the same men Felicity might be interested in." It was a weak excuse, but I couldn't very well tell her what I thought of her 'any guy with a warm body and a pulse will do' attitude.

Meredith looked first at Felicity, then back to me. "Oh, I'm so sorry... I didn't realize... How about I set it for 55 to 85? Will that make everyone happy?"

"Then there's still three of us in competition for all the same guys between here and Fort George," said Nadine.

"You could arm wrestle for them," said Orpha.

I was beginning to think I should have sent Orpha home with Nova.

"Let's cast a wider net," I said. "You three, change your distance settings to 150 miles. That way it's less likely you'll be tripping over each other for dating opportunities."

"But I don't want to drive 150 miles to meet someone," said Goodie.

"You won't have to," said Meredith. "You can meet halfway the first time, then decide if you want to see them again. And if you do, then you might be lucky enough to get a boyfriend who likes spending time at the coast, along with a house you can stay in that's closer to a big city. Sounds perfect to me!"

Goodie nodded. "I never thought of it that way."

"Importing fresh meat is good," said Meredith. "I'd like to find one from Portland."

"You only say that because you've dated all the men who'd have you on the whole peninsula already," said Orpha, "whether they were single or married!"

On second thought, Orpha could be good for our comic relief, as she often said aloud what many of us were thinking to ourselves. Not having to have a filter on my mouth was something I looked forward to when I was her age—whatever that was.

Felicity sighed, then got up from her chair to stretch and walk around a little. "I think I need a break. The guys' profiles are all starting to sound the same. Long walks on the beach, yada-yada."

I followed her over to the carpeted living area and we both sat down on the couch.

"You okay?" I asked her.

"Well, quite frankly, I'm disappointed. I'm really serious about finding someone compatible, but all the profiles I've been reading are full of poor spelling, poor grammar, poor punctuation and capitalization, incomplete sentences—" She sighed again. "Some of them don't even put a picture on their profile. Are they hiding something? Are they married, and just looking for a little something on the side? Are there any good ones out there, or did most of them get married at 18 and stayed that way?"

"Wow," I said. "That's a lot to think about, and I'm glad you're doing that. But have heart, there must be a few who'd be good for a practice date or two."

"Practice date?"

"Honey, they're all practice—until they're not." I reached out and rubbed my hand back and forth across her back. "You just never know when the oyster will turn out to have a pearl inside."

Felix laughed. "I thought you were going to tell me I'd have to kiss a lot of frogs to find a prince."

"That, too!" I laughed with her. "Have you found one you kind of think might be good practice for you? I know you haven't dated in a while, so it might be a good idea to just jump in and get your feet wet. Try not to overthink it."

Felicity laughed again, then stood up from the couch to return to the table. "You make it sound so simple, but you're right. It's time to just pick one and see how the date plays out."

"That's the spirit!" said Orpha from her position at the end of the table. "Get out there and put your line in the water, Lexi!"

For an old broad, there was certainly nothing wrong with Orpha's hearing.

CHAPTER 5

By group consensus, Felicity chose to contact a man who went by the less-than-attractive screen name of "O-fer." In his favor, O-fer was local, he was age appropriate, and he was employed. In his photo he was wearing a suit and tie, and his smile, which was a little too big and too goofy, according to Meredith, seemed to light up his whole profile page.

"This is the spaghetti approach to dating," said Orpha, bobbing her head enthusiastically, and hoping to encourage Felix. "You throw a noodle against the wall and see what sticks."

Meredith harrumphed. "I'm sure Felicity is looking for a lot more than a limp noodle, Orpha."

"Aren't we all?" Nadine muttered under her breath.

"I'm just saying," insisted Orpha. "You have to try on a lot of shoes to find a comfortable fit."

"So now we're back to the stone ages and the prince is out looking for Cinderella's foot to fit the glass slipper?" teased Merri.

"Whoa there!" Felix shook her head as if to clear it. "Enough with all the analogies, mixed metaphors, and unsolicited advice, already! I'm not looking for oysters with pearls, frogs who are princes, princes with glass slippers, or spaghetti for lunch!"

Her uncharacteristic outburst was met with stunned

silence. Even Jimmy, who was usually quick to pick up the torch of banter, had no glib retort to bounce back at her.

Felix took a deep breath, forcefully blew it out, and continued in a much softer tone. "I'm just looking for one guy nice enough to have a conversation with over coffee. Got it?"

Properly chastised, we all murmured some form of assent.

Nadine broke the tension with one more bit of practical information. "First dates are usually kind of weird anyway, Felix, so make sure you're comfortable with where you'll meet him. Make sure it's a very public place."

"And check ahead of time to make sure they have good coffee!" said Merri.

Felicity, back to her good-natured self, thanked them all for caring so much. It was already late afternoon, and I directed the remaining three dating site subscribers to keep looking through the profiles at home, but not to contact anyone until we met again the following Saturday.

Meredith loudly complained that she didn't want to wait a whole 'nother week to meet one of these guys, but Nadine countered that another week wasn't going to kill any of them, and if it did, then there'd be more men left for the other two.

That seemed to placate Merri, and she brightened considerably when I reminded her that by next Saturday morning, with any luck, Felicity would have had a first date with O-fer and we could all look forward to hearing a detailed report.

The ladies left first, and I stayed for a little while to help Jimmy put away the folding chairs and wash the coffee cups. By the time I left the Clamshell, I felt like I'd put in a very hard day at the office, and I decided to stop on the way home for a burger to go. On impulse, I ordered a strawberry shake as well. After all, I'd certainly earned it!

My cell phone rang while I was still sitting on the wooden bench inside the High Tide ordering area, reading all the business cards tacked to the bulletin board. Since my phone display screen showed it was Felicity, and not some telemarketer trying to catch me at dinnertime, I was happy to answer it.

"Sylvia! You'll never believe what happened!" said Felix.

"Try me," I replied, already knowing by the excitement in her voice what she was going to say, but allowing her the added joy of saying it herself.

"Well, I did just as you said, Syl. After I dropped Orpha off at her apartment, I came home and wrote O-fer a short message. I said I thought he wrote a nice profile, and since we were both here on the North Beach Peninsula, I'd be interested in meeting him for a cup of coffee."

"And?" I prompted her while she caught her breath.

"*And* we're going to the Rusty Rudder for dinner next week! Can you believe it? I have a date! Seriously! I have a date! I. Have. A. Date. Can you believe it?"

Well, no, I couldn't believe a guy she hadn't met yet was willing to spring for a nice dinner on the very first date, but I wasn't about to say that out loud!

"That's truly wonderful, Sexy Lexi," I teased her. "So what are you going to wear?"

Meanwhile, Nadine had gone home and had immediately tweaked her profile to make sure any prospective suitors would know, without a doubt, that she was a dyed-in-the-wool environmental activist who loved smoking a little weed to relax.

Meredith, on the other hand, had gone home and changed her main profile image back to the one she'd originally wanted to post where she's wearing her red spangled belly-dancing costume. She was proud of her looks and her fitness level and she'd be danged if she was going to let her daughter dictate what she could and could not do on her own profile page!

And as long as she was going to go rogue, Merri decided she might as well change her preferred date's age range too. She clicked on 45 again as the lower age, but had second thoughts about that 95 she'd checked while they were over at the Clamshell.

A 50-year range really was quite a spread, so she changed it to 75 as the upper limit. That way, the men wouldn't think she'd be happy with just anyone, and she was hoping that the guys would take a hint from her photo that she was the type who liked to dance the night away.

Goodie had also gone home and immediately booted up her laptop. She was excited to continue looking through the men's profiles. There hadn't been anything like this back when she was young, or, now that she thought about it, when any of them had been young, except maybe Felicity, who was still on the shorter side of middle aged.

Goodie had her list of 'relationship requirements' firmly in mind, and she knew what she didn't want, as well as what she did want.

"Nope. Nope. Nope. Nope," she muttered to herself, as she found something undesirable and/or irreconcilable in each profile she read. "Nope. Nope. Nope. Nope."

Goodie sighed. "What's the use!" she said aloud. At the sound of her voice, Hans, the ancient German Shepherd she'd brought home from the Humane Society to temporarily foster, left his hiding place in the closet and laid at her feet. She reached down and gave him a good scratching between his ears.

"Did you come out to give me some moral support?" she asked him. His tail thumped twice on the floor. Goodie smiled. *If he were a cat, he'd be purring about now,* she thought. She moved her hand on down his back, scratching the length of him, then gently tugging on his tail.

Hans had been found abandoned in a house where the tenants had skipped out without paying months of overdue rent. Apparently, they also hadn't had the money to keep feeding a dog of this size, either, and he was brought into the shelter by the kind and gentle-hearted landlord in a semi-starved condition.

The poor dog was frightened, weak, and extremely timid, and Goodie's heart had immediately gone out to him. She named him Hans, and decided on the spot to foster him, allowing him time to rehabilitate and become more social and outgoing.

When Hans chose the bottom of the coat closet as his "safe place," Goodie understood, and left the door propped open for him to come and go from there as he pleased. It was going to take some time to get him to trust humans again.

Turning back to her computer screen, Goodie clicked on the next profile. "Might as well check out a few more of these men," she said to Hans. "Miracles do happen."

And as luck would have it, the very next profile gave Goodie a good reason to sit up and pay attention. "Listen to this, Hans," she said. "He lives in Portland, but he loves spending time on the coast. He says he's a God-fearing man who regularly attends church. He loves animals. He doesn't smoke or drink. He's 70—" Goodie paused, and looked down at Hans. "He's 70, Hans. Do you think that's close enough to my age?"

Hans dutifully replied with a few more solid tail thumps.

"Yes, I thought so too." Goodie took a deep breath. "It's

not a very good picture, though. I can't really see his face. He's turned sideways to the camera and he's got a beard." She sighed. "What do you think, Hans? Shall I put this guy on my favorite's list?"

At the sound of his name, Hans again thumped his tail twice more, and softly whined.

"I'll take that as a 'yes'," said Goodie.

Goodie was in the kitchen fixing dinner for both Hans and herself when she heard her email notification bell. She set Hans' food bowl on the mat next to his water, wiped her hands on a dish towel, and went back into the living room to check her messages.

"Oh my gosh, Hans!" said Goodie excitedly. "It's from the man I just put on my Favorites list!" She read his message, then thought for a few minutes before carefully typing a few lines back to the man who used the screen name 'Danny Boy.'

"This is it, Hans." She giggled. "Sylvia never said one cotton-picking thing about not replying to a guy who wrote to me first. She only said not to initiate contact." She giggled again. "Are you ready, Hans? I'm pressing the Send button!"

Goodie and Danny exchanged several emails over the next few days. He told her that he'd been able to see that she had put him on her 'Favorites' list, and that he hadn't been patient enough to wait for her to contact him first.

By the following Friday, Goodie felt she was brave enough to meet him for lunch "halfway," at Pier 19, a waterfront restaurant over in Fort George. Fort George was really a lot closer to her house than his, but being a gentleman, he said he didn't mind driving a little farther in order to have a face-to-face conversation.

Goodie arrived at the restaurant, found a parking spot right out on the dock next to the entry door, and nervously went inside. There were no men already there sitting alone, so she got a table for two on the lower level, with an expansive view of the Columbia River.

"Would you care for a glass of wine?" asked the waiter.

"Wine?" said Goodie, "Oh, no, thank you, I'd better not." She nervously giggled. "But I'd love some unsweetened iced tea."

"Very well," said the waiter, and he quietly retreated.

Goodie looked out over the sun-sparkled water. Upriver, a few ocean-going vessels were moored. She wondered if they were coming or going, if they were waiting for the tide to change, or for a bar pilot to take them safely out to sea, or if they had simply put down anchor to rest for a day or two and take on more supplies. Downriver, she could see the mammoth four-mile long bridge, nicknamed "The Bridge to Nowhere," connecting Oregon to Washington.

"Excuse me," said a deep male voice.

Goodie, who'd been lost in her thoughts, visibly jumped in her seat. Then she looked up into a very handsome man's bearded face and managed a tentative smile, despite her scare, but was suddenly struck mute and unable to figure out what she was supposed to say. She really should have rehearsed a little on the way over.

"I'm so sorry. Please forgive me. I didn't mean to startle you." Danny touched her on the shoulder. "Are you GiGi?"

"Yes," she breathed, finally finding her voice. "Please sit down." She motioned to the chair across from her. She noted that his eyes were watering and wondered if perhaps he had allergies, like Larry had to animals, but that wasn't something she needed to know right at the moment. If they decided to see each other again, there'd be plenty of time for those kinds of questions.

Goodie smiled as Danny took his seat. "I was just considering whether I preferred the view looking upriver to the east, or downriver, to the west."

Danny sat in the chair across from her and smiled broadly. "I kind of like the view I have right now," he said, intently looking deep into her eyes.

Goodie momentarily considered that maybe she should have ordered some wine after all, as the butterflies took flight in her stomach and made her nerves a little unsteady. She couldn't remember ever swooning in her life, but there was always a first time.

The waiter came with an iced tea, and set it before Goodie. Danny said he'd like an iced tea as well, and the waiter recited the daily lunch specials as he handed them their menus.

"Have you eaten here before?" Danny asked Goodie.

"Oh yes," said Goodie. "That's why I chose this place to meet. The food is very good."

"Then what do you recommend?" he asked.

If I were as bold as Merri, thought Goodie, *I'd recommend we skip lunch and head straight for the nearest motel.*

Goodie's thoughts, the ones her priest would have to hear about in confession next week, made her nervously giggle again, and Danny asked her what it was she found so amusing.

"I was just thinking that you can't really go wrong." She quickly covered. "Everything I've eaten here has always been absolutely wonderful."

Once the ice had been broken, they chatted amicably through a leisurely lunch. Danny told her he lived in a nice apartment in northwest Portland, very close to the very same river they were watching go by right now. Goodie replied that she owned her own home in Tinkerstown. When Danny told her he'd been divorced for several decades, Goodie, in turn, told him she'd been widowed about a year, and that her husband had died from complications due to Alzheimer's. This wasn't the time to tell him all about Larry thinking he could walk out to Elk Island, and getting stuck in the mud on the way out there and drowning. Some things were better left unsaid.

And Goodie was proud of the fact that she hadn't told Danny anything about her husband's generous life insurance policy, either. No way was the sheriff going to be mad at her for disclosing too much about her financial status.

By the end of their meal, the two of them were getting along well enough that they even decided to split a decadent dessert. The thick slab of chocolate fudge cake was placed in the middle of the table and the waiter handed them each a dessert fork. Goodie thought for a moment that she might be in heaven, and it had little to do with the cake. But still, there was something niggling at the back of her brain.

"Danny?" she asked softly between bites of chocolate fudge cake, vanilla ice cream, and topped with a swirl of chocolate sauce and plenty of whipped cream, "May I ask you something?"

"Ask away," said Danny, without the slightest hesitation. He took another bite of dessert and licked his lips in a way that came across as totally seductive.

"You look so young," said Goodie. "What's your secret?"

Danny set down his fork, and sighed. "I'm afraid I have a confession to make, GiGi."

Goodie's stomach knotted into a tight ball, and she, too, set down her fork. "A confession?" She wondered if it was also something her priest would soon need to hear about.

"Yes. When I filled out my profile, my clumsy fingers accidentally hit a 7 instead of a 6, and I didn't notice my mistake until it was too late to change it."

Goodie looked thoughtful. "So you're really 60 and not 70?"

"That's correct."

"Well," said Goodie, taking a deep breath, "I *didn't* hit the wrong number, and I'm really 77, so that's a 17-year age difference."

Danny smiled. "I did the math before I agreed to drive from Portland to meet you, GiGi. I actually prefer more mature women, and may I say, you look extremely fit for your age."

Goodie blushed. "It's the belly dancing that keeps me in shape."

"Yes, the belly dancing," said Danny, smiling. "It intrigued me no end when I read about that in your profile." He reached over and took her hand. "But back to the age difference…"

Goodie realized she was holding her breath.

"I sincerely hope that silly clerical error of mine won't dissuade you from seeing me again," he said, his brown eyes looking deeply into hers.

Boy howdy! If Meredith could only see me now! thought Goodie.

She cleared her throat. "As long as we're making confessions," she said, "I'd prefer in the future you'd call me Goodie and not GiGi."

Danny smiled ear to ear. "Thank you," he said, "both for forgiving me, and for trusting me enough to tell me your real name." He squeezed her hand. "Danny is my real name, by the way. Danny Smith. And before you ask, I'm not Irish. My mother loved the song Danny Boy so much, she just decided to name me Danny."

Happily, they both picked up their forks and finished dessert.

When the waiter brought the bill, Danny reached for his wallet and suddenly looked stricken. "Oh my gosh!" he said, "In my haste to leave Portland, I must have left my wallet sitting on the dresser! Oh my goodness, this is so embarrassing!"

Goodie shook her head and reached for her purse. "Please don't give it another thought," she said, "I have plenty of money." She pulled one of several platinum cards from her wallet and set it on the tray with the bill without even checking the amount. "You can buy next time."

"Agreed," said Danny, with a sigh of relief. "And thank you." He reached over and gave her hand another squeeze.

Ever the gentleman, Danny walked her to her car, took the keys from her hand, and opened the driver's door for her. But before she could get in, he took her by the wrist, and in one smooth motion pulled her, almost roughly, but in a good way, straight into his arms.

Dangerously close, Goodie tilted her head to look up into his handsome face, and his deep brown eyes, and she involuntarily held her breath again, not daring to hope for what she hoped would come next.

"Honey," Danny said huskily, pulling her still tighter against his chest, "If you haven't been expecting this kiss, you haven't been paying attention." And then he bent his head and covered her lips with his, and if he hadn't been holding her so tightly, Goodie was sure her knees would have buckled beneath her.

His kiss was at first soft, and surprisingly tender, yet his tongue sought for her to allow him deeper access, which she willingly gave. Somewhere in the back of her mind, Goodie was thinking she might not go to confession this week after all, so she could hang on to this delicious moment, without any guilt, for just a little while longer.

When he finally broke the kiss off, Goodie looked around, momentarily disoriented. "Where's your car?" she asked, desperately grasping for a safe topic.

Danny released his grip on her and pointed to a dark-colored Lexus a few spots away. "It's right over there," he said, "but I think I'd better go back in and use the restroom before I start the drive home." He settled Goodie in her car, then leaned in and gave her a kiss on the cheek. "Drive safely, Goodie dearest."

Had Goodie been the suspicious type, she would have waited nearby for him to come back out and drive away. But Goodie wasn't thinking about anything but the way her heart was wildly pounding, and the tickle on her cheek from his beard as she headed back across the bridge.

Danny scanned the area for her sea green Toyota Corolla when he returned to the parking lot. He'd changed out of his slacks and button-down shirt in the bathroom and now wore a comfortable pair of jeans, a sweatshirt, leather chaps, and a vest. He had a backpack of his good clothing slung across one shoulder. Not seeing Goodie's car anywhere around, he deemed the coast was clear, walked over and straddled the seat of an older motorcycle, and kickstarted the machine into life.

Danny smiled as he strapped on his battered helmet. He looked forward to the ride home along the river almost as much as he looked forward to seeing Goodie again. Perhaps next time, if he played his cards right, the rich old widow would let her guard down a little more and invite him to her home, where he would reel her in, hook, line, and sinker.

CHAPTER 6

Saturday morning, I decided to splurge a little and treat the group gathering at the Clamshell to a large box of assorted donuts from the Buoy 10 Bakery and some freshly ground coffee from the Sandy Bottom Coffee Cup. The service was quick and efficient at the bakery, but at the Sandy Bottom, it took more time than I'd hoped to purchase a pound of their North Beach Blend.

"Is this for the big online dating meeting over at Jimmy's today?" asked Bim, a co-owner of the coffee shop and the barista working the front counter today.

It didn't surprise me that she knew the who, the what, and the why of the meeting. The Sandy Bottom is a primary stop on the peninsula grapevine, and in our small towns, there are virtually no secrets. Hoping she would be satisfied with a simple acknowledgement and hurry with my order, I nodded, and murmured "Uh-huh," but offered no additional information.

Not to be dissuaded, Bim offered some information of her own, and then asked a question that couldn't be answered with a nod, shrug, or single word. "Sheriff Donaldson is none too happy about The Veiled Rainbow putting themselves out there with what he calls the 'unknown quantities' they're meeting on the Internet. How do the ladies feel about him directing an undercover cop to tail them on their dates?"

Had I been drinking coffee at that moment, I would have spewed it all over the display stand by the cash register. "Don't believe everything you hear, Bim."

"But the sheriff said it himself," she insisted.

"But the sheriff doesn't have the budget or the manpower to actually do such a thing," I countered. And in my heart of hearts, I certainly hoped that was true. Most likely, Sheriff D had purposefully proclaimed that the dates were all under surveillance so that the word would get out that nobody had better try anything 'funny' with the ladies. It was a reasonable ploy, given the situation, and I almost smiled at the sheriff's strategy.

Bim finished bagging up the coffee, and I paid and left as quickly as I could. If the ladies had gotten wind of this rumor, it was sure to be one hot topic at the meeting this morning, and I didn't want to miss a minute of it. I hopped into my mustang and it's possible I might have driven a few miles over the speed limit on the way north. Fortunately, I didn't run into Sheriff D during my three-mile sprint, or I might have had to give him a good piece of my mind.

I was last to arrive at the Clamshell, and since I'd called Jimmy from the bakery to tell him to hold off on making any coffee until I got there, the ladies were all trying to function without caffeine. Well, function as best as could be expected.

"About time," glowered Meredith.

"Good morning to you, too, Mother," I replied.

"What took you so long?" asked Nadine.

"Now, now," said Goodie. "Let's all practice a little forgiveness, girls."

"Hallelujah!" said Orpha. "Syl brought donuts!"

Jimmy hurriedly put on a pot of 'the good stuff' while I passed out two paper towels to each of the ladies—one to use as a plate and the other as a napkin. Like vultures to a road kill, they immediately converged on the box of pastries.

Between bites of my apple fritter, I realized one of the rainbow gals was missing. "Did Nova decide not to join us anymore?" I asked.

"She went with Rich to a Northwest Sportsmen's Show in Portland," said Nadine.

"Oohhh…" Several in the group knowingly nodded and smiled.

"I knew it!" said Orpha, slapping her hand on the table. "I just knew those two would get together sooner or later! They have so much in common!"

Our coffee cups full, and our stomachs filled with enough sugar to keep the hangries at bay, we eagerly reconvened.

"I noticed when I came in that you were glowing," I said to Felix. "I take it things went well with you this week?"

Felicity grinned from ear to ear. "Much better than I ever imagined," she said, "but not in the way you think."

Intrigued, I immediately hushed the group so we could hear all the juicy details of Felicity's first date adventure with O-fer.

"It's about time," Orpha piped up. "All the way here from Unity, I kept asking her questions and she kept saying she wanted to tell the story just once!"

"There's nothing wrong with that," said Goodie.

"But I'm old!" said Orpha. "And age should have some privilege! What if I'd died on the way here? What if I never found out about her new hottie?"

Her protests were met with more knowing smiles and nods, and since she couldn't find a single one of us to agree with her, she gave up and took another donut to pick at.

"So, Felicity," I began. Then I smiled at her fondly. "Or should we call you Lexi?"

"Felicity is fine," she said, her face slightly flushed. "Orville Anderson and I both came clean right away about our real names."

"Well, you couldn't very well call him O-fer in public," said Meredith.

Meredith's statement prompted Jimmy to jump in with his own question. "So what does O-fer stand for, anyway?"

Felicity sighed. "Apparently, *Orville* has been trying to find a girlfriend on Sole Mates for a very long time. A few weeks ago, he was so discouraged he changed his screen name to O-fer because he was O for 22 in getting a second date."

"Oh dear," I said sympathetically. "Was he really that bad?"

"Let's have her start at the beginning," said Orpha. "I want to hear all about the date, step by step, inch by inch, moment by moment. I'm living the wild life vicariously, you know."

The others readily agreed, not with vicariously living, but with wanting a full-blown account, and Jimmy came around to top off our coffee as Felix began.

"I got to the Rusty Rudder about five minutes before 5 o'clock," said Felix. "And I got a seat across from the bar—you know, up the step to the little alcove in the back—so our conversation would be a little more private."

We all nodded; the restaurant was one of our favorites, and we knew it well.

"Don't they call that the lover's corner?" asked Orpha.

Felicity blushed. "Yes, well, I didn't see that sign on the wall until later, when O-fer—I mean Orville—happened to mention it."

I'd made the same mistake myself with Rich a few months ago, but now was not the time for sympathetic disclosure.

"Orville works till 5," continued Felix. "But he said he'd come straight from work, and since he worked almost right across the street, we agreed we'd meet a few minutes after the hour."

"Makes sense," said Orpha. Apparently, she thought it was her job to comment on every single thing Felicity told us.

"He works across the street?" asked Jimmy. "Where? At the bank, or the optometrist's, or that place that fixes roofs, or…" He abruptly stopped talking. "Why don't I just let you tell your story without interrupting?"

"Great idea," said Merri.

Felicity nodded. "You were in the right neighborhood, Jimmy. The next business along the highway is the mortuary."

Merri, Goodie, Nadine, Jimmy, and I all gasped.

"Ain't that a pip?" said Orpha. "He'll never be unemployed!"

Felix smiled. "Well, that's certainly one way to look at it."

"But he was wearing a suit in his profile photo," said Merri. "We all assumed he was in his work clothes."

"Not exactly true." Felix chuckled. "Orville had borrowed the suit jacket from the wardrobe at the mortuary for his picture."

"They have a wardrobe at the mortuary?" asked Nadine.

"Well, as Orville explained it, they have suit jackets available that are spit up the back, which they tuck around the corpses of the men who are going to be cremated after the public viewing, which takes place in a borrowed casket."

I nearly choked on my coffee. "At what point did you tell him this was way too much information?"

"I hope you had him pay for dinner before you bolted for the door," said Merri.

"So what did he wear to dinner?" asked Goodie.

"Coveralls," said Felix, choosing to answer Goodie's question first. "They were fairly clean coveralls, but he admitted he'd driven the white mortuary van straight to the restaurant from his 'worksite,' and I did notice he had a little dirt under his fingernails."

Goodie shivered, and looked at me. "That really *is* too much information."

"He brought me flowers." Felicity must have felt she needed to defend poor O-fer.

"Flowers?" Now it was Meredith's turn to choke. "Did you consider where he had most likely gotten those flowers?"

"Eeewwww!" said Goodie. "That's horrible!"

The look on Felicity's face told me that no, she had not considered where or how her bouquet might have served before they were repurposed and given to her.

"What day did you meet him?" asked Nadine.

"What?" asked Felix, confused by what she thought was an abrupt change of subject. "We had dinner on Tuesday. Why?"

"I thought so." Nadine nodded. "Thelma Olson's funeral was on Tuesday afternoon, so maybe those flowers were hers first."

Felicity's face was turning paler by the moment.

"I'm not so sure recycling funeral flowers is a bad thing," said Jimmy, trying to throw Felix a lifeline. "And if it makes you feel any better, I'm positive Mrs. Olson won't miss them."

"Forget about the flowers for a minute, Lexi." I hoped I could salvage this date review gone south by gleaning some useful information for all of us. "Did Orville truthfully represent himself in his profile?"

"Well, it didn't say he was a mortician's assistant," said Felix.

"And you didn't say you were a teacher," I countered. "Was his age correct?"

"Oh! Yes, it was. He even showed me his driver's license so I'd know for sure his real name." Felicity seemed to regain a bit of her composure, but then scowled. "But he had put down 'some college' as his level of education, and he's only taken one class at the community college in Fort George, and that was on how to make home beer and wine."

"A very handy skill," Orpha said cheerfully.

Felix ignored her. "And the height on his profile was definitely wrong."

"How do you know?" asked Goodie.

"Because his profile said he was five foot eight, but when we walked out of the Rusty Rudder, we were eyeball to eyeball, and I'm only five-five."

"Pish-posh," said Meredith. "All men lie about their height. That's a given. They lie about their height and they lie about the length of their—"

"*Mom!*"

"Well, they do, dear," said Merri, shrugging. "Men are such sensitive little creatures."

"Are you going to see him again?" asked Nadine.

"Actually, he's not such a bad guy, but no, we won't be dating." She paused, and looked thoughtfully around the group. "I told him it was nice to meet him, but that I didn't think we were such a good match, and he readily agreed. He said I was very nice, but he actually preferred much older women." She shrugged. "He asked if I had any older, more established friends I could introduce him to."

"How much older?" asked Orpha.

I detected a bit of a lilt in Orpha's voice when she asked that, but Merri squashed any hope Orpha might have had of becoming a genuine cougar.

"He's probably got a Mommy Complex," said Merri. She exaggeratedly shuddered. "Those kind of men give me the creeps."

Felicity laughed. "I suppose that's possible, but he just wasn't at all what I'm looking for."

"That's why they call it dating," I countered. "Although they could call it shopping, I guess. Anyway, you're one down, and lots to go."

Felix shrugged again and turned to Goodie. "When I got home, I started considering getting a companion cat for Walter," she said. "And I thought I'd name him Two-fer."

That got the desired laugh out of all of us, but I still thought Felicity was a little too cheerful for a woman who'd come up empty after what she thought might be a promising date.

"Time to get your line back in the water," said Orpha. "There's sure to be another guy out there just waiting for you to reel him in."

"Maybe you just didn't use the right bait," said Meredith. "What did you wear?"

"It wasn't about what she wore," I interjected. "It just wasn't a good match!"

"You're not going to give up, are you?" asked Nadine.

"Did anyone notice that I didn't bring my iPad today?" asked Felicity.

"Oh dear," said Goodie. "That's not a good sign."

"Actually, it's a very good sign," said Felix, now grinning again from ear to ear.

"Alright, Felix, it's time you told us what's really going on," I said.

"I met someone," Felicity began.

"When did that have time to happen?" asked Meredith, her penciled-on eyebrows shooting up toward her hairline.

"At the staff meeting on Wednesday morning," replied Felicity. "The principal announced that due to the fall high school student enrollment exceeding projections, we were able to hire another teacher."

"You mean to tell us that Magpie hired an age-appropriate single male teacher for you?" asked Jimmy incredulously.

"Jimmy, the principal's name is Margaret Anderson," said Felicity. "And nobody's called her Magpie since you were in high school."

"Anderson?" asked Goodie. "Any relation to Orville?"

"As it turns out, the answer is yes," said Felix. "Orville is Margaret's son."

"Wow!" said Nadine. "Small world."

"You mean small peninsula," corrected Merri. "That's why we have to look farther afield and plan on importing some new men. The peninsula's all tapped out."

"You should know," said Orpha. "You're the one who tapped it out."

"Now that I think about it," Jimmy said quickly, to keep Merri from attacking Orpha's comment. He pushed his glasses up with his middle finger. "I think Orville graduated just a year or two ahead of me."

"And you didn't think to tell Felicity about it before now?" asked Goodie.

"Hey, cut me some slack," said Jimmy. "I didn't know his name until today."

"Oh, right," said Goodie. "Sorry."

"But once you heard it, you still didn't say anything," I said. "It's not like there are a whole lot of Orville Andersons, you know."

Jimmy shrugged. "It's water under the bridge now, anyway." Turning to Felicity, he said, "So tell us about this new teacher."

Felicity blushed. "His name is Mark, and I have my first date with him tonight. Only we're not calling it a date. It's more like I'm helping him acclimate to the North Beach Peninsula. He's divorced, but that's okay. I can't expect a guy in his mid-40s to have never been married."

"I'm sincerely happy for you," said Goodie.

"Thank you, Goodie. I've deactivated my Sole Mates profile—for the time being—and we'll just have to wait and see how this turns out."

And with that, Felicity abruptly picked up her car keys and left the building, calling out over her shoulder, "Tootle-loo! And best wishes, everyone!"

The door had barely closed when Orpha crowed, "Hot diggity-dog! This online dating thing really works! One down, three to go!"

"Well," said Goodie tentatively, picking at her cruller and not meeting anyone's eyes, "maybe there's actually two down and just two to go."

All heads whirled in her direction.

"What are you saying?" I asked her. "Didn't we all agree you three would just look through the profiles, perhaps mark a few favorites, and we'd put our heads together and vet them before anyone met in person?"

"To vet," said Jimmy, "is to make critical and careful examination."

"You mean the way you all vetted O-fer?" asked Goodie.

She had us there, but I wanted to argue that it was different for Felicity and O-fer, as Felicity was not elderly, not wealthy, and not prone to making rash decisions. I wanted to argue that, but I didn't. Instead, I said, "So who did you meet, Goodie?"

"And where?" asked Jimmy.

"And when?" asked Meredith.

"And what's his stand on saving the whales?" asked Nadine.

"Was he hot?" asked Orpha.

Goodie smiled, accessing her laptop. "His screen name is Danny Boy, and he lives in Portland. We met over in Fort George at Pier 19 for lunch yesterday."

"Danny Boy?" I felt my stomach clench, and a wave of nausea hit me like a Mariner's bat when he's swinging for the fence. But Merri reacted before I could.

"Danny Boy?!" Meredith stomped her foot in agitation. "I picked out Danny Boy for myself on Sunday. I put him on my Favorites list." She glared at Goodie. "How dare you! You little tramp! You jumped the line and went off on your own instead of following Sylvia's instructions not to make contact!"

I wanted to take issue with Meredith that it was probably the only time in her entire life that she'd actually followed directions, but I managed to hold my tongue. The look on Goodie's face was clear evidence that she'd never been called a little tramp in her entire life, but she wasn't about to take Meredith's attack lying down.

"You think you're such hot stuff!" I imagined I could see fire coming simultaneously from Goodie's eyes, ears, and nose. "You think Danny Boy would have chosen to meet you and not me if he'd been given the chance? No, he would not! He has manners! He's a gentleman! He wouldn't want to date anyone who's slept with every male on the peninsula over the age of 23!"

I looked over at Jimmy, who was leaning against the

kitchen counter, his arms folded across his chest. He shrugged and smirked. "You want me to make some popcorn or something?"

"It's a little early in the day for popcorn," said Orpha, "but I've suddenly got a hankering for some jujubes or licorice whips."

Meredith's eyes flashed right back at Goodie. "Just because I'm not a Catholic prude like you doesn't mean I'm a bad person. I like sex! What about it?"

Nadine joined the fray to defend her friend. "Goodie likes sex, too! We all like sex! We just don't flaunt our sexuality like you do! Some things are better left in the bedroom!"

Meredith snorted. "My point exactly! Goodie, who thinks sex is only for the bedroom, and not for the picnic table down at the overlook at Swiftstone Lighthouse, swooped in and took the one man I was interested in before I could! She's a little wrinkled up, sexless little tramp!"

We'd crossed the line between too much information and downright discomfort. I felt like putting my fingers in my ears and start saying "La-la-la-la-la-la-la-la-la-la-la-la" to drown out what Meredith was saying. And so I did.

"La-la-la-la-la-la-la-la-la-la-la-la!" I raised both the volume and the pitch and trilled the sound, the best I could muster, to mimic a zaghareet.

Jimmy caught on right away. "A zaghareet, or ululation, is an expression of joy, excitement, or encouragement for belly dancers. It lends an air of excitement and charges the room, and/or dancers, with lively electric current."

Meredith and Goodie instantly ceased their bickering. Goodie's lips were pursed and she looked like she was about to cry. Meredith had her hands on her hips and looked like she was about to pounce on Goodie and turn this into a good old-fashioned cat fight.

"Ladies," I said sternly. "Let's not be mean to each other. It's unbecoming, and beneath you."

"I didn't think anything was beneath Meredith," said Orpha, "unless it was a mattress."

I wasn't sure if she was intentionally trying to keep the pot stirred up, but I needed to shut her down quickly. "That's enough, Orpha," I said. "Show's over."

"Spoilsport," said Orpha. "This was just getting fun."

Meredith glowered at me for a moment, then sighed. "I suppose now you want us to kiss and make up?"

"That would certainly help," I said.

"I wouldn't kiss those lips, if I were you, Goodie," Orpha interjected. "You don't know where they've been!"

"Orpha! Stop that!" I admonished her. "Unless you want to be banned from coming here—"

Orpha made a show of pantomiming zipping her lip, locking it tight, and throwing the key away. It was a bit of an overkill, but I'd take it as a win.

"I'm sorry I didn't wait for us to vet Danny Boy," said Goodie, looking everywhere but at Merri. "But he contacted me first, and I didn't want to be rude by ignoring him."

"And I'm sorry I called you a sexless little tramp," said Merri. "Even if it's true."

"That's it!" I said, standing up. "I've had it! I'm out of here!"

"*NO!*" Everyone in the group yelled at once.

I froze, already headed for the door, and quickly considered my options. If I left, there'd be no one to keep an eye on them—on who they met, where they were going, or be there to help if things went south. On the other hand, this was the toughest volunteer job I'd ever had, and I didn't like having to be a referee on top of everything else.

"This is your final notice," I said, sitting back down. "We have to have some definite ground rules. Break them, and I'm gone."

Goodie, Nadine, and Meredith all solemnly nodded.

"Cross my heart and hope to die," said Orpha, swiping her index finger across her chest in a big sign of an "X."

Jimmy leaned down and stage-whispered to Orpha. "You know she's not talking to you," he said. "So I'd suggest you just stay quiet."

I turned to Goodie. "Would you please bring Danny Boy's profile up on your screen? We may be a day late and a dollar short, but there's still some vetting to be done."

CHAPTER 7

We all gathered around Goodie's laptop screen. Well, everyone except Meredith, who definitely had her trademark pout going on and refused to join in.

"Yep, he's a cutie!" said Orpha, as soon Goodie accessed Danny Boy's profile photo.

"How can you tell he's cute, Orpha?" asked Nadine. "He's turned away from the camera, so you can't really see his face."

"Oh, he's handsome, all right," sighed Goodie. "Tall, dark, handsome, and with the most impeccable manners. He's such a gentleman!"

"Ok," I said, feeling the knot in my stomach loosen a little, "he's got a full gray beard. No glasses. And he's 70, thank God." I breathed a sigh of relief.

"Why did you say 'thank God', Sylvia?" asked Goodie. "What's God got to do with Danny Boy's age?"

"Well... uh..." I looked around at the group, wondering how much of my paranoia I should share with them. "Well, to be honest, when I heard his online name, I thought I might have known him in a previous life."

Meredith walked up behind me and gently put a hand on my shoulder. "I totally understand, Syl. I thought the same thing for a minute myself."

"Thought what?" asked Jimmy.

"Thought Danny Boy might be Sylvia's ex-husband,"

said Merri.

"You thought Danny Boy might be Mr. X?" asked Goodie, incredulously.

I nodded. "Yes, I'm afraid I did." I smiled sheepishly. "Mr. X sometimes went by Danny Boy, or Dangerous Dan, but he wore glasses, didn't have a beard, and he'd only be…" I paused, searching my memory for Mr. X's birthdate. "Well, I can't remember exactly how old he'd be right at the moment, but I know he wouldn't be 70 yet."

"And for all we know," added Merri, "Sylvia's Danny Boy is still locked up in the prison in Salem."

"What's he doing time for?" asked tactless Orpha.

"Embezzlement," I replied. "He stole from his employer. Figured out a way to write checks on the company account that were going for his personal business. Even used the company credit card to put gas in his car and eat at the best restaurants. It added up to well over a hundred thousand dollars before he was caught."

Jimmy whistled. "That's a heck of a lot of Happy Meals, alright."

I sighed. "It made the Portland newspaper, but it's been quite a while ago. We were already divorced, and he was living in Oregon by the time he was arrested and convicted. I try not to think about him, but when his nickname came up, I couldn't help myself."

Nadine, Goodie, Orpha and Jimmy all nodded.

"So do you see now," I continued, "how important it is for these guys to be vetted? If it turns out that one of us knows the guy, or if there's something hinky about his profile, another pair of eyes might be just the ticket for spotting any potential problems."

"I said I was sorry," said Goodie. She didn't tell them that Danny Boy had shaved 10 years off his age. There had to be hundreds of guys named Dan, or Daniel, or Danny out there, and they probably all went by "Danny Boy" at one time or another. And since Sylvia had already cleared this one, why mention his confidential age confession? It would only stir the pot with both Sylvia and Meredith, and Goodie had had enough bickering for today.

"So I suppose you're going to be seeing him again?" asked Meredith, tersely.

"Oh, yes," said Goodie, nodding and smiling enthusiastically. "I certainly am."

"Then I'll take him off my Favorites list," said Merri, returning to her seat, "and see what else is out there."

Within minutes, Meredith announced she was going to go out with a guy who went by the screen name of "EarltheSqwearl." When she told us that, I kept from laughing out loud, but bit my lip and broke my resolve to stop rolling my eyes.

"Whatever are these guys thinking when they come up with dumb names like O-fer and EarltheSqwearl?" I asked of no one in particular.

"I thought it was kind of clever," said Merri, "the way he spelled squirrel to look like Earl. S-q-w-e-a-r-l."

"Maybe he just can't spell," said Orpha.

I shot her yet another warning look, wondering how many warning looks she was entitled to before I booted her out of here, and she silently mouthed "Oops" before she rezipped her lip.

"Earl is well-off," said Merri, "so I know he's not a gold-digger."

"How do you know that?" asked Nadine.

"He's into multi-level marketing, and he's standing next to a Tesla in his photo," said Merri. "A guy with a Tesla has to have more than two nickels to rub together."

I scowled. "Isn't multi-level marketing another name for a Ponzi scheme?"

Jimmy cut right in. "A Ponzi scheme is a fraudulent investing scam promising high rates of return with little risk to investors. The Ponzi scheme generates returns for older investors by acquiring new investors. This is similar to a pyramid scheme in that both are based on using new investors' funds to pay the earlier backers."

Meredith sighed. "I suppose it could be, but just look at that car!"

"How do we know it's his car?" I asked.

"You're so darned suspicious!" retorted Merri. "Can't we just cut him a little slack until… or unless… we know differently?"

"I suppose we could do that." I didn't want Meredith to suffer another hit so close to her disappointment over Goodie meeting Danny before she could. "Does he live around here?"

"Also Portland," replied Merri. "The North Beach Peninsula doesn't exactly have the type of investors he'd be looking for."

"Except, of course, for you wealthy widows," I said.

"Sylvia! Stop raining on our parades! Have a little faith!" Meredith admonished me.

"You're right, Mom. Why don't you go ahead and contact him? Who knows? Mermaids and squirrels might be a match made in heaven. Just don't give him any money!"

"I'm ready to contact a new friend too," said Nadine. "I've got his profile right here, and I'm anxious for you all to tell me what you think of him. His screen name is Paranormal Patrick."

Seriously, these guys needed to take lessons in creating better screen names. What woman in their right mind— I stopped my train of thought right in the middle of that track. "Please tell us about him, Nadine," I prompted.

"Patrick lives in Gresham," said Nadine, "but he's willing to relocate, and he's 420-friendly."

"Remember now, you don't want to be a one-issue dater," I said.

"What does that mean anyway?" said Orpha.

"A one-issue dater is someone who—" I began, but Orpha cut me off.

"No, not that, Sylvia. I want to know if he has afternoon tea every day at 4:20, or what?"

Goodie giggled. "When someone says they are 420 friendly, it means he or she enjoys smoking marijuana. Gee, Orpha, I thought I was the most naïve one here."

"You are the most naïve," said Orpha. "I'm just the oldest and the most out-of-touch with the younger generation."

Her statement brought a smile from each of us, but no one said a word. Orpha was the one who always insisted she was neither old, forgetful, nor out-of-touch.

"Well," said Nadine. "Patrick's also sober, so that's also in the plus column."

"He's sober, but he smokes pot?" asked Merri, rhetorically. "In AA they call that the marijuana maintenance program, right Sylvia?"

"Right," I replied. In my Child Protective Services social work, I'd referred a lot of their parents to drug and alcohol treatment centers, and I was very familiar with the 12-step programs. In fact, I so strongly believed in the principles of the programs, that I'd chosen not to drink myself, although I'd never thought I had an actual problem with alcohol.

"Patrick's a bit younger," said Nadine. "In his profile he wrote that the speed limit is 55, and that's the highest age he's ever planning to admit to."

"A man after my own heart," muttered Orpha.

"It looks like his hair is totally gray," continued Nadine, ignoring Orpha, "but I think he's probably Irish, since he put 'red' down as his hair color."

"He's perfect for you," said Orpha, a little louder. "You haven't known what your real hair color is in a couple decades!"

"I thought you were supposed to be zipping your lip?" asked Merri.

Orpha didn't answer Merri. Instead, she addressed the group, "You two can go on and make your dates with these guys, but be sure to leave next Saturday night open!"

Okay, I decided to bite on Orpha's obvious bait. "What's next Saturday?"

Meredith dramatically cleared her throat. "The Spartina Point Casino and Resort has graciously offered to let The Veiled Rainbow perform there one Saturday evening a month, and next weekend is our first regular night to come out and strut our stuff."

Goodie, Nadine, and Orpha were all smiling and bobbing their heads.

"That's right, and all five of us will be ready, willing, and able," said Goodie, clapping her hands in front of her excitedly.

"And you'll be there too, won't you Sylvia?" asked Merri. "We could use your help.

"My help?" I looked from one to the other. "You're not still trying to rope me into putting on a violet costume, are you?"

"You'd make a great Violet," said Orpha.

"Yes, you would," said Merri, "but I understand that no means no." She took a breath. "But would you be so kind as to run sound for us?"

"Run sound? Me?" I was about as technically challenged as they come, so surely the members of The Veiled Rainbow belly dancing troupe must be up to something.

Jimmy raised his hand. "Oooo! Oooo! Oooo!" he said. "I'll do it!"

Meredith smiled. "Thank you, Jimmy. That will be wonderful. All you need to do is cue up the tape player for us as we come onto the floor." She looked at me. "It's really very simple."

Okay, so maybe they weren't up to something—this time.

Orpha harrumphed. "I don't know why you're so dead set on not joining us, Sylvia," she said. "We really need a Violet. I wish we could get Grandma Mazur to dance with us. I know she'd do it in a heartbeat."

"Grandma Mazur?" I looked into Orpha's eyes, wondering if she'd suddenly gone around the bend. "You mean like in Janet Evanovich's Stephanie Plum novels?"

"Yep," said Orpha. "That's the one. She's a real hoot. She'd be a perfect BFF for me, and she'd definitely add some violet spice to our group!"

"Orpha…" I spoke slowly and carefully. "You do realize that Grandma Mazur is a fictional character, right?"

"Of course I do!" Orpha looked deeply annoyed. "I'm not losing my grip on reality, Sylvia, I'm just saying it's too bad she's not available."

The others in the group seemed to be taking Orpha's declaration in stride. Not a one of them was batting an eyelash. Perhaps it was me who was losing my mind.

"So as I was saying," said Orpha, turning now to Nadine and Meredith, "be sure to make your dates for earlier in the week."

"No problem," said Meredith. "I have no intention of waiting that long to meet Earl."

Nadine, feeling like it was some sort of competition, piped up with a "Me, too!"

"You're meeting Earl, too?" asked Orpha.

Before their conversation could evolve into a remake of "Who's on First?" I said, "Merri is meeting Earl, Orpha, and Nadine is meeting Patrick."

"And if the first date goes well, I just might invite Earl to be my date on Saturday night when we perform!" said Merri.

"Me, too!" said Nadine.

"Earl's turning into a real popular guy," said Orpha.

I shook my head and just gave up. "Yes, Orpha, he certainly is." I looked at Jimmy's wall clock and suggested we disband for the day. "Who's giving Orpha a ride down to Unity now that Felicity has left the group in hot pursuit of her colleague Mark?"

"I can't today," said Nadine. "I have to get right home and let my dog out."

"Your dog?" asked Meredith. She looked incredulously at Goodie. "Did you know Nadine has another dog?"

Goodie shrugged. "We on the North Beach Humane Society board have voted to allow Nadine to foster a special needs dog on a temporary basis."

"A special needs animal," said Jimmy, "is an animal that has physical or emotional disabilities. They often benefit from being in a private home, in which they are protected from other animals and receive one-on-one attention from human caretakers until they are deemed ready for adoption in a forever home."

"Are you going to feed this one to the bears, too?" asked Orpha.

"*ORPHA!*" we all shouted.

"I'm just saying, I hope the Humane Society knows what it's doing." Orpha shrugged.

"Nadine is fostering Stella as part of her amends for not protecting poor Claudette," said Goodie. "We don't have enough people fostering pets—especially special needs pets—and Nadine will be closely monitored to make sure she's doing a good job."

"Stella?" asked Jimmy. "You mean like in The Streetcar Named Desire?"

"Exactly," said Nadine.

"What's her 'special need'?" I asked.

"She actually has two," said Goodie. "Stella was terribly abused, and she is partially blind. On top of that, she appears to be almost totally deaf. The vet tried out doggie hearing aids on her, but they weren't successful; she still wasn't responding to anyone. The bifocals are working a little better."

"Whoa!" said Merri. "So... Help me understand.... If Stella is out in the backyard, and Nadine wants her to come back inside, Nadine will be out standing on her porch yelling 'STELLA!' to a deaf dog?"

Goodie smiled. "That's kind of why we named her Stella."

"I like it!" said Jimmy.

"You're all nuts!" said Orpha.

"Stella's been with me a couple weeks now," said Nadine, "and I have a feeling she's not as deaf as she pretends to be." She looked at Goodie. "Is it possible she just has a well-developed case of 'selective hearing'? Because she certainly seems to hear the crinkling paper when I'm opening the box of dog treats, no matter how quiet I try to be. She's just Johnny-on-the-spot whenever there's any food involved."

"Interesting," said Goodie, smiling. "I'm glad you've noticed that. It means you're paying good attention to her and her habits."

"What kind of dog is Stella?" asked Meredith.

"A Papillon," said Nadine.

Jimmy raised his hand and waved it around again, but as usual, he didn't wait for anyone to call on him. "Papillon means 'butterfly' in French," he began. "The Papillon is also called the Continental Toy Spaniel. Its name comes from its characteristic butterfly-like look of the long and fringed hair on its upright ears."

"So if she's a toy, she's not very big," I said. "No bigger than Claudette was."

"Nadine has taken precautions to keep Stella safe," Goodie hurried to say. "She isn't feeding the bears on the back porch any longer."

"That's right," said Nadine. "I have a couple of hummingbird feeders hanging out there, but nothing else, so the bears have moved on."

"Okay, I believe you. But I'd like to know more about her bifocals," I said. "Has Stella been fitted with glasses?"

"Yep," said Nadine. "She looks so cute in them. There's a strap that goes over her ears and under her chin. She looks like she's wearing Snoopy's flying ace goggles."

"Don't they call those 'doggles'?" asked Jimmy.

"Not these," said Goodie. "Doggles are more for eye protection, like if the dog likes to ride on a motorcycle or something. Hers are prescription eyewear."

There was so much more I thought about saying, but I decided to just close my mouth before I could get myself into trouble with either Goodie or Nadine, and the group fell uncharacteristically silent.

"I'll give Orpha a ride home," said Goodie, grabbing the

window of opportunity to change the subject. "I want to go down and remind Nova about our dancing gig next weekend."

Also taking advantage of the pause in conversation, Nadine gathered up her laptop and hurried for the door. "See you later!" she called out as she left the kitchen.

Almost in unison, we all yelled out, "Good-bye Blanche!"

True to their word, Nadine and Meredith both set their dates for earlier the following week. Coincidentally, they both chose to meet on Tuesday, at 11 a.m., which meant I had to make a decision about which woman I was going to discreetly shadow on her date.

Normally, I would have chosen to stick close to Meredith, as blood is still thicker than water, but Monday morning Nadine actually called and requested that I "be nearby" when she and Patrick met out on the boardwalk Tuesday.

"Of course." I said it without hesitation, because I already knew Merri was going to meet Earl at the Sandy Bottom Coffee Cup, and I was sure Bim and/or Geri would be only too happy to eavesdrop on their conversation and give me a full report later.

"Thank you so much, Sylvia," said Nadine. I could hear her take a deep breath before she continued. "I don't know why, but I'm kind of nervous, and I know we're supposed to meet the first time in a public place and all, but since his profile said he liked taking long walks on the beach, I thought it would be okay as long as someone kept an eye on us."

"I totally understand," I told her. "Don't you worry. Dates are supposed to be fun, and you can relax and enjoy yourself knowing I'm not too far away."

I got a wild idea the moment I hung up, and picked the phone back up to call Mercedes, who lives in her motorhome in the back parking lot of the Spartina Point Casino and Resort.

"It better be important," Mercedes grumbled when she answered on the fifth ring.

I looked quickly at the clock. "It's after 10, I know you didn't work last night, and Carter didn't stay over, because Freddy has Mondays off, and the sheriff has to cover the entire south end today."

Silence.

"Mercedes?" I said softly. "Did you hang up on me?"

Mercedes sighed. "I just can't figure out how you can rattle off the comings and goings of so many people on the peninsula, and you don't even own a police scanner." She sighed again, for good measure. "Okay. So now I'm awake. What do you want?"

Her grumpiness made me momentarily reconsider why I'd called, but I plunged on ahead. "Want to come with me to do some undercover surveillance tomorrow morning?"

"I'm listening."

"Nadine has a date with a guy named Patrick, and she asked me to keep tabs on her without being too obvious, and I know how you love being involved in covert operations."

Merc snorted. "Yeah, I get it—you need someone to talk to while you're doing a stake out."

"Okay, so you saw right through me." I laughed. "But we work so well together…" I silently recalled a few times I'd been ready to kill her in the middle of several escapades she'd gotten me into, but I chose to overlook them at the moment.

"How early tomorrow morning are we talking about?" asked Merc. "And if we'll be following Nadine around on your end of the peninsula, how would I get there?"

Merc's only mode of transportation was her motorhome, and at eight miles to the gallon, she wasn't fond of driving it off the casino lot.

"Her date's not till 11, so you could ride with Deputy Freddy Morgan to my house because Sheriff D has staff meetings at 10 a.m. on Tuesday mornings. So you'd probably need to leave there about 9:15 or 9:30."

"You've got this all figured out, don't you?" asked Merc. "Including the fact that you'd get to see Freddy when he delivers me to you on our way down Sandspit Road."

"Well?" I asked. "Can I count you in?"

"I have two conditions," said Merc. "One, that we can stop for some good coffee at the Sandy Bottom, which includes a couple of their biscotti, and two, that you let me choose my own wardrobe for this stake out."

"Seriously, Merc?" I asked. "Since when have I ever kept you from covering yourself in sequins, spandex, and oversized sunglasses?"

I didn't tell Mercedes that I needed to stop at the Sandy Bottom anyway to talk to Bim and Geri about keeping an eye on Merri and her date. Merc could keep thinking that I'd caved in to all her conditions.

"See you in the morning, then," said Merc, "providing my boss says he'll be able to give me a lift in tomorrow."

The fact that Deputy Freddy Morgan had inherited the casino from his Uncle Harry, and was now technically Mercedes' boss, seemed kind of like inbreeding. Of course, on the North Beach Peninsula, the degrees of separation were always a very small number.

"See you in the morning, Merc," I replied. "Bright-eyed and bushy-tailed."

"I'm not promising nothing!" she said. "You'll get what you get."

CHAPTER 8

As it turned out, what I got was totally over-the-top, even for Mercedes, who was the undisputed queen of over-the-topness!

"So what do you think?" she asked, twirling around on my front porch so I could take in every angle and sparkling facet of her garish outfit.

"I… Uh…" I looked at Freddy, hoping he'd say something to rescue me.

"I told her you'd love it," said Freddy, standing in his uniform at the bottom of the porch steps. He gave me one of his big, beaming smiles.

The combination of Freddy's uniform and the boyish "just for me" smile made my knees a little weak. The thought crossed my mind that if Mercedes hadn't been here—

"You told her I'd love it, huh?" I couldn't help but return that smile. "Well, then, I guess I love it. And it's good to see you, Deputy Morgan."

"It's been too long, Syl." He sighed heavily. "We've both been so darn busy."

Busy wasn't the half of it. What with him trying to work two full-time jobs, and me trying to ride herd on The Veiled Rainbow's online dating escapades, we hadn't seen each other—alone—in a couple weeks.

"What do you say we have a date night tonight?" asked Freddy.

"Great idea!" Mercedes butted in. "We can double date. It's Taco Tuesday at the Rusty Rudder, so I'm sure Carter won't mind eating out. Tacos! Yum! My mouth is already watering."

Freddy climbed the four porch steps and gave me a quick hug and a peck on the lips. Then he whispered in my ear, "I won't have to take her back home if she's riding with Sheriff D."

I wasn't totally sure of his intentions, but I liked the way he'd nuzzled his words into my ear.

"I'll look forward to it," I replied. "Now you'd best get to work. You don't want to keep Sheriff Donaldson waiting."

Freddy started for his car. He opened the door, blew me a kiss, and winked. The butterflies in my stomach instantly took wing. Two weeks was definitely too long to go without seeing this man, whether we had chaperones with us for dinner or not.

Mercedes and I arrived at the Sandy Bottom Coffee Cup just about 10:30. I knew Meredith and Earl were due there at 11, and I wanted to be sure we'd already come and gone before they arrived. I didn't want Merri thinking I was here to check her date out, even though I would have done exactly that if I hadn't already committed to keeping an eye on Nadine.

"Well, aren't you a glorious sight for sore eyes!" said Bim to Mercedes, coming out from behind the counter. She wiped her hands on the towel hanging from her belt, and gave Merc a tight squeeze.

"So what am I, chopped liver?" I asked.

Bim dutifully gave me a hug as well. "You're different. I see you every few days, but I haven't seen Mercedes since the film crew was here last spring."

"Apology accepted."

Merc and I ordered our coffee and biscotti to go, and while Bim was fixing it for us, I filled her in on Meredith's upcoming date, and asked that she check the guy out for me. "If there's anything hinky about him, call me right away," I told her. "I'll be nearby, just down at the boardwalk, and I can be here in a matter of minutes."

Bim was happy to oblige. "But why don't you just check him out yourself?" she asked. "Surely you and Mercedes can hang out here a little while."

"Because we're going to the boardwalk for a very specific reason," Merc interjected. "We're going undercover to keep an eye on Nadine and her first date with a guy named Patrick, and we can't be in two places at once." She pulled herself up to her full five-foot, four-inch height. "Couldn't you tell by my specially-made-for-the-occasion surveillance outfit that we're officially on the job?"

"Oh, so sorry," said Bim, "I just thought those were your everyday clothes."

Mercedes had truly outdone herself. From her green and gold bedazzled tennis shoes to her copper and earth-toned sequined ball cap, she looked like she was auditioning for a celebrity cameo spot on either Honey Boo-boo or Duck Dynasty.

Mercedes' hot pink binoculars hanging around her neck seemed inconsistent with her camouflage flak jacket, despite the fact that it sported beaded fringe, but otherwise I was sure she could blend right in with the military on patrol. Not *our* military, of course, but with some other military, maybe on another planet, in a galaxy far, far away.

"You like?" Mercedes asked Bim, doing her little twirl again. "It's my recon apparel."

"I don't just like, I love!" said Bim enthusiastically.

Naturally, Bim loved anything bright and glittery. The more bedazzled, the better she liked it. She and Geri owned an Oscar-worthy closet full of sparkly duds to die for, whether you dressed as a wannabe Hollywood starlet or needed a tailored tux for a black-tie event.

We took our coffee and goodies, and I drove us down to the beach approach. Nadine had said she wanted Patrick to see the welcoming beach arch spanning the roadway before they walked, so I knew they'd be starting from the north end of the quarter mile, wooden boardwalk.

I parked my blue and green chameleon painted mustang along the approach, right along the edge of the sand, where we would be able to see almost the entire length of the boardwalk paralleling the ocean. Then I got out and opened the trunk to retrieve my own binoculars. They were Bushnell Black, so I thought we'd have no trouble telling them apart.

Promptly at 11 o'clock, Nadine's black and white smart car with the glamor eyelashes added above the headlights came slowly down the approach, followed by a non-descript white van. Both vehicles parked right next to the boardwalk on-ramp, and we watched as the two of them got out and awkwardly shook hands.

"Huh," said Merc. "I'm so glad I'm done with all that first date stuff. It's like going on a job interview."

I had to agree. Watching Nadine and Patrick climb the ramp to the corner where it turned south, I couldn't tell if they were doing much talking, but they were keeping quite a distance between themselves.

They stopped at the turn, and Nadine was gesturing to the north and south, possibly telling Patrick some of the history of the sand accretion along the shoreline, or about the infamous visit from Captain William Clark and a few men from the Corps of Discovery in November, 1805.

Then Patrick reached inside his jacket to a concealed pocket, and pulled something from it that I couldn't quite make out. Apparently, Mercedes couldn't see what it was from her vantage point either.

"What's he got there?" Merc asked, looking through her own set of binoculars.

"Can't quite tell," I replied. "Could be most anything. A snack, maybe."

"Or a knife, a gun, a hand grenade, a poisoned dart, a box cutter—" added Mercedes, lowering her binoculars and reaching for the car door handle. "Sylvia! We gotta go save Nadine! Isn't that what we're here for?"

"Not just yet." I put my hand on her arm. "Let's give it another minute or two."

And another minute was all that was needed for me to start chuckling as I watched intently through the lens. I took my first big breath of the stake out and relaxed a little. Patrick had obviously lit up a joint, presumably of marijuana, and the two of them were passing it back and forth as they continued their walk.

"Oops," said Mercedes. "I guess Nadine doesn't need any saving right at the moment."

"Not at the moment, but we still need to keep an eye on them."

We took turns watching their progress along the shoreline while we sipped our coffee and munched biscotti.

"These cookies are so good," said Merc. "I wonder if they bake them there."

"I think they're imported," I shamelessly lied. I'd promised Bim some time ago that I'd never give up her "Grandma Costco" secret recipe, and I certainly wasn't going to give it up to Mercedes and her big mouth!

"Well, they're good, whoever made them," said Merc,

licking her fingers. "But one thing I know for sure; I've had way too much coffee. I gotta pee something fierce."

I turned to my left, and focused my binoculars on the restrooms. "Uh, Merc... The restrooms are closed for remodeling."

"Wouldn't you know it?" said Merc. "Well, I guess I'll just have to use some of these here napkins from the Sandy Bottom to make sure I don't get no sandy bottom myself."

"What are you saying?" I asked, as if I needed clarification.

"I ain't proud, Syl, and I really got to go. I mean *now*! I'll just step around the side of the car here. No worries, it's just pee, and it will soak right into the sand."

And before I could tell her I could see one of the county's patrol cars coming slowly down the beach approach from town, she had jumped out, closed the door, and, I assume, wrestled out of her spandex slacks.

Freddy was driving the cruiser, and as he made a wide loop before parking next to me, I couldn't help but take a glance in the mirror and fluff my hair. Then he positioned his open driver's side window next to my open window and winked at me.

"Good morning again, beautiful. You keeping an eye on Nadine?" Freddy asked.

"How did you…" I began, then took a quick glance out my passenger side window. "Oh. Of course. You know what her car looks like."

"There aren't many smart cars on the peninsula, and it's kinda hard to miss those glamour eyelashes she added," said Freddy, grinning. "So don't blame Mercedes for telling me on the way to your house this morning what you two were up to today."

Mercedes! Oh fizzle! I quickly twisted around in my car

seat to see if her naked fanny was exposed out beside the car.

"You can get back in the car, Mercedes!" Freddy called out. "I don't want to have to resuscitate you if you get asphyxiated by the car fumes." He'd left his car still running, and it was now facing back down the approach in case he needed to leave in a hurry.

Mercedes sheepishly got back into the passenger seat of the mustang. "How did you know I was…" she began, but Freddy stopped her.

"Deductive reasoning," he said, and let it go at that.

"Is that Nadine and Patrick over there?" he asked, pointing to the only couple on the boardwalk.

"Yep," I said. "Just follow the cloud of pot smoke."

"Oh," said Freddy, grimacing. "Smoking pot isn't exactly legal out in public."

"You may not have noticed," said Merc. "But this beach, on a weekday morning in the fall, ain't exactly public, either."

"I doubt your reasoning would hold up in court," said Freddy, "so I'll just pretend I didn't see them, and you didn't tell me, and I couldn't smell it from here, anyway."

"Good deal," said Mercedes. "You need to cut Nadine some slack. The poor girl's got enough on her rap sheet already."

I thought Mercedes was referring to the trouble Nadine got into for feeding the bears in her backyard, but now that Merc was sleeping with Sheriff D, she might be privy to all kinds of things about Nadine, who had worked for Greenpeace for many years. Come to think about it, Merc might have the goods on any one of us.

Freddy put his car in gear. "I guess I'll be seeing the both of you at dinner tonight," he said. "The sheriff thought Taco Tuesday was a great idea." And with that, he went back up the approach road, letting Nadine and Patrick have their uninterrupted time together.

By now, the couple on the boardwalk had become quite chummy, and they were walking arm-in-arm, heading slowly back toward their vehicles.

"Let's get out of here, Syl," said Mercedes, "before they spot us."

"Patrick doesn't know us, doesn't know what we drive, and doesn't know we know Nadine, so we can just sit here and continue to watch," I said.

But Nadine had other ideas. She marched Patrick right up to my car and introduced him to both of us! Then she said they were heading down to Unity to have fish and chips at Pier 103, before Patrick headed back to Gresham, because they were both suddenly starving, and she didn't want to send him away hungry.

Merc and I watched as they left in their separate vehicles, then Merc said, "I know we're having tacos later, but I could use a little something to eat before then myself."

I picked up my cell phone and called Jimmy. "What's for lunch?"

Since it's Jimmy's responsibility to keep the motel office open as many hours as possible, we decided that Merc and I would pick up some mini-tsunami burgers at the High Tide and head over to his place.

On our way past the Sandy Bottom, I noted that Meredith's car was not parked in front of the coffee shop, so either her date hadn't been so hot, or they'd moved on to another location—hopefully not her house. I was half-tempted to stop in to get the scoop right then from Bim, but I was sure Jimmy had already called our burger order in.

When we arrived at the Clamshell, Jimmy took one look at Mercedes, and I saw him bite his lip to keep from laughing. "I guess it's safe to say you're not in WitSec, huh, Merc?"

"I'm not in what?" asked Mercedes, unloading our lunch onto the kitchen table.

"Seriously?" I asked, grabbing the roll of paper towels from the wall by his sink. "All the crime TV you watch, and you don't know what WitSec is?"

"Oh, right, WitSec," said Merc, nodding. "I just didn't hear him."

Jimmy looked at me, then said to Mercedes, "WitSec stands for Witness Security Program."

"So what's this WitSec thing have to do with me?" she asked, stretching up to her full five foot, four inch height.

"Never mind," said Jimmy, shaking his head. "I've just never seen anyone out on an undercover recon wearing a fringed flak jacket before."

Merc twirled to give him the full effect of the beaded fringe in motion, then plopped down in a chair at the table while I retrieved three diet sodas from Jimmy's always well-stocked fridge.

"Flak is actually a German contraction for Fliegerabwehrkanone," Jimmy continued, matter-of-factly. "The jacket was designed to provide protection from case fragments, or frags, from high-explosive weaponry, such as anti-aircraft artillery. The original flak jackets were made from ballistic nylon and were bulky and ineffective against most rifle and pistol fire, but they were widely used, as they provided at least a little protection and allowed soldiers to feel secure."

Neither one of us rose to the bait, although I would have liked to ask him to pronounce Fliegerabwehrkanone one more time, and more slowly. I was sure if either one of us asked so much as a single question, Jimmy would launch into the complete history of World War II, and we'd never get to enjoy our lunch.

"Oh, well," said Jimmy, suddenly realizing we just

weren't that interested in his topic. "Ever since Sylvia called, I've been jonesing for a mini-tsunami, so I'm too hungry to explain it further."

Thank goodness! We all tore into our burgers and fries, Merc and I discovering we had worked up quite an appetite while sitting in the car watching Nadine and Patrick out walking.

Between bites, I filled Jimmy in on our morning's mission. "I think it's safe to say that Nadine and Patrick, despite their possible 10 to 15-year age difference, might want to see each other again."

Jimmy nodded. "I guess that's something you and Nadine have in common."

I felt my face flush, but said nothing. How could I protest when what Jimmy said was true? Freddy was about 15 years my junior, but that hadn't kept us from developing a strong bond. I guess you just can't fight chemistry, not that I'd ever want to!

As if on cue, a knock at the door announced Kanji's arrival. I knew it was Kanji before he entered the room, as no car had come up the driveway while we'd been eating. Obviously, he'd seen my car parked out there, and being in competition with Freddy for my attention, he couldn't resist the opportunity to say 'hello' when there were fewer people in the room to distract me from appreciating his advances.

Jimmy glanced up at the clock and hollered for him to come on in, and I must admit, the sight of Kanjirappally Kumera, dressed in black slacks, white shirt, striped tie, and polished shoes, started my heart doing a little tap-dance. Boy howdy, he was one fine-looking man!

"Right on time," said Jimmy. "Would you like some of my fries?"

"Thank you for the kindness of your offering, but no. I

do not wish to interrupt your meal," said Kanji, bowing slightly, "and yet I must deliver Elvis to your care before I depart for my shift at Spartina Point."

Okay, so maybe Kanji hadn't come over to the motel office to try to woo me after all. Elvis, his six-month-old bundle of energy, bounded into the room, went straight to Priscilla's cat dish, sniffed the empty bowl, then jumped up on the couch to curl up next to her for his afternoon nap as if he owned the place.

"Elvis is quite at home here," Mercedes observed. "My Brutus isn't so well-adjusted."

That was quite an understatement, as Merc's long-haired dachshund was the most timid 'fraidy cat dog I'd ever met, and spent most of his time hiding behind her couch.

Kanji's eyes met mine, and his smile deepened. "Miss Sylvia," he said, "it is a pleasure and an honor to see you again."

"Good to see you, too, Kanji." And I knew I was telling the truth. I was quite fond of both the men in my life, and was grateful that neither one of them had pushed me to make a decision about exclusivity. "Are you working full-time now?"

"Almost," Kanji replied. "I work today because I'm filling in for the regular bartender. Most often I work four days a week—Friday through Monday—and my duties are confined to those of the Hospitality Specialist."

And speaking of inbreeding and/or incest, Freddy was boss to both Mercedes and Kanji at the casino. Yep, we were all just one big happy family, although Freddy's decision to hire Kanji had originally been to keep an eye on him when he learned Kanji was his primary competition for my affection.

"I very much enjoy interacting with all the people at the

resort, both visitors and staff," Kanji continued. "I have made many good friends here."

"I do certainly hope that includes me," gushed Meredith, coming in the door behind him.

I don't think any of us had heard Merri's car pull in, but none of us were too surprised to see her. Most of us knew she'd been on a coffee date in Tinkerstown, and the Clamshell was on her way back north to Ocean Crest.

"Certainly, Miss Meredith," said Kanji, with that endearing little half-bow of his. "Making your acquaintance has been one of my true delights."

Before their mutual admiration society could get any more embarrassing, I quickly asked, "How was your date, Mom? Did you and Earl have a good time?"

"Oh, now, I wouldn't want anyone to jump to any conclusions, but I'm bringing him with me Saturday night when The Veiled Rainbow performs at the casino," said Merri.

"I was most pleased to see your belly-dancing troupe listed on the entertainment schedule," said Kanji. "And I look forward to seeing all of you on Saturday." And with a quick kiss on the hand for each of the three women there, Kanji left for work.

"So spill it," said Mercedes. "What's this Earl fellow like? I got some catching up to do."

But Meredith steadfastly refused to give out any of the juicy details. She just told us that after having coffee at the Sandy Bottom this morning, they'd gone to lunch.

"I just took a chance you'd be visiting with Jimmy this afternoon, so stopped in, since it's on my way home, and all. I didn't know you'd be out and about with Mercedes, but it's always a pleasure to see you, Merc." Meredith nodded in Mercedes' direction.

"I knew you'd be worrying about me until you knew I was safe and sound, Sylvia. So suffice to say, I had a nice enough time, I'm seeing him again, and you can judge for yourself if he's step-daddy material on Saturday." Then she bent down and kissed me on top of my head, and left without sticking around to be grilled any further.

Step-daddy material? Good grief and gravy, Merri definitely had something up her sleeve. I sighed. I'd just have to wait and see what it was she had going on, but I was already pretty sure I wasn't going to like it one little bit.

CHAPTER 9

Meredith knew she'd dodged a bullet getting in and out of the Clamshell before Sylvia had had a chance to weasel any more information about Earl out of her. The truth was, that she was only using EarltheSqwearl as a decoy to keep any of the women from knowing which man on Sole Mates she was really interested in. And once the troupe had met Earl, they'd be falling all over themselves with gratitude that Merri quickly moved on to someone else—*anyone else*—she'd found on the website. That was the plan, right from the get-go, and she was sticking to it.

There was something not-quite-right about Earl Jones, but she would have to do a little more sleuthing to put her finger on it. He'd arrived at the Sandy Bottom a few minutes after she did, pulling into the parking lot in a small, blue-and-bondo pickup truck with the passenger door duct taped shut. *Strike one,* thought Merri.

Earl came in to the Sandy Bottom, glanced nervously this way and that, and finally made eye contact with Meredith, sitting at a small table tucked off to one side of the main room. To his credit, his profile photo looked just like him, minus the suit, the tie, and the Tesla, of course. Merri lifted her fingers and wiggled them at him. "Hi Earl."

Earl was wearing jeans and a t-shirt that said, "Got Crabs?" that Merri found downright offensive, but she held her tongue. He moved the second chair at the table from the spot across from her to sit much closer to her, with only the table corner between them. He then sat down, and despite his thick, black-framed glasses, Merri could see his eyes darting this way and that, taking it all in, not missing anything. He caught her reading his t-shirt and grinned.

"You like my shirt? I wore it especially for you, since I was coming to the coast and all."

For all the world, Earl behaved a lot like a real squirrel, not sitting still for longer than a minute or two, crossing his legs first this way, then that, and Merri wondered if she should point out where the restrooms were located. But then Earl asked Bim if he could smoke inside the coffee shop, and Meredith couldn't hold her tongue any longer. "Your profile said you were a non-smoker."

"I'm trying to quit," said Earl. "And I knew I'd get more dates if I said I didn't smoke."

Strike two, thought Merri.

After several cups of coffee, Meredith decided EarltheSqwearl might be an acquired taste, and suggested they go someplace for lunch. After all, she needed to build some kind of actual rapport with him if she was going to invite him to accompany her on Saturday.

"I *am* a bit hungry," said Earl, "And I saw a good place not too far from here when I was driving in." He nodded. "Okay if we take your car?"

"I was going to offer that suggestion," said Meredith.

"Great," said Earl. "I'm never sure if 'Little Blue' is going to give up the ghost and strand me someplace too far from home to walk, so I drive it as little as possible."

Strike three, thought Meredith. She absentmindedly wondered how many strikes she was willing to allow him before she, too, gave up the ghost. *Maybe that was just a foul tip,* she thought, *after all, I need him to be my Saturday night date to set my plan in motion.*

Unbelievably, they'd only driven a few blocks before Earl had Merri turn into the McDonald's parking lot.

"You want to have lunch *here*?" she asked.

"Is this okay?" asked Earl. "I've got a coupon."

Meredith, bless her heart, didn't tell Earl she hadn't eaten at a McDonald's since she was in junior high school, and good-naturedly followed him inside.

"We'd have saved a lot of money if we'd had our coffee here, too," he told her. "It's only a dollar. I should have thought of that."

Merri stared at the lighted, moving screens of fast food as they rotated in front of her, and had no idea how to select what she wanted to eat. Inside, she shrugged. It didn't matter what she ate today, it was only one meal. "How about you just order for me, would you please?" She looked at Earl in her most adoring way and smiled. "I'll find us a table."

At the counter, he handed the cashier his coupon. "We'll take two of these chicken sandwich meals," he said, reaching for his wallet, which was chained to his jeans.

"Uh... Sir?" said the cashier. "Sir, I'm afraid this coupon is for another fast food place."

"Oh?" Earl looked around like he didn't know where he was.

"This coupon is for a restaurant that's not on the North Beach Peninsula."

"Really? Are you sure?" Earl took back the coupon and examined it carefully. "Then will you match the offer?"

"I'm afraid I can't do that, sir," said the cashier. "Would you like to order off our Value Menu?"

At long last, Earl arrived at their table carrying a tray with two happy meals on it. "I figured a woman as trim and fit as you are doesn't eat very much, so I got the smaller-portioned lunches."

"That was very thoughtful of you Earl," Merri said graciously.

Over lunch that Merri barely picked at, she asked Earl about his multi-level marketing business.

"Well, no... I, uh, gave that up a little over 10 years ago."

"Gave it up?" asked Meredith. "Why?"

"It was all a misunderstanding," said Earl, "but I ended up being falsely accused and convicted of fraud, and going to prison for a few years. If I so much as think about helping someone invest, I violate my parole."

Yep, thought Meredith, *if there's one squirrel in the whole bunch, there's no doubt I'll be the first to pick out the nut jobs.*

"I think you're a real nice lady," said Earl. He reached out and took her hand, and it was all Merri could do to keep from jerking her hand away. "Are you willing to give me a chance, despite my unfortunate background?"

Merri didn't directly respond to his question. Instead she asked, "So what do you do now for a living, Earl?"

Earl smiled widely, and Meredith almost cringed at his lack of dental hygiene. "My wife divorced me while I was in prison," he said. "So, since I didn't have anywhere to live, I became a professional house sitter. I don't have to pay rent, and I get to live in a new home every few weeks or months, depending on how long the owners are away.

"It's never boring, and I get lots of referrals because I'm good at what I do. I water their plants and mow their lawns, and for a little extra, I'll take good care of any pets they have—except snakes. I won't housesit snakes for any amount of money."

"So you have no permanent address?" asked Merri.

Earl grinned again, but this time he kept his mouth

closed. "I am free to relocate anywhere," he said. "And I'm sure when I finally meet my true soul mate, she'll want me to move in with her right away, so living this way saves me the stress of having to sell my own home and combine household furnishings."

In an odd way, what Earl said made at least a modicum of sense, but Merri wasn't the least bit interested. Earl was only in his 50s, a fact she'd carefully hidden from Sylvia and other gals, and she doubted he'd be dying of natural causes any time soon. Unless, of course, he had high cholesterol, which was certainly a fast-food possibility.

Meredith took a leap of faith. "Earl, would you like to come back to the peninsula next weekend and accompany me to the Spartina Point Casino and Resort Saturday night?" She batted her eyelashes. "I'd like you to meet some of my friends."

Earl's eyes got wide. "You mean like a real date?"

"Yes," said Merri. "Exactly like a real date."

Meredith had given him her address, and assured him that they would take her car on to the casino from there. She would die if anyone saw her arrive in his old beater, but she didn't let on how she felt about that. She returned him to his truck in the Sandy Bottom parking lot, and deftly turned her cheek when Earl attempted to kiss her good-bye.

"See you Saturday!" he said.

"See you Saturday," Meredith echoed, and tootled her fingers at him as he drove away. *What have I gotten myself into?* she thought. Then she remembered. After everyone got a good look at Earl Saturday night, anyone else she decided to date was going to look really good to the troupe. *Anyone.*

Since Felicity was no longer searching for her Sole Mate online, there was no need for the other gals, all retired, to meet on Saturday morning, but we did anyway, at least a few of us.

Orpha had begged off, saying she was saving her strength for The Veiled Rainbow's return performance that evening. Nova had offered to drive them both up to the casino in Orpha's car late that afternoon, and I can't say I didn't think it was a darn good plan. I knew for certain it would speed up our morning meeting, not that I didn't love Orpha dearly.

So when we gathered, it was supposed to be just Jimmy, Nadine, Goodie, Meredith and me. The three women would report on their dating adventures the past week, and unless we needed to vet another possible candidate for anybody, I planned to be out of there long before noon.

But when I pulled into the Clamshell parking lot, another familiar vehicle was already there, parked beside Jimmy's ancient green Pinto, Meredith's red Saturn, Nadine's black and white smart car, and Goodie's sea green Corolla. Sheriff Donaldson had backed his black and white Inceptor in right next to the motel office, primed, I assumed, for a quick get-away.

I took a deep breath, and braced myself. No doubt the sheriff had more "good advice" for the ladies to take on their dates with them. So far, no one had had to use the pepper spray, so I took that as a good sign, and hoped he'd back off a little.

"Welcome, Syl," said Jimmy as I came through the door. He handed me a cup of his strong, black coffee and whispered, "You're probably going to need this."

I took a big gulp before pasting a phony smile on my face and addressing the group. "So what have I missed?"

Sheriff D decided that I'd posed the question directly to him, which I kind of had, and he cleared his throat. "Well,

Sylvia, it seems that your Rainbow Girls are a little hesitant to give me any information about the fellows they've met."

My Rainbow Girls? I almost laughed. Almost. Instead, I kept my mouth closed, and took my eyes off Carter, looking from person to person around the table. Nadine, Goodie, and Meredith. Senior women I loved and deeply cared about. They looked back at me, waiting, I suppose, for me to tell the sheriff he could go pee up a rope.

I took another swig of coffee. "Ladies," I said, "I'm afraid I agree with the sheriff on this one. We don't know these men, and it's totally possible they're all just regular nice guys looking for love online. But it's also possible that one of them could be up to no good, and I'd really rather error on the side of caution."

I turned back to Sheriff D. He was tipped back in his chair, using his thumb and index finger of his right hand to smooth his mustache out from the center to the ends. I managed to keep from smiling at his frequent gesture during concentration, and waited until he sat up straight in his chair before I said, "What would you like to know?"

"We can start with first and last names," said Sheriff Donaldson. "I don't suppose anyone knows their date's birthdate, but I'll take it if you've got it, along with addresses, license plate numbers, anything that might help me run a background check."

Merri opened her mouth to protest, but I held up my hand in the universal "stop" signal. "No, Mother, I will not give in on this. I want to be as sure as I can be that you're all safe. I'd never forgive myself if something happened to any of you because we weren't prudent."

Sheriff D took his notebook and stubby pencil out of his shirt pocket and turned to Nadine. "You first," he said.

"Patrick O'Leary. I know he's somewhere past 55, but

I'm not sure how far. He's an Aquarius, so that's late January, first part of February. He drives a white van with no side windows, which is currently doubling as his residence because he's between apartments." I think even Nadine heard how sketchy that sounded.

"And that's all you know about him?" asked the sheriff.

"Well," said Nadine, "I know he's against offshore drilling."

The sheriff didn't jot that particular bit of information down in his notes, but moved on to Goodie. "And you?"

"Danny Smith," said Goodie. "He lives in Portland, and he drives a dark-colored Lexus. It's either midnight blue or black."

Sheriff D snorted. "Smith," he said. "Right. And how old is he?" asked Sheriff D.

Goodie looked down at the sleeve of her gray cardigan sweater and picked at a fuzzball on the cuff, not meeting the sheriff's eyes, or answering his question.

"Goodie?" repeated the sheriff. "Do you know Danny Smith's age?"

"Yes," said Goodie. She didn't meet anyone's eyes. She took a deep breath and continued, "His profile said he was 70, but when we met, he admitted that he'd accidently hit the 7 instead of the 6 when he typed his age in."

"So he's 60?" asked Sheriff D.

"I guess so," said Goodie in a small voice. She didn't look up from her sweater cuff.

I felt my stomach knot as tight as my Uncle Jay's wallet whenever it came time to pay the dinner bill.

"Danny Boy is 60?" I asked Goodie.

She lifted her head and nodded. "I'm sorry Syl. I didn't want any of you to think I was a cradle robber. I know he's 17 years younger than me, but I don't want anyone to judge."

"Good for you!" said Merri, clapping her on the back. "We've already outlived all the men our own age, might as well be on the lookout for someone a little younger."

I think I was still in shock. "Danny Boy is 60?" I repeated.

Goodie finally grasped what I'd been thinking. "He's not your ex-husband," she insisted. "He's kind, and funny, and smart, and I'm sure there are hundreds of men named Danny who are single and looking for dates on Sole Mates, and…" her voice trailed off.

I turned to Sheriff D, and tried to swallow the lump in my throat before speaking. "Carter, could you please do me a favor? Could you check to see if Mr. X, also known as Daniel Gardner, aged 60, is still incarcerated in Salem?"

"Oh, Syl," Meredith jumped in. "We both looked at his picture. It couldn't be him. This guy didn't wear glasses, did he Goodie?"

Goodie shook her head no.

"You need to relax, my dearest daughter," continued Merri. "Not everybody nicknamed Danny Boy is a bad guy."

"Carter?" I said again. "Will you do this for me? Please?"

Sheriff Donaldson agreed to my request, and I appreciated him for not rolling his eyes or shaking his head when he made a note to check on Mr. X's whereabouts.

"Your turn, Meredith," he said when he finished writing.

"Oh, would you look at the time!" said Meredith, rising to her feet. "You will all just have to come meet him tonight at the casino."

"Meredith Avery!" the sheriff's bark was all business, much louder than required to get Merri's attention, and she froze in her tracks. "His first and last name, please."

"Oh, all right." Merri said, and she sat back down. "Earl

Jones, fifty-something, five foot seven, brown eyes, brown hair, but he's balding, so it's just a fringe, really. He's currently housesitting in Gresham, I think, drives an older light blue pickup that's had some fender damage, and wears black-rimmed glasses like Jimmy's."

All eyes turned to look at Jimmy's glasses, as if we didn't know already exactly what they looked like.

"That's a pretty good description," said Sheriff D. "So what are you holding back?"

Merri scowled. "What makes you think I'm keeping anything from you?"

"I'm a trained investigator," said the sheriff, as if that answered her question. "So what are you hiding, Meredith? I need to know everything you know about him."

Meredith sighed and shrugged. "I guess you'll find out sooner or later. Earl was a financial investor a few years back and has done a little time in prison for fraud." She looked up at me and her eyes narrowed. "And don't you dare say 'I told you so!'"

"Fraud, huh?" said Sheriff D. "No other crimes?"

"Not that I know of," said Merri. Obviously, the wind had been taken out of her sails, but she wasn't going down without a fight. "Hey, I only just met him," she said, looking around the group. "If you're coming to the casino tonight, you can all just check him out for yourselves."

Sheriff Donaldson nodded. "I'm on duty at the south end tonight, but I'll have Freddy ask him a few questions, if you don't mind."

"I *DO* mind!" Meredith's eyes flashed. "I don't want tonight to be ruined by any lame-ass interrogation in the middle of the ballroom! That's just not fair!"

Sheriff D stroked his mustache again and looked at the ceiling. "Alright. I'll give you tonight. But watch your purse, and don't invite him back to your place after the show."

"Carter," said Merri, more calmly than I knew she felt, "Earl's truck will be at my house, so we'll have to go back there together."

"Then don't invite him *IN*," said the sheriff. "Can you do that?"

"Yes, sir!" said Merri, her arms now crossed over her chest and her face about the color of her bottled hair. "If you say so, sir!"

I had to give her credit for not saluting, but I think her crossed arms were actually holding a lot of her rage and indignation in.

"I say so," said Sheriff D. Then he closed his notebook and stood up. "Have a good time tonight," he said. "Break a leg, or whatever you belly dancers say for good luck."

After he'd left, Goodie reported that Danny Boy wasn't able to come down tonight to join us at the casino, but they had plans to go night clam digging the following weekend.

Nadine was all atwitter about Paranormal Patrick. "This could be the one!" she said. "He's got some great shh--." She stopped herself and looked apologetically at Goodie. "Sorry. He's got some great pot, and he's a leftover Greenpeace hippie freak, just like me!"

Then Nadine looked a bit uncomfortable. "Patrick was hit head-on by a drunk driver a couple years ago," she said. "He says it was the best thing that ever happened to him. Now he makes a living giving seances and delivering messages from the deceased to their loved ones."

"He does *WHAT*?" asked Goodie.

"He sees dead people," said Nadine. "And he makes sure their loved ones know their dearly departed family and friends are thinking of them."

"For a price," Merri said flatly.

"Yes, for a price," said Nadine, defending him. "That's how he makes money for food and gas and eventually rent, when he's able to save up enough."

"Right," said Merri. "You told the sheriff he was living in his van."

"If things work out on our next date, I think I'm going to let him park in my driveway for a few weeks. I can run an extension cord out there and he can use my shower in the house and —"

"WHOA! Just whoa!" I gave the referee's signal for a time out. "You're getting the cart way, way out in front of the horse, Nadine! Way, way out there! That poor horse is going to need a telescope before too long!"

Nadine changed direction, and told us that Patrick wouldn't be there at the casino tonight either, but they had plans to meet in the middle of next week, and she had invited him to come to her house for a visit before an early dinner.

"You invited him to your house?" asked Merri.

"Hey! Sheriff D didn't put any restrictions on *me* inviting a gentleman caller over," said Nadine. "You're the one who's dating an ex-con."

Meredith stood up and put her coffee cup into the sink. "I'll see you all tonight?" she asked, unnecessarily. "And Jimmy! You're still going to be running sound for us, right?"

"Right," said Jimmy. "Can't wait!"

And I couldn't wait to meet this peach of a guy that Mom was dating. She had invited him to Spartina Point as her date tonight, but I secretly hoped to high heaven that it didn't mean she was anywhere near being serious about him.

CHAPTER 10

"I am most sorry I will not be able to sit with you tonight, Miss Sylvia," said Kanji, placing a glass of diet ginger ale in front of me, and a signature Spartini cocktail in front of Mercedes.

The two of us were sitting at the very same table where we'd officially met Kanji just six months ago. How time flies! Tonight Kanji was not only the Hospitality Specialist, but also assisting the woman waiting tables in the casino ballroom.

"That's ok, Kanji," I replied. "This is a show, and there won't be an opportunity to dance, like when Mercedes is playing."

"You're rootin-tootin right about that!" said Merc. "I doubt there's even one waltz on their entire play list, although how can anyone really know? It's hard to find the beat with all those weird Middle Eastern instruments and—." She stopped without finishing her diatribe, but it was already a little late.

Kanji laughed. "No offense taken, Miss Mercedes. The rich culture of Middle Eastern music is not for all preferred tastes." Then to me, he added, "But if anything sounds like it might turn out to be a waltz, Miss Sylvia, I would be most honored if you save that dance for me." He bowed, kissed my hand, and walked to the next table for their order.

"Oh, girl, you're going to have to make up your mind

about him one of these days soon," said Mercedes. "That man is H-O-T, hot, and the women are practically lining up for him."

I didn't need to ask how Mercedes knew that, because she was, as she called it, "an invisible lounge singer, who saw all, and told no one," unless, of course, the gossip was just too juicy to keep to herself. Then she spread it all over town, bless her little pea-picking heart.

Promptly at 7 p.m., Jimmy appeared onstage, dressed head-to-toe in various shades of violet costuming. And I mean literally, from head to toe. He wore a sequined turban, billowing blouse/shirt open to the waist, flouncy, embroidered harem pants, and satin slippers with the tips curling up. He looked for all the world like he was auditioning for a role in the Broadway production of "Aladdin."

"Holy moly and Hay-soose to boot!" exclaimed Mercedes. This was as close as she ever came to swearing. "Would you just look at Jiminy Cricket!"

I was pretty sure everyone in the room was looking at Jimmy, and counted my blessings that it was him, and not me, who agreed to "run the sound" for The Veiled Rainbow tonight. The gals might not have convinced him to dance with them—yet—but it sure looked like they finally had a Violet to complete their rainbow.

Jimmy checked the boom box, making sure it held the right CD, discreetly tapped the wireless microphone a couple times to be sure the mic and both speakers were working properly, then motioned for the overhead room lights to be turned down in the ballroom, leaving only a spotlight on the area designated as the stage.

Rich Morgan, Freddy's father, and owner of Captain Morgan's Deep Sea Fishing Charters in Unity, suddenly appeared at our table, and slid into the chair next to me without asking permission until he was seated. "Ok if I sit here?"

"Of course!" I said. I gave him a genuine 'happy to see you' smile, and reached over to briefly squeeze and release his hand. I'd always been quite fond of Rich, although a good friendship had been the total sum of our involvement.

"A handsome man is always welcome to join us," said Mercedes.

"Rumor has it, Rich is taken," I chided her.

Rich smiled. "Nova's one hell of a woman, Sylvia, and she's savvy to the unpredictable lives of fishermen." He took a swig of the bottled beer he'd brought to the table with him. "I'm no fool. I'm smart enough to recognize a good woman when I see one," he said. His eyes rested on mine for just a second too long, and I almost squirmed, remembering more about our platonic, but only at my insistence, history.

Fortunately, before either of us could say anything more, Jimmy started the intro music. The varied sounds of the flowing music filled the room as I considered the recent twists and turns of Rich's life as a charter fisherman. Technically, it hadn't been his fault that his step-brother, Harold Rodman the Third, had used Rich's high school deckhand to unknowingly transport drugs up the North Beach Peninsula. Rich was now doing community service for his unwitting role in past events. Fortunately, he received no jail time, and he was actually enjoying teaching special needs high school kids how to fish.

My thoughts were interrupted as The Veiled Rainbow took the stage and Merri introduced the dancers. When their name and color was announced, they each did a wiggle, or turn, or hip flip, and waved to the crowd, just as they'd done six month ago in this very same venue.

Meredith was all dressed, except for her jingling gold coin belt, in shades of red, Orpha was in orange, Goodie in yellow, Nadine in green, and Nova in blue. And then Merri introduced their "sound man," Jimmy, who, she said, was not dancing—at least not tonight. Then she winked conspiratorially at the onlookers.

The Veiled Rainbow had drawn a big crowd, with lots of family and friends, of course, but also with plenty of North Beach Peninsula tourists and local looky-loos, wondering what this geriatric belly dancing troupe was all about.

With respect for their "advanced age," the rainbow gals were scheduled to do two sets of just 3 songs each, showcasing different movements in different songs. After their introductions, the first full-length song Jimmy cued up was one I was vaguely familiar with, though I only knew it by its abbreviated name, "Habibi, Habibi."

As the ladies began twirling and swirling, Kanji deftly rearranged the chairs at our table, and pulled up a seat between Mercedes and me.

I turned and smiled. "Taking a break?"

He nodded. "I could not miss the opportunity to watch the peninsula's veiled treasures perform once again," he said, "if only for a few minutes."

Kanji had been there last spring when The Veiled Rainbow first took this stage. Although he'd arrived on the peninsula under false pretenses, he was a welcome addition to our growing retirement community.

He leaned in to whisper in my ear, "This song's full name is 'Habibi Ya Nour El Ain' by Diab Amar, which means, 'my darling, you are the light of my eyes.'"

I don't know if it was the proximity of Kanji's lips to my ear, or that the room had suddenly become too warm for me to breathe, but I felt a flush tingle its way clear through me. I was afraid to face him, instinctively knowing that any movement in his direction was going to put our lips dangerously close to each other. So I did the safest thing I could think of—I kept my eyes firmly fixed on the dancers and just nodded.

Habibi, Habibi, I thought to myself. *My darling, my darling.*

"Pretty catchy tune, isn't it?" Freddy shouted above the music as he took the seat next to Mercedes. He nodded to Rich across the table from him. "Good to see you, Dad."

Of course, as the sole owner of the Spartina Point Casino and Resort, Freddy had every right, and responsibility, to mingle with all the guests in the ballroom tonight, but I found his timing was just a little suspicious, arriving only moments after Kanji had joined us.

The ladies finished their first song, and both Kanji and Freddy stood up to leave. Kanji bent down to kiss my hand as he departed, but Freddy just gave me an indecipherable look as he left us. Was that jealousy? Or annoyance? Or maybe he was just as confused about our relationship as I was. The time was quickly coming when we'd both have to figure out what it was we wanted from each other, but I hoped it wouldn't be too soon.

After two more songs, Meredith took the microphone while the ladies caught their breath. "And now, a special treat." She smiled broadly. "I know many of you are surprised, and maybe even inspired, by our performance. So we've decided to bring a few of you up here with us and show you how to do some classic movements yourselves."

I closed my eyes and willed myself to be invisible. Please no, please no, please no. She wouldn't dare! Would she?

Mercedes reached over and squeezed my arm. "It's okay, Syl, there are plenty of crazies here, waving their arms in the air and hoping to be chosen to make fools of themselves."

I opened my eyes, and saw that the rainbow ladies were jingling and shimmying through the audience, each of them choosing a volunteer to join them onstage.

Nova approached our table, and seductively motioned with one hand and then the other for Rich to come with her as she backed away from our table. It surprised me no end when Rich set down his beer and stood up to follow her.

"Well, would you look at that?" said Mercedes.

Merc had not known that Nova and Rich had become quite an item on the south end of the peninsula, but it was obvious she approved. The five ladies each found someone brave enough to participate in their demonstration, and Merc and I both breathed a huge sigh of relief.

"I'm glad they didn't try to get me up there," said Mercedes. "I get all the exercise I need doing step aerobics at home."

I gave her a quizzical look. "Step aerobics? Do tell."

"Yep. Every time Brutus is lying on the floor where I want to walk, I just say, "Don't get up," and I step right over him!"

I laughed. "With a program like that, you'll probably live forever."

"Oh, I got myself an insurance policy for a long life," said Merc. "I decided that the last thing I want to taste before I die is white chocolate raspberry cheesecake. So it stands to reason that as long as I don't indulge in another piece of white chocolate raspberry cheesecake, I'm sure to live forever."

I chose not to challenge Mercedes' logic, and watched the dancers and volunteers practice a few hip flips, snake arms, and veil work to an innocuous little tune. None of the audience members were any good at it, but everyone seemed to be having a great time.

Freddy returned, and sat in the seat Kanji had left. He put a proprietary arm across the back of my chair, and I didn't know whether to be pleased or irritated.

"The sheriff is none too pleased about the online dating adventures of Goodie, Nadine, and Meredith," he said.

I looked directly at him and exhaled pointedly through my nose. "So tell me something I don't already know."

"Well," Freddy began, "do you know how you, and the other women, can learn to be quite adept at becoming human lie detectors?"

"Oh," said Merc, "that skill could come in mighty handy when a guy's lying his tushy off, just trying to get himself into a lady's knickers."

I might not have said it as eloquently as Merc did, but she definitely had a point.

I wasn't sure if Freddy was more concerned about my personal welfare, or the ladies who had profiles up on Sole Mates, but I knew the bottom line was that he wanted everyone to stay safe, so I said nothing, and he went on.

"Okay, Sylvia, since you're not getting your feathers all ruffled, I'll assume you're not going to fight me on this, I'll give you the two-minute crash course," Freddy began. "And you can fill the rest of the gals in on it the next time you meet up at Jimmy's."

I nodded.

"Okay. When a guy is using pronouns instead of names, talking more slowly than normal, pursing his lips, scratching his nose, leaning back in his chair, blinking more, and then less, he might be spinning a yarn," said Freddy.

Merc and I both nodded.

"But maybe his nose just itches," said Mercedes. "You know like when you're about to sneeze, and it tickles, and you scratch it because you don't want to sneeze just then."

"One or two of these might not be a problem," said Freddy, "but it's prudent to be on high alert, especially if there's a definite lack of eye contact."

I wondered if Sheriff Donaldson had put Freddy up to coaching us in lie detection, but I decided it didn't matter. Good information was still good information, and I wanted to keep the ladies out of harm's way no matter who was the messenger, or even if his bottom-line intentions were somewhat self-serving.

Meredith returned to the microphone, thanked the volunteers for being such good sports, and had them all give their names and take a bow as they left the stage. Then she announced that The Veiled Rainbow was about to take a short break. "But don't y'all go anywhere," said Merri. "We'll be back before you know it!"

Rich returned to our table, while four out of five of the gals disappeared to the restroom that tonight doubled as a dressing room. Merri, however, wandered through the tables along the far wall, then headed back in our direction with a gentleman in tow.

"Hello, everyone!" said Merri. "I'd like you to meet my friend Earl."

It took everything I had to keep from blurting out "Hello, EarltheSqwearl," but for once I was able to control my mouth.

"Earl Jones," said Merri, "I'd like you to meet..." and she motioned to each of us as she introduced us around the table. "...Mercedes, who plays music here on the nights we're not performing, Freddy, who owns and runs this place when he's not at work as a county deputy, Sylvia, my daughter, and Rich, who is both Freddy's father and a charter boat captain in Unity."

I was proud of Mercedes for not jumping down Meredith's throat for not introducing her as the main musical attraction three weekends out of four in the ballroom, and the fact that Freddy shook Earl's hand and then moved on to another table.

Earl set the drink he'd brought with him down on the table, let go of Merri's hand, and held her chair for her. He wasn't much to look at, but at least he had a few manners.

The other four dancers soon joined us at the table, coincidentally arriving just as Kanji showed up with a full tray of champagne flutes. I knew the flutes were filled with nothing stronger than ginger ale, so I helped myself as he came around with the tray.

Merri introduced the dancers to Earl, and then the real interrogation began. Orpha started it off, by asking how much money he had, then Goodie asked about his religious beliefs, and Nadine wanted to know if he'd voted for the legalization of marijuana.

Nova, bless her heart, was too busy making goo-goo eyes and talking quietly with Rich, her arm looped snuggly through his.

I wanted to let the troupe satisfy their curiosity, as they were Merri's closest friends, after all, so I just sat back and watched Jimmy changing the discs in the player and setting out an array of brightly colored scarves for the next number.

Nevertheless, I was still tuned in to what was being said, and tried keeping a straight face as the girls were grilling Earl. Orpha was right; this was much more entertaining than reality TV.

We'd all scooted over to squeeze everyone in—all nine of us, plus an extra chair for Jimmy when he finished setting up the next set, at a table for eight, so when Mercedes dug her elbow into my ribs, it wasn't much of a stretch.

Merc leaned over and whispered, "Do you think Earl has to sneeze?"

I looked at him over there, fielding the more-than-polite personal questions right and left, and in the space of only a few minutes, Earl scratched his nose, pursed his lips, leaned back in his chair, blinked his eyes as if to rid them of some invasive debris, and started talking like his life was in molasses-bound slow motion.

I excused myself with the pretense of using the restroom, and went looking for Freddy. "I hate to ask you to do this," I began, "but would you mind discreetly collecting Earl's glass in an evidence bag so you or Sheriff D can run his fingerprints?"

"I'm way ahead of you, Sylleegirl," said Freddy. "He calls himself Earl Jones?" He shook his head. "I'm just not buying it."

Back at the table, the focus of the conversation had shifted from Earl to the idea that since Freddy had allowed The Veiled Rainbow to perform, perhaps he'd be willing to consider hosting at least one evening of classy male strippers, "just to keep the balance between the genders."

Jimmy had joined the group, and he was all smiles. "Yeah, well, maybe that wouldn't keep things totally even," he said, "since there are those of us men who'd appreciate seeing some shirtless male dancers here as well."

"I'm just saying," continued Merc, "that the 'Thunder Down Under' has been touring the casino circuit, and I don't see why Freddy couldn't invite them to perform here, too."

"Mercedes!" Merri admonished her. "Don't you have your hands full with the sheriff, already? What would he think if he caught you ogling a bunch of scantily clothed men?"

"I think he'd appreciate whatever, or whoever got me in

the mood!" said Merc, laughing.

It was totally too much information, and I was beginning to think at least some of them may have had a nip or two of a private alcohol stash in their dressing room.

Goodie giggled, Nadine belly-laughed, and Jimmy literally bounced in his chair. "Sylvia... Oh, Sylvia..." The way Jimmy said it made my name sound like it did in the song from Dirty Dancing. "Why don't you ask Freddy if he'll find out about hiring them? It wouldn't hurt to ask."

It was obvious why they'd ask me to do their dirty work, but before I could decline the honor of embarrassing myself by asking my part-time boyfriend if he'd bring in strippers for the entertainment of me and my gal pals, plus Jimmy, Orpha suddenly knocked over her ginger ale.

Several of our group instantly grabbed for the glass, and others threw their cocktail napkins in Orpha's direction to attempt to mop up the mess. But Orpha herself didn't move. Her suddenly pale face displayed an expression of total surprise as she softly said, "Oh dear," put both hands up to her chest, and slid from her chair right onto the floor beneath the table.

"*MEDIC!*" bellowed Mercedes in her loudest opera-trained voice.

Rich and Earl jumped up and pulled the table out of the way, as both Freddy and Kanji arrived on the scene. Freddy had the first-aid kit, and Kanji carried the defibrillator. After a quick triage assessment of the situation, it turned out that Kanji carried the most useful cargo.

Thankfully, Freddy was well-trained in using the "jump starter," as he called it, and he'd insisted that all his employees be able to run the portable apparatus.

Orpha, eyes closed, lay deathly still, a very poor choice of adverb, and I couldn't see if her chest was moving up and down enough to indicate breathing. I felt a rush of tears stinging my eyes. I looked around the group, and saw similar expressions of disbelief and grief.

But within minutes, the men had administered an electric shock, and Orpha took a huge, gasping breath. "Where am I?" she said, and made a half-hearted attempt to get to her feet.

Kanji held her hand and told her to lie still, while Freddy used his cell phone to order a medivac helicopter to come take Orpha to the hospital in Portland. It was the first time I'd been grateful the casino came equipped with a helipad on the roof, and thankfully, Orpha's ride was quick to arrive.

By then, she was a little more herself, saying she'd never ridden in a helicopter before, and asking if she was going to have to pay more to get a window seat.

As they took our dear friend away, the group consensus was that since Nova had Orpha's car keys, having driven them both to the casino, that I'd drive us all in Orpha's Crown Vic to Portland. The Crown Vic was a little like driving a tank, but it was big enough that all us women could ride together. We decided to make quick stops at each of our residences, including Orpha's, to pick up a few overnight essentials and a change of clothes.

Only Meredith dissented. "I'm not going," she said. "There's nothing we can do, and I don't think it's necessary to dash to Portland in the dark tonight. Tomorrow we'll know a lot more about her condition."

Even though Merri was a retired nurse, and knew more about such things than the rest of us, I wasn't sure if her reasoning was valid, or if her interrupted date with Earl caused her to decline our road trip, but I didn't have time to debate her decision. We needed to get going, and we needed to get going *NOW!*

CHAPTER 11

If Merri had considered inviting Earl in, despite the sheriff's warning not to, it wouldn't have mattered. Earl headed straight from Merri's red Saturn to his dilapidated pickup, without even walking her to her door. "I know with Orpha's collapse, you've got a lot on your mind," he said, unlocking his truck door. "I'll call you." He hopped into the truck and roared out of Merri's driveway without so much as a backward glance.

Meredith didn't know whether to be grateful or perturbed that Earl had not even attempted to kiss her goodnight. She put her key in the lock, but discovered the door wasn't locked. Thinking she must have just forgotten to turn the button on the knob when they'd left, she went on inside, and flipped on the light switch next to the door.

"Holy mother of—" Meredith froze in the doorway. Her living room had been ransacked. Drawers and cupboards stood open, the couch cushions were all on the floor, pictures hung crookedly on the walls.

Merri started to go on inside, then took a step backwards, turned, and ran to her car. She locked herself inside, then dug through her purse for her cell phone.

"9-1-1," said the operator. "What is the nature of your emergency?"

Despite considering herself a woman of substance and determination, Meredith burst into tears. She managed to choke out her address, and the fact that she wasn't sure if the burglars were gone, or even where her three cats were.

The operator instructed her to stay on the line until the police arrived, but Merri insisted that she had to make one more call, promised to stay locked in her vehicle in the driveway, disconnected from the dispatcher, and punched in another number.

"Meredith?" asked the concerned voice on the other end of the line. "Is everything alright?"

"Kanji!" said Meredith. "I need help! I know you're working, and Freddy's not on deputy duty tonight, but I need you both to come over right away. My house has been broken into!"

And as Merri predicted, Freddy and Kanji, still both wearing tailored suits, arrived in Freddy's police cruiser nearly 15 minutes before Sheriff Donaldson, who'd been working in Unity, on the south end of the peninsula. Meredith immediately threw herself into Kanji's arms and sobbed without reservation, while Freddy, Glock in hand, went inside, making sure the small house contained no hiding criminals.

"All clear," said Freddy, rejoining them in the driveway. "I located Harlan, Chuckie, and Bob, all hiding in various small places, but they seem unharmed."

"Oh! My poor cats!" said Merri. "They must have been terribly traumatized! Is it okay to go inside now?"

"Not yet," said Freddy. "Let's wait for the sheriff to get here and dust for fingerprints. And I'll help him check for other evidence, as well."

Freddy took a good look at Meredith, wearing a wool pea coat over her full red satin belly-dancing costume, additionally wrapped in Kanji's arms. "Uh... Is there something you two would like to tell me?" he asked.

"There is nothing of any particular consequence to tell," said Kanji, speaking for the both of them. "Miss Meredith and I have discovered we both share a love of classic movies. We have attended many matinees at the theater in Fort George together over the summer." He looked fondly at Meredith. "We have become dear friends."

Meredith lifted her head from Kanji's chest. "Kanji and I are good friends, Freddy." She looked Freddy straight in the eye. "And Sylvia doesn't need to know a thing about it."

Freddy said nothing. He could hear the sheriff's siren coming up Pacific Highway and he opened the trunk of his car, parked right next to Meredith's, withdrawing rubber gloves and evidence bags. "We should be through here in less than an hour," said Freddy to Meredith. "Then you can come in and start making a list of missing items."

Meredith's fear turned to rage when the men finally let her back inside her house. "Those lousy sons-of-a-" she stopped herself from the stream of swear words that came quickly to her lips, but her anger kept building as she took in all the destruction and chaos inside the sanctuary of her usually tidy home. "When you catch these jerks, Sheriff, I want 5 minutes alone with them, and I don't mean in that room at the station with an observation mirror!"

Sheriff D ignored her outburst, and instructed her to complete her inventory and come in to the station in Tinkerstown to make a statement the next afternoon. Then he handed her a business card. "You might want to look into installing a security system," he said. "We've worked with these guys before."

Meredith took the card and stared at it blankly. "You mean the robbers might come back?"

"Maybe not the *same* guys," said Freddy, "but unfortunately, there are more than a couple crooks on the peninsula. There are plenty of drug addicts and tweakers looking for cash or jewelry they can quickly pawn to get their next fix."

Meredith bent over and ran a hand along the backs of Harlan, Chuckie, and Bob, who were all rubbing against her legs, clamoring for attention. She swiped at the tears on her face before turning back to the men. "Kanji?"

"I would be most honored to stay and help you reorganize your home," said Kanji. "And if you would feel more secure tonight, I shall stay until the morning."

Meredith nodded. "Yes. Please. I've never felt so vulnerable in my own home."

"That's quite understandable," said Sheriff Donaldson. "Besides your tangible items, they have stolen your feeling of safety." He squeezed her shoulder as he headed for the door.

Meredith nodded, deep in thought. "Sheriff?"

Both Sheriff D and Freddy turned back to hear her out.

"You all know I was at the casino tonight."

They both nodded.

"So my car was not in the driveway."

They both silently nodded again, waiting for her to formulate her thoughts.

"But Earl had ridden with me, and his truck was in the driveway," said Merri. "Why didn't that keep the thieves from breaking in? How could they have been sure no one was home?"

"I hate to say this," said Freddy, "but we advertised the belly dancing event all over Facebook, so anyone on social media could have known you weren't home tonight."

"It is true," said Kanji. "The advertisement contained all the ladies' photos and names."

"But there was a vehicle in the driveway," repeated Merri.

Sheriff D cleared his throat. "They could have just knocked on the door, Meredith. If anyone had answered, they could have pretended to be asking for directions." He shook his head. "Please try to get some rest tonight."

Rest was the last thing on her mind at the moment, but Meredith nodded weakly.

Again, Freddy and Sheriff D started for the door.

Again, Meredith said, "Sheriff?"

And again, both men stopped and turned and patiently waited for her to speak.

"What about canvassing the neighbors? Maybe one of them saw a vehicle or something."

Both men smiled. "You watch too much crime TV," said the sheriff, not unkindly.

"I watch *some*," Meredith protested, all but stamping her foot, "but not that much!"

The radio crackled on Sheriff D's uniform collar. Although the words were all but indecipherable to those not trained in the fine art of radio speaker crackle, the sheriff immediately turned to Freddy and said, "I've got to get down to Tinkerstown. Can you take this from here?"

The sheriff left, and Freddy diligently went to check with the two neighbors who might have seen any vehicles coming or going from Meredith's driveway. It was a long shot, and they all knew it, but Freddy also knew that Merri might sleep a tiny bit better after he asked them anyway.

Kanji, bless his heart, put the kettle on for tea while Meredith fed the cats. Then together they methodically went room to room, both of them straightening things up as Merri made a list of missing items, most of which had been in her bedroom. And as Freddy had predicted, jewelry was the main thing missing, her earring racks ripped from the wall and her own suitcase used to transport the stolen items.

Fortunately, all her "good" jewelry was in a safety deposit box at the bank, and the robbers got only her costume earrings, but that was bad enough.

Freddy soon returned, and politely knocked on the door. "Turns out we may have gotten a lead after all," he began. "Your neighbor to the north—Mrs. Carpenter?— she said that a couple hours ago, two men in a white van pulled into her driveway, then just turned the van around and left, without knocking on the door or anything. She didn't get a good look at them, other than to know that they were men, and of course, she didn't think to get a license plate number, but it could give us a hand up in this investigation."

"I knew it!" said Meredith, almost sounding like her old self. She narrowed her eyes and said, "You be sure to remind the sheriff it was my idea to canvass the neighborhood."

Freddy said he'd be happy to do that, and left Meredith in the company of her good friend Kanji. He wondered if he should tell Sylvia about Merri's overnight guest when she returned from Portland, but thought better of it. It really wasn't any of his business if Kanji and Meredith were dating, but if they were, that meant Kanji wasn't a threat to Freddy's own growing affection for Sylvia, and that made him smile as he drove back to Spartina Point alone.

Nadine, Goodie, Nova, and I arrived at the hospital in Portland a little more than five hours after Orpha had arrived by helicopter. Although Nadine kept urging me to "step on it," Orpha's ancient Crown Vic would only go so fast up the hills in the coast range, and although I tried to make up some time going down the hills, it still seemed to take forever to get there.

We'd have been there two hours sooner if we hadn't stopped at all of our houses as we careened down the peninsula, but it couldn't be helped. At each of our homes, we picked up a few necessities to spend a night or two in town. Nadine, Goodie, and Nova, of course, had all changed into street clothes and shoes.

Our last stop before heading east was Orpha's apartment, where we put enough cat food out to keep her cat named Cat happy for at least a week, gathered her reading glasses, cell phone charger, bathrobe and slippers, and a set of clothes that were a lot less conspicuous than the orange belly dancing costume she'd been wearing when they life flighted her away.

Orpha's collapse had taken place right around 7:30 p.m., so it was going on 2:00 a.m. when the four of us hurriedly approached the admissions desk in the hospital emergency room.

Naturally, I figured the HIPPA privacy rules were going to prevent us from knowing if she'd even survived the helicopter ride, as none of us were related to the unstoppable Orpha Starr. But Orpha, bless her heart, had had the presence of mind when they brought her in to put me down as her emergency contact, so we knew that she was still breathing when she got here, and we were privy to her medical status after all.

The admissions clerk, after carefully checking two pieces of my photo ID, paged the doctor on call, and told us to take a seat.

Dr. Swanson, still in his scrubs, met with us a few minutes later. "Orpha is doing well," he said, right off the bat. "We put in a stent, and she should make a full recovery."

We all expelled a collective sigh of relief, and Goodie started quietly crying.

"When can we see her?" I asked.

Dr. Swanson smiled. "There are a couple of motels close

by. I suggest you all get some sleep and come back in the morning—say about 10:30 or 11 o'clock. By then we'll have done the morning rounds, and we will have a lot more to tell you."

"Ten-thirty or 11 o'clock?" I repeated. "Not until then?"

"You can have breakfast in the hospital cafeteria. It's quite reasonable, and the food is much better than back in the not-so-good old days." He chuckled. "Now, if you'll excuse me—" And he quickly walked back through the double doors to the trauma center.

I turned to the other three ladies. "Let's all make a pact not to tell Merri she was right," I said, holding out my pinkie finger. "Let's pinkie swear to keep this to ourselves!"

"I just hate that she's at home sleeping in her own bed tonight, while we're going to be sharing a motel room, and probably a bed, too," said Nadine. She sighed. "And I didn't even think to bring any weed to help us all relax."

Nova handed the satchel we'd packed up at Orpha's house over to one of the ladies at the desk, and she said she'd call an orderly to take it right up to her. "And please be sure she tells Orpha that her belly-dancing friends will be here to see her in the morning," said Nova.

The woman smiled. "I sure will."

Promptly at 10:31 the next morning, we entered Orpha's room. The bed was empty, and I know at least one heart that leaped to one of our throats, because that heart was mine. I looked at the empty bed, and then at the others, and I could tell they were thinking the same thing I was thinking, and I knew none of us wanted to say it out loud.

Fortunately, the fear passed as quickly as it came when we heard a familiar voice call out, "Hello out there! Nurse? Is that you?" from the bathroom.

Goodie blew out a breath and smiled. She reached over

and pressed the call button on Orpha's bed, and a nurse promptly came to assist our eldest friend.

"Well, well, well," said Orpha, seeing us all gathered around her bed. "Why all the long faces? Did you think I'd gone to meet my maker?"

"As long as you're already up and toileted," said the nurse before any of us could mumble out a reply, "would you like to take another walk around the nurse's station?"

"Another walk?" asked Nova. "You mean she's been up and walking already?"

"Don't talk about me like I'm not here!" said Orpha. "Of course I've been up and walking already," she continued. "You saw that for yourself when I came out of the bathroom!"

Obviously, the surgery had taken none of the spunk out of her, and we dutifully agreed to walk a hall lap or two with her. The nurse wheeled Orpha's IV pole next to me, so I took charge of it as Orpha held her bright-red heart-shaped pillow against her chest.

"They give one of these to everyone in the cardiac ward," she said. "Isn't that nice?"

The five of us went out into the hall and Orpha stuck her head into the very next room. "Grandpa Beebops!" she called out. "Want to join our purple penis parade?"

Goodie gasped. "Oh, dear."

Orpha turned to Goodie. "Well, it's not my fault," she defended herself. "Just take a good look at the heart diagram on this pillow." She held it straight out from her chest for us to view.

We all stared at the heart. We could see the chambers, and the arteries, and the valves, all of various colors, and sure enough, right there—in purple—was what certainly looked like an upward curving penis!

Goodie gasped again. "Now I'll never be able to unsee that."

Nadine took a closer look, tracing it with her finger as she examined it. "And *everyone* here gets one of these pillows?"

"That's right!" said Orpha, bobbing her curls up and down. "Men and women both! Ain't it a hoot?"

Nova said nothing, but quietly reached over and took Orpha's pillow. I thought she was going to turn it around, so the design didn't show, but she quietly turned it upside down instead. The effect was that the purple penis now curved down instead of up. "That's more natural-looking, don't you think?" she said to Orpha.

Grandpa Beebops chose that moment to emerge from his room, his IV pole in one hand, and his rather obscene pillow in the other. His knee-length blue bathrobe was tied tight at his waist, and he wore slippers to match. I guessed his age to be about 75 or 80, and his face lit up like an LED flashlight as he beamed at Orpha.

"I'm all packed up and ready to go, honey," he said in a voice much too loud for a hospital hallway. "Except for my hearing aids. Can't seem to remember what I did with them when I took them out last night." He laughed. "So if you'll just talk loud when you introduce me to your friends, Orpha, I won't have to ask you to repeat yourself."

I shot a look at Orpha, who was looking adoringly at the bald little man in the blue bathrobe. "Orpha?" I could feel my eyebrows vaulting toward my hairline. "You've been here less than 24 hours, had a stent put in just last night, and you've already found yourself a honey?"

Orpha pursed her lips and rolled her eyes. "Time is of the essence, Sylvia" she said. "Surely you're of an age now where you can appreciate that. None of us are going to live forever!" Then she pointed to each of us in turn. "Bill," she said, nearly shouting at him, "I'd like you to meet Nova, Goodie, Nadine, and Sylvia. Gals, I'd like you to meet my friend Bill."

"Bill?" I whispered to her. "You sure his name is the same as your deceased husband?"

"Ain't it a hoot?" asked Orpha in her normal speaking voice. "I won't ever have to worry about calling him by the wrong name!"

I couldn't begin to argue with that logic, and since the other gals were too stunned to have anything to contribute to the conversation, the six of us started shuffling as one down the hallway, like in the opening credits of "The Golden Girls."

"Hi Orpha!" called out one of the men in the next room. "Are you going home today?"

"*Home?*" Goodie and Nadine said together.

Orpha took two steps backwards and waved to the man in the first bed. "Not today, John," she answered. "They want to keep me one more day for observation. They must think I'm old or something."

John laughed. "Maybe they just want to keep you here to improve our morale!"

"I charge by the hour!" said Orpha.

John's roommate, sitting in the chair by the window, called out to Orpha, "Do you know the difference between cardio surgeons and God?" He paused briefly, then answered the question himself. "God doesn't think he's a cardio surgeon." Then he laughed at his own joke.

The rest of us laughed politely, then walked on. A nurse, whose hospital ID said Ms. Simmons, joined us to take a look at Orpha's IV. "As soon as you finish this lap around the nurses' station, we'll come in to remove this," she said. "You wouldn't have needed it at all if you hadn't been so dehydrated when you arrived."

Nova stepped forward and asked Ms. Simmons the question I'm sure was burning in all our brains. "How long is the usual stay after a stent has been put in?"

Ms. Simmons smiled. "Most angioplasty or stent placement patients go home in 12 to 24 hours." She lowered her voice. "We're keeping Orpha here overnight so that she and Bill can watch a movie on TV together this evening. It's their date night." She winked at Orpha.

Orpha winked back.

There were at least four of us who knew the nurse couldn't be serious about Orpha and Bill having a date night, but if it made them happy to think so, then who were we to say otherwise?

Bill, for his part, hollered at the nurse, "I hope we're having red Jell-O for lunch. I'm not so fond of the green kind. It makes me think it's gone bad and spoiled."

Orpha looked at him and giggled. "Isn't he just adorbs?" She reached over and took his free hand. "He's going to be here a few more days. After he gets home and feels a little stronger, he's going to see if his daughter will drive him down to Unity for a visit."

We completed our walk, dropped Bill off at his room, and found that a couple extra chairs had been placed around Orpha's bed. True to her word, Ms. Simmons came in and removed her IV, and asked us if any of us wanted coffee or tea or anything.

"Wow," said Nadine. "Hospitals sure have changed since the last time I was in one."

"When was that?" asked Orpha. "The last time you gave birth?"

And with that first bit of fun poked at Nadine, we all

settled in for a day of lighthearted banter and convivial conversation, and I'm ashamed to say it wasn't until almost dinnertime that I thought to call Meredith to report on Orpha's medical status.

CHAPTER 12

"Hi, honey," said Meredith when she picked up the phone. "How's Orpha?"

As I filled her in, I couldn't help but sense something was wrong on Merri's end. She asked no follow-up questions, murmured no more than a word or two to let me know she was still there and listening, and never once interrupted me. Finally, I came right out and asked her what was wrong.

"Now, don't you go getting upset," Merri began. "But when I got home from Spartina Point last night, my house had been broken into."

I think I gasped, but in hindsight, my gasp might have had a small shriek attached to it. The women in the hospital room all became silent and stared at me, waiting for me to tell them what was going on with Meredith.

"Uh, Mom? Can I put you on speaker phone?"

Putting our conversation on the speaker saved me from having to repeat everything to the gals after I hung up, but it sure didn't help communications for the five of us to all be asking her questions at the same time. Finally, I held up my hands for everyone in the room to stop talking.

"We'll do this one at a time," I said. "Starting with me."

Meredith was a little hesitant to admit she hadn't spent the night alone, but I don't know if I was more peeved or relieved when she admitted it was Kanji and not Earl who'd spent the night with her. But my radar went on red alert when she kept adamantly insisting that Kanji had slept on her couch. The lady did protest too much, me thinks, but I kept my thoughts to myself.

"Now don't you worry," said Merri as the questions wound down. "The sheriff recommended a security company, I called them, and they have already been here. They're coming back to install my alarm system when it gets here in a few days."

"Isn't that like closing the barn door after the horses are out?" asked Nadine.

"Are you afraid they might come back?" asked Goodie.

"Would you like someone to stay with you until it's installed?" asked Nova.

"Why don't you just get a gun?" asked Orpha.

Meredith sighed so heavily I almost felt the breeze come through the phone. "No, no, no, and hell no," she said emphatically. "Statistics show that most often a gun is taken away from the homeowner and turned on them. A gun would only make me feel more fearful."

I kept my mouth tightly closed. She knew I had a 9mm Glock, and she knew I knew how to use it. And Mercedes had a gun, if you could call her little pink .22 pea shooter a gun. And I was willing to bet Nova kept one on the boat. But there was no way I was going to get suckered into any discussion about the pros and cons of gun ownership right at the moment.

"Are you sure you're okay?" I asked. "If you need us to come home tonight, we will. Otherwise, we're planning on one more night in town, then bringing Orpha back with us tomorrow."

"I'm fine, Sylvia," Merri insisted. "I wasn't even going to bother you with any of this until you got back. What's done is done, and there's nothing you can do."

Merri was right, of course, but I couldn't keep from feeling a bit guilty that I wasn't there to hold her hand.

"Stop by tomorrow when you get back," said Merri. "That's all I need right now, just to see my daughter and spend a little quality time with her."

It seemed like there was more to it than that, but before I could press the issue, Orpha's dinner tray arrived, so we all said our good-byes to Meredith, and I hung up.

Goodie lifted the cover off the tray and I looked at the generous portion of salmon alongside a fresh green salad and dinner roll, and my mouth started salivating.

"Would you look at that?" said Orpha, lifting a piece of her salad with her fork. "The menu said 'argumentative salad,' but this looks just like plain old curly lettuce."

Nadine picked up the slip of paper with Orpha's order on it and laughed. "You should try wearing your glasses when you order your meals, Orpha. It says arugula salad, not argumentative!"

We all had a good laugh, then Orpha booted us out of her room so she could eat in peace before her big date with Grandpa Beebops. "See you in the morning," she said as she waved good-bye. "But don't come back too early!" And she winked again.

I'm not sure any of us knew, or even wanted to know, exactly what she meant by that, so none of us ventured to ask. *Culpable deniability*, I thought wryly, as we left the hospital.

The next morning, Nurse Simmons flagged our entourage of four down before we got to Orpha's room. "We had a little excitement last night," she began.

"Is Orpha okay?" I quickly asked.

"Oh, she's fine, and Bill's fine, too, but one of the young orderlies wanted to insist that Bill return to his room at 9:30, and Orpha got quite loud, and was borderline verbally abusive, saying Grampa Beebops wasn't going anywhere until the movie was over."

"That's our gal," said Nadine, matter-of-factly.

"Oh, but it gets worse," said the nurse. "The orderly came out of her room quite shaken up and called a 'Code Gray' on the intercom."

"Code Gray?" I asked.

"A combative or abusive person, but with no visible weapons," said the nurse. "Security came running, but there won't be any charges pressed, as Orpha promised she would apologize right after the movie was over, which she did."

Good grief and gravy! Orpha sure knew how to keep the pot stirred!

"Anything else we need to know?" I asked, hoping the answer was no.

"Well, we'd like her to stay through lunch, so we can give our favorite patient a special little send off," said Ms. Simmons. "Since it's her birthday and all."

Her birthday? I looked at Nova, Nadine, and Goodie, and I could tell they were as clueless as I was, but I didn't let on to the nurse that we had no idea of either her birthday or year. "And what kind of a surprise did you have in mind?"

"Pudding cups for everyone!" said Ms. Simmons. "And we'll free up as much staff as we can to sing her Happy Birthday, of course."

"Of course," I said. "So, Ms. Simmons, I assume you saw her birthdate on her chart?"

The nurse nodded.

"And how old did it say she was today?"

Ms. Simmons smiled. "Your friend tried her best to

convince us that the year written on her chart was wrong and that she's turning 85 today."

I laughed. "She's been saying she'll die being 85, but we really don't know if she's above or below that number, but we suspect she's a few years above." I gave her my best smile. "So would you mind telling us just how old she is today?

"Well," said Ms. Simmons, "I don't think I'll get into any HIPPA trouble if I hint at her age, since everyone on this floor already knows." She smiled conspiratorially. "Your inspirational belly-dancing friend became a nonagenarian today."

"A what?" asked Nadine.

"She's 90?!" said Nova.

"Oops," said Ms. Simmons, briefly putting her hand over her mouth. "I guess the cat's out of the bag!"

"No worries," I assured her. "Our lips are zipped. We won't tell anyone who told us." But I wondered just how long any one of us would actually be able to keep that promise.

As it turned out, we didn't have to keep mum about Orpha's age at all. After a nice-looking lunch of soup, salad, and half a sandwich, Nurse Simmons wheeled in Grandpa Beebops, and the staff all gathered to sing, modifying the middle line of the song to be, "Happy 90th, dear Orpha."

Orpha looked like she was going to deny her age, but when she discovered Grandpa Beebops still didn't have his hearing aids in and hadn't heard that part, she just smiled and shrugged. "I guess since I've honestly earned all those years, I might as well claim them."

After pudding cups all around, Orpha insisted that the staff get back to work and the rest of us turn our backs or at least close our eyes so she could collect a decent birthday kiss from Bill. "One never knows how many more men I'll get to kiss while I can still remember their names," she said with a gleam in her eye.

The ride home in Orpha's car was a little cramped, but otherwise congenial and uneventful. We spent most of the drive catching Orpha up to speed concerning the online dating exploits of Deenie, GiGi, and Mermaid, otherwise known as Nadine, Goodie, and Meredith.

Nadine was still all atwitter about seeing Patrick again, as, according to her, they were definitely on the same wave length. I had to force myself to exercise extreme self-control to keep from asking if they were going to wear matching foil helmets to keep the aliens from reading their minds, but somehow, I managed.

Goodie was planning on seeing Danny Boy the next Friday night, and they were going out to dig clams, something she hadn't done in many years. I was relieved to hear her say it was Danny's idea to go out on a night clam dig. That was something I don't think my own "Danny Boy" would ever have suggested for a second date.

Orpha had met Earl at the casino, and like the rest of us, was none too thrilled about Merri's choice of dates. "There's something shady about him," said Orpha. "I just don't trust him."

It was as good a time as any to share Freddy's advice about becoming human lie detectors, so I did, although I rather wished Merri had been there with us so I wouldn't have to explain it twice. I also shared how Mercedes and I had witnessed Earl demonstrating almost all of the "tells" that indicated he was lying when we first met him.

"I think your instincts are right on about that guy," I told Orpha. "I hope we're able to steer Merri in another direction." I sighed. "I just hope she's open to looking at someone else on the dating site. I don't want to have to fight her on this."

By the time we got back to the North Beach Peninsula, the consensus was that we'd hold off on our judgment of Patrick or Danny until Nadine and Goodie had another date or two, but EarltheSqwearl was going to have to go. Period.

The return logistics weren't as simple as when we'd left the peninsula. I dropped Nova off at her place to get her car and meet us at Orpha's apartment. I wanted to leave the Crown Vic with Orpha, and that meant all of us cramming into Nova's Outback.

We dropped off Goodie in Tinkerstown, and then Nadine, who lived out on Sandspit Road, just a couple miles south of me. Normally, I would have been next, but my car was on up at Spartina Point, so we went right past my driveway without stopping in.

At the casino, Nova deposited me at my car, then headed back down to Unity on the main highway. I went in and spoke briefly with both Freddy and Kanji, and hoped I was keeping a poker face when I thanked Kanji for staying with Meredith Saturday night. Then I headed over to Mom's place, despite the fact that I was tired to the bone.

"Oh, honey, I'm so glad to see you!" Meredith about squeezed me in half when she met me at the door. "How's Orpha?"

"Orpha's on top of the world," I told her. "She had a stent put in, then found a boyfriend in the room next to her in the cardio ward of the hospital."

Meredith narrowed her eyes and peered at me. "You're telling me the truth," she said.

"Uh, yeah. Why would I make something like that up?"

Merri nodded. "Freddy told me about being a human lie detector. I think his suggestions were good advice, and I was just trying it out."

I was grateful that Freddy, and not I, had been the one

to tell Meredith about detecting lies from potential dates. I'm almost positive she would have thought I had an ulterior motive if I'd suggested any such thing myself.

"So I passed?"

"Yes, honey, you passed with flying colors, but I'm afraid EarltheSqwearl did not." She sighed, and looked over at her laptop, open on her dining room table. "So I've gone back to Sole Mates, and I've been looking through the profiles again."

"Oh?" I dared not say anything more, as I couldn't believe my good fortune in not having to tell Merri that the rainbow gals had collectively, and quite adamantly, decided she would not be seeing Earl again.

"Come see what you think of this one guy." She moved two chairs close together so we could both see the screen.

"He's got a ponytail," I said.

"So?"

"So, I'm just surprised that anybody…" I peered at the age on his profile. "…that any guy 75 years old would still have enough hair for a thick, gray ponytail."

Meredith shrugged. "Hair is one of the only things we can change about our appearance," she said. "And I should know!" She laughed as she tossed her flaming red hair back with a flip of her hand. "Women are the masters of color, but men can change their whole appearance with the addition or subtraction of a mustache, beard, toupee, or ponytail."

"Geez, Mom, for someone who had their house broken into, you're sure in a good mood."

Merri looked at me as if she were going to say something important, then apparently changed her mind. "It's only stuff, Sylvia. Stuff can be replaced."

"But what about the memories that went along with that stuff?"

Merri smiled a sad, soft smile. "Oh, I still have plenty of those." She sighed again, but this time it sounded almost wistful.

I looked more closely at the man's profile. "Les is 75, 5'11", has blue-green eyes, and wears wire-rimmed glasses. Hmmm... It says he's widowed." I read his personal bio to myself, then asked, "Hey! He worked for Greenpeace! Small world! Do you think he knows Nadine? They're about the same age."

Meredith quickly turned the screen toward her and bent over it. "I musta missed that detail. I was pretty taken with his subject line though: 'Les is More.' Isn't that cute? And he sings and plays guitar. I've always had a sweet spot in my heart for musicians."

"You have?" I'm sure my brow furrowed. "Were you a groupie or something? Cause I sure don't remember you mentioning if Harlan, Charles, or Robert were musicians."

"They weren't," said Merri. "They also weren't the only men I was ever intimate with, Syl. Surely you must know that."

I cleared my throat, silently willing her not to tell me anything else about her sexual escapades. I'd had a hard enough time coming to grips with my mother as a femme fatale, or maybe a black widow would be more apropos, during her brief tête-à-tête with poor Walter.

"It says here he lives just south of Fort George. That's not very far."

Merri nodded. "He's probably within about an hour's drive. Maybe less."

"Les is More," I said, contemplating my next words very carefully. "Mom? Why don't you write this guy? It certainly sounds like he's worth at least a cup of coffee."

Meredith smiled. "I already did," she said. "But thanks

for your approval."

I should have known. Merri had always been a rule breaker, and the one time she hadn't broken the rules, Goodie had swooped in and nabbed Danny Boy before she could contact him. Why would I have expected her to wait for the group to check this guy out, especially after her earlier disappointment?

"So when are you meeting him?"

"Tomorrow," said Meredith. "In Fort George. And no, you can't go with me, and no, I'm not going to tell you where, or what time."

I stood to leave, giving her a quick hug at the door. "May I say one thing?"

"Just one thing?" asked Merri, arching her eyebrows in mock surprise. "Sure. Why not? Knock yourself out."

"Promise me you'll take your pepper spray."

Merri rolled her eyes. I really think eye rolling must be an inherited thing. She sighed again, this time quite noisily. "Fine. I'll take my pepper spray."

I rolled into my driveway just before dark. What an unbelievably long day it had been! The only thing I wanted to do was take a hot shower, get into one of my velour sweat suits, and eat a big bowl of ice cream while watching a Hallmark movie until bedtime.

But the Universe had other plans. When I pulled into my garage, I saw the interior door to my rec room standing open. Without even getting out of the car to investigate, I called Freddy.

"I know for certain that door was closed and locked," I told him. "I know because my car was at the casino all weekend I didn't come in that way when we stopped to pick up a few things before heading to Portland. I grabbed a change of clothes, and left through the front door, the same way I came in. I am 100% sure nobody went near the door that's now standing open."

"Stay where you are," said Freddy. "We're on our way."

I didn't have time to ask who "we" were, but I really didn't care. The cavalry said they were on their way, and that was good enough for me.

It seemed to take forever, but Freddy, with Kanji riding shotgun, blazed into my driveway no more than 15 minutes later. I kind of figured Freddy would bring Kanji, but what I hadn't known was that Sheriff Donaldson was visiting Mercedes that night, and he and she arrived in a second whirlwind of lights and sound right behind Freddy's cruiser.

The men made sure the house was clear before Mercedes and I went inside. The hair on my arms stood straight up as I walked from room to room, taking a quick assessment of any damage and getting some idea of what was missing.

Mercedes, bless her heart, made coffee, and the five of us gathered around the dining room table after my walk-through.

"Well?" said Sheriff D. He had out his pocket notebook and pencil stub.

"Well…" I took a deep breath to steady myself. "Well…" The rest of my words came out in a rush. "There is food missing from the refrigerator. There are dirty dishes I didn't leave in the sink. The TV remote control is on the wrong end of the couch. My washing machine is set for large load instead of small, and the dryer is set to cotton instead of permanent press. There are damp towels on my bathroom counter. The toilet seat has been left up. And worst of all—my bed's been slept in."

A shocked silence followed my report, and I took advantage of the brief pause to pull out my cell phone and call Felicity. "Did you, or anyone you know, stay at my house over the weekend?"

It wouldn't have been the first time Felix had taken advantage of having a copy of my house key, but she denied even being on the peninsula since Friday afternoon. Her new teaching colleague Mark had taken her to a concert in Portland. Did I want to see their ticket stubs? And what was this all about?

I assured her I'd call her later to completely fill her in, hung up, and set the phone down on the table. "It wasn't Felix," I said. "But someone definitely broke in here."

And then, despite my determination to be tough, I burst into tears.

"Oh my goodness! It's just like the story of Goldilocks and the Three Bears," said Merc, putting her arm around me. "They ate your porridge and slept in your bed."

"I seriously doubt that it was a 'they'," said Sheriff Donaldson. "I suspect it was a single 'he', and that he probably knows you, and that he definitely knew you were going to be out of town for at least a few days, and that he may not know that you're back yet."

"There's no sign of forced entry," added Freddy. "Who besides Felicity has a house key?"

When the light suddenly dawned, it was as if a spotlight illuminated my whole face. I dashed from the dining room, through the living room, out the front door, down the porch steps and grabbed the fake rock key holder residing in my planter box.

Then I collapsed on the bottom porch step, and my stomach clenched as if a prizefighter had suddenly pommeled the wind out of me.

The house key I kept hidden outside for emergencies was gone.

CHAPTER 13

Oddly enough, Mercedes was the only one who didn't volunteer to stay with me that night, after I'd steadfastly refused to go bunk with Jimmy over at the Clamshell.

"You know my .22 is in my purse," Merc whispered, while the men were busy discussing my immediate security needs. "But I'm not really a very good shot, and I also snore, so I probably wouldn't hear anyone come in."

"Don't worry, Merc," I whispered back. "I think Freddy and Kanji are going to arm wrestle for the pleasure of sleeping on my couch."

Mercedes' eyebrows arched toward her hairline, which wasn't an easy feat, considering the amount of Botox she'd had injected into her brow. "If Freddy stays, he wouldn't necessarily be sleeping on the couch, would he?"

"You think I'd be in the mood to fool around with anybody when I'm listening with both ears for someone to be helping themselves to my involuntary hospitality?"

If the guys heard any part of what we'd said, they discreetly kept it to themselves.

"Sylvia," said Sheriff D, after the men had finished formulating a plan. "Kanji will be staying here with you tonight, all day tomorrow, and tomorrow night. It would be best if you didn't use too many lights in the house, and laid low until Wednesday morning.

"Freddy's going to take the glass and silverware from the

sink, and we'll see if we can lift a few usable prints from them.

"*IF*, and please remember it's a big if, Sylvia, the guy actually comes back, it would most likely be during the day tomorrow. Meanwhile, limit your outgoing calls. The fewer people who know you're hiding out at home, the better."

"Can I call my mother?" I asked in a small voice.

Sheriff D shook his head. "I'd rather you didn't. We don't know if these two break-ins are connected, and like I said, we need to keep a tight lid on all of this as we sort things out."

The sheriff pushed his Stetson up a little, perhaps waiting for me to protest, which I did not, surprising everyone, including me. Then he continued. "Freddy and I are the only ones authorized to drive the county's police vehicles, so we're going to be leaving in them shortly, leaving no sign that you've come home."

"Gee, thanks," I muttered. "You're leaving me here like a sitting duck."

"I beg your pardon," said Kanji, bowing his head slightly, "but I held several titles as a championship marksman in college, and Freddy will be leaving me his back-up revolver."

"And," said Freddy, "you still have a 9mm Glock, don't you?"

I nodded. "It's in my trunk."

"Well, go get it," said the sheriff, "so we can clear out of here before our police presence becomes known. Freddy will be staying at the Clamshell, which is only five minutes away. It's unlikely you'll have any problems tonight, but if you do, call first, and shoot only as a last resort. Only if it's in self-defense."

I looked at Kanji. "Any chance you'd like to watch a few Hallmark movies tonight?"

Kanji smiled. "I am quite familiar with what you call made-for-television Chick Flicks. Your mother introduced me to them Saturday night."

Yeah, well, that didn't make me feel all that much better, but at least I knew he wouldn't insist on watching a shoot-em-up action flick, or any type of horror show, before bedtime. "Thanks, Kanji. I'll make some popcorn."

When morning came, I wondered how I was going to explain to Freddy that Kanji and I had, indeed, slept together. For I had awakened with my head on his chest, and my hand resting in the bowl of popcorn on his lap. We were still on the couch, and still fully dressed, but I wasn't sure that was the way I wanted to tell the story. A little rivalry isn't necessarily a bad thing.

Tuesday morning dawned sunny and unseasonably warm. Meredith smiled. It was a perfect day to drive over the bridge and into Fort George to have coffee with Les. She kept a close watch in her rearview mirror for any car she might recognize, thinking that she might pick up a tail somewhere along the way. In fact, anywhere along the way. And knowing Sylvia, she might have borrowed a car that Merri wouldn't recognize and be waiting at the south end of the bridge.

She shook her head as if to clear those thoughts from her mind. "I'm too suspicious," she said aloud. Then she lowered the visor in front of her and flipped open the mirror to check her image. "Not bad, for an old broad," she said aloud.

Massive numbers of butterflies took wing in Meredith's stomach as she parked around the corner from her coffee shop destination. She was a half hour early on purpose, so she could pick a good place to sit where she could watch the door for Les's arrival. For just a fraction of a second, she wondered if she should go through with this meeting at all.

The short walk cleared any doubts, and she arrived with renewed confidence. Stepping through the door, she glanced over to her favorite spot, on the couch by the window, and saw that spot was already taken. By Les.

As if he sensed someone watching him, or maybe because he had been keeping an eye on the door himself, he looked up from his newspaper and their eyes met. He smiled. She smiled. And Merri felt a frisson of excitement course through her entire body.

Les rose to his feet and they quickly moved toward each other to embrace.

"You look wonderful, Merri," said Les, wrapping his arms around her.

"You don't look so bad yourself, Woody."

Still holding her, Les leaned back, studied her face for a moment, and his smile deepened. "You're the only one who's ever called me that with such tenderness."

Then his lips met hers, right then and there in the middle of the coffee shop, and Meredith happily returned his kiss, not caring if the entire Veiled Rainbow, her daughter, and half the town of Fort George were watching. Not even the whole town watching could make Merri any less happy to be participating in public displays of affection with this man.

When Les reluctantly broke off the kiss, they ordered coffee and sat down on the couch, thigh pressed to thigh, wanting to be as close as possible.

"That belly-dancing photo you put up on your profile," said Les, with a shake of his head. "The minute I saw it, I was hoping with all my heart that it was really you."

"And you—" Merri reached over and playfully flipped her hand under his ponytail to fluff it. "You haven't changed much at all. As soon as I saw your smile, the way your laugh-lines crinkle around your blue-green eyes—well, I was certain our paths had finally crossed again."

Les nodded. "And I'm so grateful." He reached over and squeezed her hand. "So where shall we start? We have a lot of catching up to do."

Merri laughed. "Fifty-five years, give or take."

And for the next two hours, downing more coffee than it would take to float a small boat in dry dock, they did their best to fill in the half-century plus gap that had separated them.

Les told her about his work in the Peace Corps, his time with Greenpeace, his retirement move to the north Oregon coast, his wife who'd died of cancer, and his regret that he'd never had children.

And for her part, Meredith told him about becoming a registered nurse, working for literally decades at the North Beach Hospital in Unity, and the three cats she currently had, all named after the three husbands she'd outlived.

"Did you have any children?" asked Les.

"Just one—a daughter," said Merri. "She lives on the peninsula, too." She smiled. "If you play your cards right, perhaps you'll get a chance to meet her."

"I'd like that," said Les. "I'd like that very much."

Merri coquettishly batted her eyes at him. "The part about playing your cards right, or the part about meeting my daughter?"

"Both," said Les without hesitation. "Absolutely both."

They stood, placed their coffee cups in the dish bin at the end of the ordering counter, and left the coffee shop arm in arm. It didn't surprise either one of them that they'd both parked around the corner, right next to each other, Merri's red Saturn, and Les's silver Prius with the "Save the Whales" bumper sticker.

"So when are you going to invite me over to the peninsula?" asked Les, after giving her another resounding kiss at her car door.

"Is now too soon?" asked Merri, looking up into his eyes, and feeling her knees growing weak with the thought of them alone together at her place.

Les chuckled. "I'd love nothing more," he said. "But unfortunately, I wasn't expecting our meeting to go so well, and I have a commitment this afternoon that can't be changed."

"I thought you were retired," Merri teased him.

"I thought so too, but I do a lot of volunteering, and I'd hate to ditch those responsibilities just because I got a better offer."

"Awww…. A better offer. How sweet of you to say that." She shrugged. "Okay, I forgive you." And Merri initiated yet another deep and lingering kiss.

"I know how this is going to sound," said Les, "but I'm going to say it anyway."

"I'll call you," said Merri and Les together, and they both laughed.

Les silently looked away for a minute, and when he looked back at Merri, he had tears in his eyes. "I really mean it this time," he said. "And I'm sorry I didn't stay in touch before."

Merri put two fingers against his lips to hush him. "Water under the bridge, or over the dam, or wherever it is that water goes these days."

"But I've never stopped wondering…" Merri quickly silenced him with another kiss, this one a quick peck on the lips.

"Hand me your phone," said Merri, "and I'll put my

number in it."

Les quickly relinquished his phone. "I'm sorry. I should have thought to ask you for your number. Forgive me."

"Les," interrupted Meredith, "we have an opportunity for a fresh start, but if we don't both get into our vehicles and leave right now, we could end up standing here listing our past regrets all day." She handed his phone back to him. "Forward is the only viable direction."

Les pulled her tight to his chest. "You've always been a wise woman, Merri. I'll call you tomorrow. I promise."

"I'm sure you will, Les; I'm already looking forward to it."

On the way back across "The Bridge to Nowhere," as it was nicknamed many years ago, Merri saw the sunlight sparkling on the water and couldn't keep herself from singing. "Zippity-do-dah, Zippity-day, My, oh my, what a wonderful day…"

Tuesday was not such a happy day at my house, but it was blessedly uneventful. Kanji and I woke up together, still on the couch, my head resting on his chest, and our bodies covered with a soft quilted afghan I kept on the back of the couch for just such emergencies. Not that I'd planned to sleep with Kanji—or anyone—on my couch, but I was glad we'd had a blanket handy when it got chilly and we began to nod off.

That first night, around 4 a.m., I'd thought about excusing myself and leaving Kanji there while I slept in my own bed, but then I started to feel bad about leaving him to sleep on the couch, and for several moments, time was frozen and my brain refused to process any option other than how nice it felt to be all cuddled up with him, and wouldn't he like to stretch out and get more comfortable with me in my bedroom, and—

And right about then, Kanji had put his arm around my shoulders, pulled me a little closer, tucked the afghan around the two of us, and solved my dilemma. I had been warm, cozy, safe, and much too comfortable to get up and go anywhere till morning.

By morning, I realized that I hadn't yet changed the sheets on my bed since the intruder had slept there, and I shivered all over. Kanji helped me strip the bed and start the laundry, and even helped me remake the bed between games of Scrabble we played to fill part of our day. I felt like I was on house arrest, but the sheriff's plan made sense, in the event the perp returned.

Tuesday night, despite the fact that now there were clean sheets on my bed, Kanji and I again cuddled up and fell asleep in front of the television, and I wasn't sure if I were disappointed or relieved that we hadn't taken the short walk down the hallway together.

By Wednesday morning, all was still quiet at my place, so Kanji and I had a late breakfast at the Sea Biscuit Breakfast House before I drove him back to his apartment at the Clamshell. We'd been up most of the previous two nights watching movies on television, sitting in the dark, quietly armed with a bowl of buttered popcorn, lots of napkins, my Glock, and Freddy's service revolver, and I knew he'd need a good long nap before going to work.

Jimmy was out walking Kanji's dog Elvis when we pulled in, and he handed the leash to Kanji the moment he stepped from the car.

"I sincerely hope caring for my beloved pet was not too much of an inconvenience for you," said Kanji.

"No problem at all," said Jimmy. "Elvis is a good dog."

Kanji nodded his thanks and went straight into his unit

at the Clamshell to shower, change, and catch up on his sleep before I came back later this afternoon to take him to the casino, where he'd left his own car.

Jimmy and I entered the motel office, and on into his apartment, where I attempted to catch him up to speed concerning Orpha's surgery, Mom's break-in, and my own home invasion, but I needn't have bothered.

"Julio told me all about the break-ins," said Jimmy, matter-of-factly.

"And Julio knew about the break-ins because…?"

"Because they keep a scanner on back in the kitchen at the restaurant. I've been thinking about getting one of those myself. Then I'd always know where you were." He laughed. "I mean, I'd always know where there's trouble on the peninsula."

"Of course that's what you meant."

"Well," Jimmy said truthfully, "quite often that's the same thing."

Then Jimmy went on to explain, in length, that the Cinco Amigos Chinese Cuisine staff were using the scanner to stay right on top of the sheriff's comings and goings since ICE raids had become all-too-common on the North Beach Peninsula. Sheriff Donaldson, bless his heart, might just happen to mention over the air when the Feds were in town, and it gave our hardworking Mexican residents a solid heads-up.

There had never been an immigration issue on the peninsula, and the sheriff was quick to point that out to the men in the white immigration van when they sought to gather information from him about a specific Mexican's whereabouts. He told them he was in charge of arresting criminals who willfully broke the laws he was hired to enforce. He saw no need for them to haul away people who were contributing to our community's economy, especially when they stepped up to do some pretty undesirable jobs.

"Okay, okay," I said, when Jimmy finally ran out of air, "put the soapbox away, already. I understand how Julio learned of the break-ins, and how he came to tell you about them, but how did you know about Orpha's medical condition?"

"Oh, that was easy." Jimmy shrugged. "If she hadn't been fine, someone would have already called me. No news is good news, you know!"

I had to agree with that, and left Jimmy to go pick up Felicity at the high school in Unity. When I had stopped by Merri's on Monday, she'd told me about how Freddy had reluctantly canvassed the neighborhood, and how he'd gotten a solid clue to follow up on, nevertheless.

So I'd called Felicity first thing this morning, and she had agreed to come with me right after school when we could do a little canvassing of our own.

Across from my house was a cleared but empty lot where the steamer clam harvesters parked their cars. Then they used a short, well-worn path to get down to the bay to gather their bounty. At least ninety percent of these workers belonged to our Mexican workforce, and Felicity, the high school Spanish teacher, was a fine interpreter, if one were needed.

The tide on Shallowwater Bay was just turning to come back in as we drove up Sandspit Road, and I was happy to see a half dozen men stowing their boots, gloves, and other gear in the trunks as we arrived. The nets filled with steamer clams were piled into the back of a pick-up truck and would soon be on their way to market.

"Buenas tardes," said Felicity, stepping out of the car. "Habla inglés?"

"Sí," said one of men closest to us. "These clams not for sale."

Felix and I both laughed. It was clear these fellows had been asked many times before about buying the steamers fresh out of the bay.

The man looked longingly at my chameleon mustang convertible. "These car for sale?"

"Oh, heavens no!" I said, placing my hand over my heart. "Not till I'm 90, and maybe not even then!" We all laughed again.

Then I told him my name, pointed to my driveway, and said, "I live there."

He nodded. "Jess. Pretty lady who sometimes rides motorcycle."

I felt a slight blush coming on, but managed to ask if he, or any of his friends, had seen anyone coming or going in or out of that driveway anytime on Sunday, or maybe on Monday before dark.

He turned to the other men and spoke in rapid-fire Spanish. The men gathered together and try as I might, I could make neither heads or tails out of a single thing they said. Good grief and gravy, those guys sure talked fast!

"Felix?" I asked. "Are you getting any of this?'

Felix smiled. "I'm pretty sure I'm getting all of it."

But before Felicity could fill me in, the man returned. "You have a motorcycle, no?"

"I have a motorcycle, yes," I answered.

He looked confused, but Felicity told him something in Spanish and he grinned ear to ear.

"Did you tell him I was a moron or something?"

"Whatever would make you think that?" she asked me, feigning innocence.

I think I glowered. Another strike against keeping my

forehead wrinkle-free. I turned again to the man. "What is your name?"

"Me llamo Oscar," he said.

I lightly touched his shoulder. "Oscar, did someone see a motorcycle going in or out of my driveway during the last couple days?"

"Sí!" said Oscar. "Sunday morning. We got here to work. A very loud motorcycle turned into your driveway. Was it not you?"

"No," I said. "It was not me. Do you know what color the bike was?"

Oscar scowled and shook his head. He asked the men something in Spanish, and all I got were a few words that sounded like la motocicleta color.

The men all shouted their replies at the same time, and then Oscar shook his head. "I am sorry, some say blue, some say black, one says orange." He shrugged.

"Bummer," I said under my breath.

"But it was very loud," Oscar offered. "Very, very loud. And the rider wore a backpack."

"Gracias," I said. We'd learned a little, and it was important information, but a lot less than I'd hoped we'd come away with.

Felicity and I stopped by my house just to check the doors and then we headed over to Jimmy's so I could pick up Kanji for work. There was an unfamiliar vehicle in the driveway, and as soon as Felicity saw it, her eyes lit up.

"That's Mark's black SUV," she said. "I texted him while you were checking your house doors, and he said he'd meet me here instead of you having to take me all the way back down to Unity."

"So you two are now... an item?" I asked.

"I guess so. It's only been a couple weeks, you know.

We're just getting to know each other, but so far, neither one of us has discovered any deal breakers."

"Well, like you said, it's still very early in the relationship." As soon as I said it, I wanted to rip my tongue out. "I didn't mean anything by that, Felix, really I didn't."

"I know," said Felix, "sometimes your mouth gets way ahead of your brain."

Wow! That was as close as Felix had ever gotten to slapping me down, but I deserved it.

Mark turned out to be exactly what you'd expect in a high school English teacher. Clean cut, firm handshake, and he'd stood up as we came in. He might be a keeper, and I certainly hoped so, for Felicity's sake. She deserved a great guy.

And so do Goodie, Nadine, and Meredith, I suddenly thought. *So where are all the good men hiding, and how do we know which ones are not to be trusted?*

CHAPTER 14

On our way to Spartina Point, I slowed the car down, but Kanji and I did not stop, as we went by Meredith's driveway in Ocean Crest. I could see her red Saturn, but there was also a silver Prius parked behind it. *Must be one of her friends, checking up on her,* I thought.

I was glad for that. There are few circumstances in life that leave you feeling so vulnerable, so hopeless, and so debilitated, as having the sanctity of your home invaded. And unfortunately, I now knew the feeling firsthand.

On my way back, the Prius was gone, so I didn't hesitate to stop. I wasn't sure if I would have stopped if the Prius had still been there, but it wasn't, so problem solved.

"Hi Mom," I gave Merri a quick hug. "I just gave Kanji a ride to work, since he was gallant enough to stay with me the last couple nights, and I saw an unfamiliar car parked here."

"Are you spying on me?" asked Merri. She took my hand and guided me toward her living room. "Do you have time to come sit with me and chat for a little while? I'm still not all that comfortable being here alone."

I was pretty sure I didn't have much of a choice in staying with her for a bit, but Merri seemed to have missed the gist of what I'd just said.

"Mom! Did you hear me? Kanji stayed at your house Saturday night, and my house on Monday and Tuesday nights. Aren't you going to say something snarky about that?"

Merri smiled. "You're an adult. You can certainly make your own decisions about who you want to date."

"Whoa! Who said anything about dating?"

"Honey," said Meredith, "I'm jerking your chain. I already know about your home invasion, and the fact that Kanji was going to be your house guest for a couple nights."

"How in the world…"

"Jimmy called to say how sorry he was about both our break-ins and asked if I needed anything. He told me he was babysitting Elvis while Kanji was staying with you. If he hadn't told me that Kanji was there, I would have come right over and stayed with you myself."

"Oh." I suddenly felt a little petty, and a lot out of line. "So who owns that Prius?"

"My friend Les," said Merri.

"The 'Les is More,' Les?" I asked incredulously. "The guy you were meeting for the first time for coffee over in Fort George yesterday?"

"Yes, that Les," said Meredith. "Only it turns out that I actually met him a long time ago, and back then, he went by the nickname 'Woody.' So it turned out to be really more of a reunion than a first meeting."

"And you didn't recognize his photo on Sole Mates a few days ago?"

"I thought he looked really familiar, but honey, cut me some slack, will you? It's been many decades since I last saw him."

"So are you going to be seeing each other again?" I asked.

"Yes," said Merri, thoughtfully nodding. "I believe we will."

Nadine excitedly opened her front door to Patrick's knock just after noon on Thursday. He greeted her by blowing a big cloud of smoke in her face. "Hey, babe, how's it goin'?"

"Oh, Patrick, you started partying without me!" Nadine pretended to pout.

Patrick handed her the joint he carried. "I just lit up after I parked my van, Deenie. I never smoke weed while my brain's busy looking for an address."

Nadine took a large toke and held the smoke inside her as she motioned for him to come inside. She rather liked that he still called her Deenie. It was like a silly little secret only they shared, drawing them closer each time they spoke.

"Jamais vu," said Patrick, entering her home. "I feel like I've never been here before."

"You haven't." Nadine giggled, and reached for the joint again. "Next time you visit, you'll be able to say déjà vu."

Stella, from her dog bed by the hearth, lifted her head when Patrick entered. She tilted it this way and that, perhaps trying to focus her little vision-correction goggles, then thumped her tail and went back to napping.

The pot quickly worked its magic, and in less time than it takes to say "Hey, Deenie, let's take off our clothes," both Patrick and Nadine were enjoying the freedom of being au naturel in her living room. And then in her bedroom.

A little later, Nadine stood at her kitchen sink getting a glass of water. She gazed out the window to her back porch. Patrick came up behind her and put his arms around her. He kissed the back of her neck. "I'm starved," he said. "Let's go out and get something to eat."

"The hummingbird feeder is empty," Nadine replied.

"Uh.... Deenie? That was not exactly the answer I

expected," said Patrick.

Nadine turned around and hugged him back. "Help me refill the hummingbird feeder before we go." She gave him a peck on the lips, opened her fridge, and retrieved the pre-made sugar-water nectar for the feeder.

They went outside, still without the benefit of clothing, and Patrick held the plastic chair for her to climb up on. She unscrewed the feeder from the hook, and handed the container down to him. He filled it from the pitcher of sugar-water and handed it back up.

"We make a good, team, don't we Deenie?"

But before Nadine could answer, there was a loud volley of barking from inside the house. Stella was jumping repeatedly against the screen door, wanting to come outside to join them.

"What's got her all excited?" asked Patrick.

"She's a spaniel. Spaniels love to bark and jump, and just because she's a Papillon, it doesn't make her any different from all other types of that breed."

"She looks so funny in those goggles," said Patrick. "But you need a scarf, dude." He spoke directly to the dog, which seemed to encourage her to bark louder and jump higher.

"You silly boy," said Nadine. She bent down to kiss the top of Patrick's head from her perch still on the chair. "Stella is a dudette. Now go let her out. She just wants to join us."

But when Patrick started for the door, Stella abruptly backed up, banging into the solid wooden door in her haste. Her butt pushed it back hard, and it hit the spring stopper on the wall and swung slowly forward again, coming to a stop about half way closed.

Patrick rushed to open the screen door, but Stella saw this as a threatening advance, and lunged again, this time jumping against the interior door, as she tried unsuccessfully to focus her trifocals. The door slammed shut with a resounding "Click!"

"*STELLA!*" yelled both Nadine and Patrick. Then they both started giggling.

"Please help me get down," said Nadine, when they'd finally stopped laughing. "Thankfully, I know the bathroom window isn't locked. But one of us is going to have to go around the house and climb inside, and I'd rather it wasn't you the neighbors might observe entering my house through the window in the nude, if you know what I mean."

"My Queen of the Green, " said Patrick, wiping his eyes, and gathering his breath, "I think Stella just totally harshed my mellow."

Nadine started giggling again. "You sound just like my friend Jimmy."

Patrick gave her a funny look. "Who's this Jimmy guy? Are you just now going to tell me I have competition for your affection?"

"Jimmy's gay, Patrick."

"Oh. Well in that case, I guess I'll help you down from that chair after all."

"You mean you were just going to leave me up here if I had another beau?"

Patrick thought about that for a moment, then he helped Nadine get down from the chair. "You're barefoot," he said. Then he looked at his own feet. "Are these your socks or mine?"

Nadine went into another fit of giggles. "Those are mine, Patrick! And I'll need them to walk around the house to get in!"

Patrick gave up the socks without comment, then stood silently by the back door until Nadine went around, climbed in through the bathroom window, and let him back inside.

He looked at the wall clock in her kitchen. "Now I really am starving. I think my appetite doubled while we were out in the fresh air on the deck."

They pulled on the same clothes they had recently shed, and Patrick suggested they take Deenie's car. "I've never ridden in a smart car before," he explained. "Does it get good mileage?"

"Terrific mileage," said Nadine, "but you sure can't carry much cargo in it." And during a long, leisurely lunch, she explained how she sometimes had to have Goodie bring her dog food and other large items from Costco.

Returning to her house, Patrick said he had to get going right away, as he wanted to get back to the city before it got too late. He had a séance scheduled for midnight, and he wanted to catch a quick nap first so the spirits could start speaking to him. He gave her a quick hug and a peck on her cheek, then hopped in his van and drove away without a backward glance.

Nadine, still basking in the glow of their encounter, walked up her steps, and went inside, thinking that in all the earlier excitement, she must have forgotten to lock her front door.

"Stella!" she yelled, upon entering. "Did you get bored and just decide to destroy my living room?!"

But the living room was not the only messy room in Nadine's house. Every single room had been ransacked. Drawers stood open, clothing was strewn about, and her laptop was missing. Clearly, she could not blame Stella for all that.

Early Friday afternoon, Sheriff Donaldson paced back and forth in his office, still fit to be tied. Three break-ins this week, three older single ladies, two of them registered on the dating site Sole Mates, and the sheriff wasn't inclined to believe in such coincidences.

"Sylvia!" he barked into his phone. "I want you to get those rainbow gals of yours to immediately cease and desist meeting any more of these online dating fellows."

"And how, exactly, do you think I could manage that?" I asked him. "I didn't major in herding cats, Carter. I'm just as perplexed as you are, but I can't forbid them to stop looking for love, online or anywhere else. They wouldn't listen to me anyway."

Sheriff D sighed. "Syl," he said. "What if one of these ladies surprises a robber in their home and ends up getting hurt—or worse."

"I know you're trying to get me to promise to keep a tighter leash on them, but I'm not sure how to go about it, and neither do you, or you wouldn't be asking me to do the impossible." I decided to redirect his focus. "Have you gotten any results from the background checks?"

"Struck out all around on that," said the sheriff. "Danny Smith, Earl Jones, and Patrick O'Leary either do not exist, or they have never had a run-in with the law. Not even a parking ticket for any of them, and we know that's not true, since Earl admitted to being in prison."

"Which prison?" I asked.

"The penitentiary in Salem."

"The same one Mr. X is in?" I asked.

"About that," said Sheriff D. "Daniel Gardner was released a little over a year ago."

My stomach was getting plenty of practice clenching these days. Too bad it didn't count as exercise, like when you do a bazillion crunches on purpose to flatten your stomach.

"Do you know where he's living?" I tried to keep my voice level.

"No," said Sheriff D. "He's not a sex offender, so he's not required to register."

"Swell. So he could be anywhere."

"And in answer to your previous question, yes, Earl and Danny were most likely in the same pen at roughly the same time, but I can't say for sure whether they knew each other."

I thanked him for calling, and disconnected the call. Bim was standing at my elbow, holding a fresh pot of decaf. There's no such thing as a private conversation at a public coffee shop, and I was well aware of that when I answered the sheriff's call.

"Does the sheriff have any leads?" asked Bim. She didn't even pretend she hadn't heard my end of the whole thing.

"He's trying to connect the dots," I said. "It's possible that all these online dating guys aren't who they say they are."

I thought about Felix's encounter with O-fer, the glorified grave digger, Meredith's disappointment with EarltheSqwearl, and Nadine's apparently deepening drug connection with Patrick. Were these good guys or bad guys at their core?

Meredith now seemed quite smitten with her former friend Les. Goodie had a date with Danny to go clam digging this very night, and she seemed to believe he was the real deal.

Goodie! I gulped down the rest of my coffee, and yelled "Thanks, Bim," over my shoulder as I hurried to my car. Goodie might just possibly be able to help me shed some light on all this, as long as I could convince her to play along with my admittedly half-baked idea.

"I don't know, Syl," said Goodie after I told her what I was thinking. "I don't think Danny has been anything but honest and forthcoming, and distrusting him like this isn't a good way to start a relationship."

"You're not distrusting him, Goodie, I am," I said. "If he's a good guy, he'll never have to know that we set a trap for him, and if he's a bad guy..." I let my sentence go unfinished.

Goodie mulled it over for a few more minutes. Then she sighed. "I get it, really I do. And I know your heart is in the right place, Syl, so let's do it."

Danny wasn't due to arrive for another couple hours, so I had time to go home, pull on my jeans and a dark hooded sweatshirt, get my Glock from the car trunk, find my little LED flashlight, and get back to Goodie's. This time I took my motorcycle, the best darn gift I'd ever been given from the best darn part-time boyfriend I'd ever had.

Meanwhile, Goodie had backed her own car out of the garage so I could park the bike inside and no one would ever know I was there. I put the garage door down and went into Goodie's kitchen through the side door. "Hi honey, I'm home!" I called out.

Goodie came down the hallway dressed in what we locals call "clamming clothes." In other words, she looked like a senior model for one of our thrift shops. She had gray woolen socks with two red stripes around the top pulled up over her well-worn jeans. Instead of a jacket, she wore a red hunting vest zipped up over a thick, long-sleeved, mauve sweater. Her stocking cap was an Oregon Ducks green and gold, complete with a tassel on the top the size of a tennis ball.

"Nice outfit," I teased her.

Goodie laughed. "You won't be making fun of me when you're begging for some of my world-famous clam chowder."

She was right about that. Goodie had a secret recipe that

had won first place in the amateur division several years in a row during our Razor Clam Festival. There was talk that she shouldn't be allowed to enter this year in order to give other home chefs a chance.

"Where's Hans?" I asked, looking behind her couch for the socially shy German Shepherd I knew Goodie had been fostering. I looked behind the couch first because that's where I usually found Mercedes' long-haired dachshund Brutus. So much for having a dog for protection.

"Check the front coat closet," said Goodie. "That's where I put his dog bed. He likes having his own personal space."

Sure enough, there was Hans, surrounded by a number of multi-colored dog toys, hunkered down on his dog bed, wedged in between the vacuum cleaner and two pairs of matching clamming boots.

"Won't you be needing these tonight?" I asked, holding up the boots, which, strangely enough, being green with yellow laces, kind of matched her stocking cap.

"Yeah, I'd better go squeeze those into the trunk," said Goodie. "We'll be taking my car, so Danny doesn't have to drive his Lexus out on the beach sand."

"His Lexus?"

Goodie nodded. "Remember? I told the sheriff about it. I saw his car when we had lunch over at Pier 19. So when we decided to go clamming, I offered my Corolla as our transportation."

"And you said Danny's never been clamming?"

"That's right. He thought it might be fun. I gathered up the equipment Larry and I used to use, and put everything in my trunk." Goodie paused and traced the initials "L.G." written in red fingernail polish on the top of one of the boots.

"Larry liked to put his initials on everything." She

sighed. "I still really miss him." She sighed again, then took a deep breath and continued, "So far I've put two aluminum clam guns, two clam nets to tie around our waists, a Coleman lantern, and matches into the trunk—and now—" she said, taking both pairs of boots from me, "I'll add these to the rest of our gear."

"What about a clam license?" I asked.

"I told him to stop at the gas station on the way into town to get one," said Goodie. "And he's bringing a dry change of clothes for when we get back."

"I guess you've thought about everything, then," I said.

"So tell me again what you're going to do while I'm gone," said Goodie.

"I'll just be sitting in here in the dark with Hans," I said. "And if no one shows up to rob the place, I'll be out of here exactly two hours after you two leave."

"And if someone shows up?" asked Goodie.

"Then I'll stop them from robbing you." I didn't want to get into the specific details with Goodie, because I didn't want her worrying about me while she was out on her date. Goodie doesn't normally allow guns in her house, although she must have known I had mine with me.

"The best-case scenario is that no one attempts to break in, and you and Danny both get your clam limits, make a big pot of chowder tonight, and live happily ever after."

"And the worst-case scenario?" asked Goodie.

"Let me worry about that," I said, looking once again at Goodie's wall clock and standing up from the couch. "Now I'm just going to wait in your bedroom until you've left. Turn off your lights and lock your doors on the way out, okay?"

"Okay," said Goodie.

I got myself settled into the dark bedroom just in time. From far down the road, I heard a vehicle approaching, but it sure didn't sound like any Lexus I'd ever heard. Or any car, for that matter. There is no mistaking the sound made by a Harley Davidson Motorcycle.

Pressing my ear against the closed bedroom door, I could make out most of Danny's end of the conversation. He said he had ridden his Harley to the beach instead of bringing his Lexus because it was such a perfect fall day for a bike ride. No, he wasn't allergic to animals, it was the wind in his face that made his eyes run. Yes, he'd stopped and gotten a clam license. Yes, he'd brought a change of clothes with him, and could he leave his backpack right there on the couch?

After a few more bits of conversation, the two of them left the house. I heard Goodie start up her car, and away they went.

I opened the bedroom door and went out into the living room, using my pocket flashlight just enough to guide me to the wingback, overstuffed chair at the far end of the couch, where I could sit in the shadows. Hans soon joined me, venturing from his safe room, and sat on my feet, putting his head in my lap.

Scratching Hans behind the ears and down his back, I thought fondly about Goodie, with her big animal-loving heart, and was glad she was helping Hans regain his self-confidence.

"Hans," I said softly. "Of course she named you Hans." The big dog looked up at me when I said his name. "Hans is a good German name. It means 'God is Gracious.' Did you know that? I bet Goodie knows that."

Hans thumped his tail twice against the floor and emitted a long, drawn-out sigh, the bulk of his body still sitting on my feet as he relaxed against my legs in contentment.

At one point, I turned the light on Danny's backpack, but decided against investigating its contents. It needed to be left alone, at least for the time being. The ticking of the clock was the only sound in the room, and its regular tick-tock, tick-tock, tick-tock, soon lulled me into sleep.

I don't know what it was that woke me. It could have been a vehicle turning into the driveway, or maybe headlights flashing briefly across the front room windows. I shook my head, trying to clear the fog and get my bearings. Han's head continued to rest on my lap, so I sat still as a statue and waited, listening.

I heard the sound of two vehicle doors closing. Footsteps on the gravel walkway. Whispers on the porch. I felt the hair on Hans's neck begin to bristle under my hand.

Someone tried the doorknob. Bless Goodie, it was locked. Then I heard something I'd only ever heard before on television, and I was surprised I was able to recognize the scratchy sound coming from the other side of the front door.

Someone was picking the lock.

CHAPTER 15

Goodie and Danny arrived on the beach shortly after the sun had descended into the ocean, leaving a red, orange, gold, then deep purple hue on the water and along the sand where they drove. Goodie was looking for a good place to dig for clams, watching the receding tide for emerging sand bars.

"There's a good place to park," said Danny, pointing to an area not far ahead.

"But it doesn't look like anyone else thinks this is a good spot for clams," said Goodie. "All the other cars are farther north."

Danny reached over and squeezed her shoulder. "Wouldn't we have more fun avoiding the crowd and having a little privacy?" The way he smiled at her made her heart flutter like a hummingbird on steroids, and she was pretty sure it wasn't A-fib.

So instead of arguing, or continuing to drive, Goodie pulled right off where he'd pointed and parked the car. She turned the car so they faced the ocean, then backed it up, just like Larry used to do, to get it out of the way of passing vehicles, but not so far back as to get stuck in the softer sand.

She turned off the key, looked at Danny and smiled. "How's this?"

"Perfect!" he enthusiastically replied. "Let's go dig!"

Goodie laughed. "Not so fast, hotshot. The tide's not out far enough to uncover the clam beds. Low tide isn't for a little while yet, but the best digging will be an hour or two before it's all the way out."

Danny slumped down a little in his seat, obviously disappointed, but he recovered quickly. He reached over and took Goodie's hand. "Tell me more about The Veiled Rainbow," he said. "I can't wait to meet some of your friends down here."

So Goodie happily chattered on, telling him about her friends, and explaining how the five of them had come to use belly dancing for exercise, and how they each had their own color of the rainbow, and so forth and so on, and in no time at all, the colors had faded from the beach and it was time to light the lantern and head out to dig.

Goodie went around to the back of the car and opened the trunk. She handed Danny a pair of boots. "I'm so glad you wear the same size Larry wore," she said.

Then she kicked off her tennies, and leaned against the back bumper while she laced up her own boots. Danny couldn't believe how long the yellow laces were, and he wrapped them once around his calves before tying them, to keep from tripping over a loose lace. Goodie watched him, and for a guy who hadn't done this before, he seemed pretty at home lacing up the boots.

Then she handed Danny the Coleman lantern and was pleased that he seemed to know what he was doing there too, as he adjusted the wick and got it going, despite it being a little windy on the beach. Then he used the back of his hand to wipe across his eyes.

"Is something wrong?" asked Goodie.

"No, it's just the wind bothering my contacts again," said Danny. "It makes my eyes water."

"Like when you arrived at my house on your motorcycle," said Goodie. She also remembered that his eyes had watered when he'd arrived at Pier 19, but it was only a random thought that flitted through her mind. Sylvia was the suspicious one, not her,

They each tied a clam net around their waist, picked up an aluminum clam gun, and Danny carried the lantern as they headed toward the water—or toward where the water had been the last time they'd seen it, as darkness was now full-on, and the full moon was hidden by a sudden thick layer of clouds that had rolled in just after the spectacular sunset. That happened sometimes when the tide changed, and Goodie was glad she had dressed warmly.

"Be careful," said Goodie. "There are soft spots in the sand and holes on the beach, and you could fall if you stepped in one."

But Danny only walked faster, as if trying to outrun her, or something chasing him, and when he didn't slow his pace, Goodie had to trot along beside him, or lose the advantage of the circle of light surrounding the lantern.

Once they got near the water's edge, Goodie explained how she would stomp a circle around Danny and the lantern, and he could be on the lookout for any clam shows.

"What's a clam show?" he asked.

"It's the mark left by the clam when it pumps out the sand while it's digging deeper to get away. Some people call them little volcanoes, or donuts, or washers."

"Oh, right," said Danny, but he sounded more dismissive than interested.

"Turn around in a circle with the lantern, and you can watch the sand behind me while I stomp," said Goodie. She stomped a wide ring around him, and sure enough, there was a definite clam hole that showed up along the tracks she left.

The cold was already seeping into Danny's bones. It was the kind of chill that goes deep into one's soul in the dark winter nights of the Pacific Northwest. He shivered, wondering if he'd have the courage to carry out his plan tonight when the time was right.

Goodie positioned herself facing the ocean, and showed Danny how to rapidly pump the aluminum tube deep into the sand while chasing after the illusive little bivalves. "You put your thumb over the hole on the top of the tube when you pull back up on the gun, and the sand will stay inside because of the vacuum-like pressure."

Goodie dumped the sand from the gun, then bent over and reached down into the hole, retrieving a nice fat razor clam. "Yum!" she exclaimed. "My mouth is already watering for a taste of the chowder we'll make together later!"

Danny said nothing about the clam, or the chowder. Instead, he set the lantern on the beach and held out his hand. "Give me your car keys, Goodie."

"My what?"

"My pockets are deeper than yours. The way you chased after that clam, I was afraid you'd lose the keys out here on the beach, and then we'd never find them."

Goodie had never lost a car key on the beach in all of her 77 years, but she didn't want to argue with Danny—not about the best place for clams, a place to park, or whether she needed to relinquish her car keys. She stuck her clam gun upright in the sand, briefly wondering why it was called a gun and not a tube, then dutifully reached into her pocket and handed her keys over. She made sure her clam net was still secure on her belt, adjusted her stocking cap, and cheerily said, "You get to dig the next one!"

Danny looked up and down the beach at all the lanterns glowing— bright little dots of light all along the waterline— and sighed. "It really is like a second city."

"I knew you'd love it," said Goodie. Secretly, she wasn't

all that keen on night clam digs, but an opportunity to be out on the beach with all the flickering wicks of hundreds of lanterns seemed like such a romantic date when Danny first suggested it.

Tonight's weather was far from perfect. The crosswinds were downright cold, and Goodie could see that Danny's eyes were watering something fierce. Perhaps the wind was why there weren't as many diggers around as there usually were. The way the surf was pounding the shore often drove the clams deeper and more difficult to find.

"This spot is perfect," said Danny, nodding thoughtfully. "We've got this section of beach all to ourselves."

Goodie laughed. "That's not necessarily a good thing when you're clamming, but we've already got one, so there must be more clams around here someplace," she said optimistically. "Are you ready to try your hand at digging one yourself?"

Danny didn't immediately answer, but Goodie started stomping another circle around him anyway. Then she stood directly in front of him and scanned back over her footprints searching for another clam show. Nothing. She shrugged, and smiled as she looked up at him. "You win some; you lose some."

But Danny didn't return her smile, and there was something almost sinister in the way the lantern light grotesquely distorted his face. Who was this man, Goodie wondered. Who was this new friend who wore such an ugly air of arrogance tonight? And what was he thinking that soured his expression so? She shivered.

"Are you cold?" asked Danny.

"Probably not as cold as you are," said Goodie. "I've been moving around, working up a sweat stomping and digging. Would you like to take a turn stomping?"

Danny remained silent as a thin wave skimmed the beach, encircling their boots, erasing their footprints, then quietly pulling back out.

"Shall we try here again, or move down the beach a little?" asked Goodie.

Danny lifted the lantern as if to adjust the wick. But instead of greater illumination, the lantern suddenly went out, and they were pitched into blackness. Momentarily losing her orientation, Goodie called out, "Danny! Where are you? I can't see!"

But Goodie didn't need to see Danny, because her voice had helped him hone in on her whereabouts, and what she immediately felt was far more chilling than the ocean water seeping into her worn boots.

Danny had set down the lantern, then calculatedly taken two steps toward the sound of Goodie's voice. He'd placed his hands on her shoulders, gripping them tightly. Then he roughly pulled her head close, and pressed his mouth against her ear. "I'm right here," he grunted. "No need to yell."

Goodie tried to back away. "Danny— Danny, you're hurting me."

"The pain is temporary," he said, emitting a low, deep chuckle. His hands slid from her shoulders up to her neck and he began squeezing, the fingers of both hands behind her head, the thumbs pressing hard down on her windpipe. "Too bad about you getting swept away by a sneaker wave tonight. Such a pity."

Goodie couldn't breathe. How had he known about sneaker waves? She'd never mentioned them to him. Her thoughts swirled as she struggled against his grip, but it did no good.

She tried to drop to her knees, thinking to pull him

down with her, as she'd been taught in the self-defense class she'd taken at the senior center, but Danny was far heavier and stronger. Goodie felt the terror rising in her throat, and knew she only had a few moments left before she totally blacked out.

The sudden thought of her grandchildren passed through her mind, and the image of them all taking the giant pendulum ride at the county fair last summer. The pendulum ride, that swung them heavily back and forth, back and forth, higher and higher until it went so high it swung them all the way up and around and—

With every ounce of Goodie's remaining strength, she flung her aluminum clam gun out and away from her body, then up and around in a high arc, high over the top of her head, just like that giant pendulum. She heard the resounding *THWAAACK!* as the tube connected heavily with the side of Danny's head.

"Oooof!" Caught by surprise, Danny relaxed his grip just enough for Goodie to suck in a deep gulp of air.

But instead of pushing Danny away, Goodie reached up, grabbed the front of his jacket, and pulled him forcefully toward her. Danny flailed his arms to grab for her as he pitched forward, but being smaller and quicker, she stepped lithely aside, and he fell like a sack of cement, his face slamming into the hard-packed sand just as the next wave skimmed up the beach.

Then Goodie turned and ran, up toward the dunes, helter-skelter, heart pounding, breaths coming in short, raspy pants. And then she went down. Hard. Onto her knees. She'd fallen into a hole, or tripped over a piece of flotsam or jetsam or whatever kind of seaweed and driftwood littered the beach at the high tide line. Her right ankle screamed in pain.

Don't give up, she told herself. You've got to get away. Goodie tried to get to her feet, but her ankle wouldn't support her weight. She couldn't even touch it to the ground without the pain flashing through her like a bolt of lightning. Don't give up, she told herself again, and she forced herself to crawl on her hands and knees toward where she thought they'd left the car. If she could just get to the car, she'd be safe.

The car! The thought slammed into her harder than the sand she'd fallen on. Danny had taken her keys! Even if she found the car, she wouldn't be able to get inside, or drive away. Her cell phone was in the car, too! She'd left it there for safe keeping. *Think,* she told herself. *Think!*

It was slow going once Goodie got to the softer sand, but if she ever wanted to see those blessed grandkids again, she'd have to keep going. She'd have to hide in the dunes and wait till daylight. Yes! She could do that, and she would survive, or die trying.

The absurdity of that thought made her want to laugh out loud. "I'll survive or die trying," she muttered, vaguely understanding that it was cold, her feet were wet, her ankle was either sprained or broken, and she was rapidly descending into shock.

The lock picker trying to break into Goodie's house wasn't all that good at his job, and he scratched at the doorknob and jiggled the handle for several minutes before the door swung open. Two figures were silhouetted by the bright porchlight, and I couldn't get a good look at either one of them. One was skinny and the other one was short, but I couldn't even tell you if they were men, women, or one of each.

I tightened my grip on the gun and pointed it in their

direction. It's legal to shoot looters in Washington, but it can't be a lethal shot. That much I knew. I just hoped I wouldn't be blinded by the overhead light when they flipped on the switch just inside the door. With my luck, I might end up killing one or both of them, and end up in prison myself.

Turns out I needn't have worried. Hans, the introverted, socially shy, total love of an aging German Shepherd, started growling deep in his throat. I reached down and took hold of his collar, but he jumped to his feet, straining against my hand, barking harsh and loud and furious. Then he succeeded in pulling away from me and charged toward the intruders in the doorway.

"Holy shit!" yelled one of them, as they both turned and ran for their vehicle.

"I didn't sign up to be eaten by no dog," yelled the other.

Had they bothered to look back, they would have seen Hans, standing just inside the doorsill, as if there were an electric fence, or screen door, or something stopping him from continuing on outside.

As for me, I was still in the wingback chair just to the right of their line of sight, and still in the shadows. My left foot, the one that was most underneath Hans's body while we napped, had also fallen asleep, and even though I tried to get up and chase after the would-be thieves, the tingles rendered me useless right when I needed my foot the most.

Holy Criminitly! The least I could have done was get a good look at the make and model of the vehicle and maybe fired off a warning shot, or shoot out their tires, or something equally dramatic! Some detective I was!

I sat up as tall and straight as I could, and it was just enough to see a boxy vehicle's taillights as the bad guys skeedoodled out of the driveway.

By the time the feeling came back to my foot, Hans had

left his personal line of demarcation at the open front door and gone into the kitchen. Apparently, chasing off thieves worked up his appetite, and I heard him pushing his empty food dish around the floor with his nose.

I closed and relocked the front door, trying to concentrate on what little information I had gleaned. Two men. Yes, men. I got that from the sound of their voices. And the second one had used poor grammar. I mentally rolled my eyes. Yeah, that information probably wouldn't get them arrested by anyone other than a grammar cop.

Racking my brain, I realized they had backed into the driveway, because I'd seen only taillights when they hurriedly left, as they pulled straight away in a spray of gravel. It might have been them out there jockeying for getaway position that had awakened me, but that wasn't going to help track them down. Lots of people, including the sheriff and his deputy, backed their vehicles in. But other than that, I was pretty clueless.

I made my way into the kitchen before flipping on any lights. The least I could do was feed poor Hans. We'd both had a good scare tonight, and I hoped it wouldn't have a lasting effect on his rehabilitation. He'd been through a lot before Goodie had rescued him, and I said a quick prayer that our misadventure tonight wouldn't set him back emotionally.

"That's a good boy," I said, scratching along his back as he ate. "You were a hero tonight, you know that Hans?"

Hans's tail waved slowly back and forth, but he didn't stop eating.

"You know, Hans, I'm thinking that maybe Goodie should give you another name. One that reflects your newfound bravery. Something like Adolph."

Hans lifted his head, licked his lips, and tilted his head

at me.

"You like the name Adolph?" I asked. "Do you know that Adolph means 'noble wolf'?" I sighed. "Well, at least one of us was able to protect Goodie's house tonight."

I was still beating myself up for my stake-out incompetence when I went out and pulled my 883 Sportster from Goodie's garage. I was 99% sure the burglars wouldn't be coming back tonight, or any time soon, for that matter, and it was late enough that Goodie and Danny could be returning at any time with clams to clean and chowder to make.

Danny's bike was parked up near the garage in the driveway. Hoping in some way to redeem myself, I recited the license plate number over and over on the ride home.

I'd call Goodie—as well as Sheriff Donaldson—first thing in the morning with my full report. Sheriff D was probably going to give me hell about not telling him before going on my stake-out, but it was always easier for me to apologize than ask permission.

Out on the beach, Goodie had successfully crawled over the first line of dunes and had found a spot to at least partially conceal herself in the tall grass. She couldn't stop shivering, so she scooped some sand over her legs like a blanket, thinking that might help warm her.

Goodie knew the signs of shock. She'd learned them when she took the first-aid class at the senior center. The first aid class. The self-defense class. The kick-boxing class that she and the gals had given up at the insistence of the ER doctor, and taken up belly dancing instead. She thought fondly of The Veiled Rainbow, and wondered if her twisted ankle would keep her from participating at their next gig. She hoped they wouldn't need to replace her with another yellow if she died out here. What if she were never found? What if the coyotes ate her and left nothing to be found, or buried? What if—

She told herself to concentrate. Focus. Stay awake. Focus. Focus. Recite something! "Hail Mary, full of grace," Goodie said aloud. "The Lord is with thee… The Lord is with thee… The Lord…" Strange, that's all she could remember of that prayer, although she seemed to remember it ended with the words "in our hour of death."

Goodie's breathing and heartrate were both so rapid, she thought she might be a little bird. What kind of a bird would she be? Not a seagull. Those birds were nasty. What about a chickadee? Were there chickadees on the beach? She wasn't sure. What about vultures? No! No birds! Focus! Focus! Maybe she'd be a little hummingbird. She'd heard somewhere that those little birds ate several times their weight every day.

But Goodie didn't want to think about eating. She felt sick to her stomach, like she might throw up. And she felt chilled—chilled clear down to the center of her bones, and oh, so bone weary and tired. So very, very tired.

If I could just take a little nap, Goodie thought, *I'd feel much better.* She lay back in the sand, sighed deeply, and closed her eyes.

CHAPTER 16

As soon as I thought it was late enough for Goodie to have both eyes open the next morning, I called to confess my total failure as a home protection specialist. Her cell phone rang and rang and then went to voice mail. That was odd. It wasn't going straight to voice mail, as it would have if she had the phone turned off, so why wasn't she picking up?

I knew Goodie well enough to know she would never have invited Danny Boy to spend the night in her bed, but maybe he'd slept on her couch last night. That was possible, I guess, so he wouldn't have had to drive all the way home last night. And this morning they might have already gone to breakfast somewhere.

But wouldn't Goodie have taken her cell phone along? Maybe she had the ringer turned off so that it wouldn't interrupt their conversation. Maybe she… Oh fizzle! I could drive myself crazy all day playing this game.

I waited another half hour, in case she'd been in the shower or something, and called again. Again, I got the voice mail, so I left a non-incriminating voice mail in case anyone else heard her messages. My next call was to Nadine. After all, Nadine was her best friend, so if anyone knew where Goodie was, it would be her.

"Nope," said Nadine. "I haven't heard from her yet this morning, and I've been dying to hear all about her date with Danny Boy. I sure hope they're getting along as well as

Patrick and me."

And then she gave me a much-more-than-I-cared-to-know, complete recounting of her afternoon nude adventure with Patrick while trying to refill the hummingbird feeder out on the deck, and Stella's insistence to be included in all the fun. The story itself was hilarious, but I was anxious to steer the conversation back to Goodie's whereabouts.

"Do you think Danny spent the night at Goodie's?" I asked.

"Not a prayer of that happening unless or until our little Goodie-two-shoes has a ring on her finger," Nadine answered without hesitation. "She's not nearly as free-spirited as I am!"

I did not want to think of Nadine, or Meredith, or any of The Veiled Rainbow engaged in sexual acts, but the naked, wrinkled images came streaking into my consciousness anyway.

Good grief and gravy! My own body was not as fit and trim and soft and smooth as it had once been either, and I mentally vowed to keep the lights off in my bedroom forevermore!

"Do you think she's okay?" I asked. "Shall I go do a wellness check?"

"I live a lot closer than you do," said Nadine. "I'll run over and see if she's home. She might be outside washing the salt and sand off her car after driving it on the beach last night."

"Okay," I said. "That makes sense. Call me when you get there."

And less than 10 minutes later, Nadine called me back. "Her car's not here," she said.

"Did you look in the garage?"

"Of course I looked in the garage. I'm not a complete

ninny."

Another thought suddenly struck me. "Is Danny's motorcycle still in the driveway?"

"You must think I'm without any wits at all," said Nadine. "What kind of a moron would be peeking in the garage windows if there were a man's motorcycle parked out here?"

I didn't bother to tell Nadine we all knew how much she enjoyed smoking pot, and that unless I knew if she'd been imbibing this morning, I wouldn't have any idea what kind of a moron she might be.

"You think maybe she went grocery shopping?" I asked instead.

"Maybe," said Nadine. "But why wouldn't she have called to invite us over for clam chowder later so she could tell us all about her date?"

"You got me," I said. "She could be anywhere, doing anything, and I'm reluctant to call the sheriff and risk looking ridiculous, again, when she turns up at the hairdresser's or the post office or the bank."

"You know it's Saturday, right?" said Nadine. "The hairdresser, post office, and bank are all closed," she huffed. "And you act like smoking pot turns me into a forgetful and confused old woman! Maybe you should try some, yourself, Sylvia."

I sighed. "Well, she could still be at the store!"

"Tell you what," said Nadine. "I'm going to sit right down on Goodie's porch, smoke a joint, and wait for her to return." She sighed. "Goodie doesn't care if I smoke outside."

"Good idea," I said. "And call me the minute you see the whites of her eyes. Meanwhile, I need to call Sheriff D anyway. I got a little something I need to talk to him about, and then I'll just happen to ask him if he can put out a silver alert for Goodie."

"Silver alerts are for senior citizens with Alzheimer's, or dementia, or some other mental disability," said Nadine.

"I'll tell him she's nuts to be going out with a guy so much younger."

Nadine obviously choked on her toke, resulting in a coughing fit that continued for several minutes. Finally she gasped out, "You hypocrite! You also qualify for a mental disability based on that particular parameter, you old cougar!"

I hadn't thought about that. Freddy's age had become more and more irrelevant as we enjoyed each other's company, and I was almost ready to consider it a non-issue. Almost.

I conceded Nadine's point, but still had to call the sheriff to explain what I'd been up to at Goodie's last night, and then I'd report that we couldn't find her this morning.

"Have you considered that Goodie doesn't want you to find her?" Sheriff D asked, after I'd filled him in on my nearly fruitless stake-out.

"But she doesn't even know about the guys who attempted to break in! I was going to tell her all about that first thing this morning. Something's fishy with these guys from Sole Mates, Carter, and I'm afraid Goodie might be in over her head with Danny Boy."

"Or maybe she just fell for him, hook, line and sinker, and they decided to elope without telling anyone," said Sheriff D. "Ever think of that?"

Well, no, I hadn't thought of that. In that case, Nadine might be sitting out on Goodie's porch for a good long time.

My silence went on long enough that Sheriff D decided to fill it himself. "Look, Sylvia, I can put out an unofficial local BOLO for her car, just to the deputies on the North

Beach Peninsula. Do you know the make, model, color and license plate?"

"License plate!" I squealed. "Oh, Carter! I got the license plate number for the motorcycle Danny was riding last night! Can you run it to see what his real name is?"

"Let's do one thing at a time," said Sheriff D. "What do you know about Goodie's car?"

I was pretty proud of myself. At least I knew the make, model, and color. Then I gave the sheriff Danny Boy's plate number and we got off the phone. For now, I'd done all I could do.

Goodie's eyes opened, but she didn't move. For a few minutes, she didn't know exactly where she was, or how she had gotten there. It was daylight, it was misting heavily, and she was covered from the waist down in sand. Slowly, the events of the past night returned to her.

Tears trickled down her face and mixed with the rain. Her Darling Danny had tried to kill her! Why would he have wanted to do such a thing?

As she lay there, she remembered that she was hiding in the dunes because he'd taken her car keys. She wondered if her car were still out there on the beach. And if so, she wondered if he were hiding inside, waiting for her to return, so he could finish what he'd started. Then she wondered if she were already dead.

Goodie's stomach growled. No. She was definitely not yet dead.

"Hail Mary full of grace. The Lord is with thee. Blessed art thou among women, and blessed is the fruit of thy womb, Jesus. Holy Mary, Mother of God, pray for us sinners, now and at the hour of our death. Amen." Goodie sobbed as she completed the prayer. It had not yet been the hour of her death! There was hope!

Filled with resolve, she started brushing the sand off her legs—the sand that had somewhat insulated her and kept her warm enough to survive the night. "Blessed be the sand," she said aloud. "And blessed be the rain." She gratefully licked some of the water off her lips, then opened her mouth wide, and tipped her head back to get a little more.

It was the rain that had probably awakened her. A soft, but all-day drizzle, had settled in over the entire north coast, and she was glad it hadn't yet soaked through all her layers of clothing.

As she tried to pull her feet from the sand, a searing pain shot up her leg from her right ankle, and she cried out. Her ankle! Now she remembered falling, and crawling a long ways—probably more than a hundred yards—to find a place to hide. But wouldn't Danny now see the crawling tracks she'd left on the beach?

"Blessed be the rain," she said again, thoughtfully nodding her head. The rain would have already obscured her path through the sand.

Still sitting on her butt, Goodie carefully extracted her left foot from the sand. Then pushing with her hands and free foot, she successfully pulled the injured foot out. Instinctively, she knew not to try to take the boot off, but when she attempted to stand, the searing pain shot through her again and nearly made her pass out.

"Okay, Mr. Ankle," she said aloud. "You win. I won't be walking anywhere, anytime soon."

She could crawl, still with some pain, but if Danny were waiting for her, she could not outrun him, and certainly not out crawl him, in her condition. So she decided it was best to just sit tight and either wait for dark, or for someone to find her. Hopefully, the next faces she'd see would be her rescuers, and not Danny's.

Goodie searched her pockets for some kind of weapon, but came up with only a package of gum and her clam license. She popped a stick of gum into her mouth immediately, and stuck the license back into her pocket. If she were to die, by either natural or unnatural causes, at least she'd have some ID on her. Which wouldn't matter at all if her body was buried in the dunes.

"You stop that!" she said aloud. "You're not going to die."

Nadine called to tell me she'd abandoned her post on Goodie's porch and was back home by mid-afternoon. In the early evening, I went over to Jimmy's to enjoy Indian food that Kanji had prepared for the three of us. I was trying hard not to think too much about where Goodie might be, and with whom, and why, when my cell phone started ringing like a siren.

"It's the sheriff," I said unnecessarily, and excused myself from the kitchen table to talk more privately in the living room side of the building, which, I realized half way there, was a rather silly notion, so I did an about face and started back for the kitchen table.

"Hello Sheriff," I answered. "What's up?"

"One of our reserve officers found Goodie's car," Sheriff D began.

My knees went weak, and I grabbed for the table's edge. Kanji, sensing my distress, immediately jumped to his feet to steady me, and held the chair while I sat back down.

"Sheriff? I'm at the Clamshell with Jimmy and Kanji; I'm putting you on speaker." I set the phone down on the table in front of me and numbly stared at it.

"Goodie's car was found out on the beach, just north of

the Sandy Flats Approach. It was empty, but Goodie's cell phone was in the glove compartment."

"Goodie and Danny were going clam digging last night." I choked on my words. "Sheriff?" I didn't know what else to say.

"Yes, it's apparent they were going clam digging, as were half the population of the peninsula, but most of the others headed farther north, where there are a lot more, and allegedly bigger, clams."

"Is there any sign of either of them?" I asked in an uncharacteristically small voice.

Sheriff Donaldson cleared his throat. "This is an ongoing investigation, and as such—"

"Was there any sign of them?" repeated Jimmy, a lot louder than I'd been able to squeak out.

"Thank you, Jimmy, I already answered her question," said Sheriff D. Then he sighed. "Okay. There was one aluminum clam gun with a rather bad dent in it and a Coleman lantern found in the debris left at high tide about a quarter mile north of the car. There's no way to know if either item belongs to Goodie."

"Wait." I racked my brain for an elusive memory. "Sheriff, do you have the items with you?"

"That's affirmative," said Sheriff D. "Deputies Bill and Bob are bagging and tagging half the garbage from this section of the beach, as we do not yet know what might be important evidence. Why do you ask?"

"Could you check to see if either the clam gun or the lantern has the initials L.G. in red fingernail polish on them anywhere?"

We waited while we heard the sheriff ask Bill, or maybe Bob, to check for the initials, and then he said the words I was hoping I wouldn't hear. "Well, I'll be damned."

Tears stung my eyes. Was it possible that Goodie, and Danny of course, had been the victims of a sneaker wave? Danny wouldn't know about such things, but Goodie would have known better than to turn her back on the ocean. But what if she had tried to rescue him, and got pulled out in the water herself? What if their boots had filled with water and they were pulled under, unable to get back to shore? What if— "Have you called for the Coast Guard helicopter?"

"I did, but the chopper is on a capsize rescue just south of Tillamook head. Since it's already getting dark, they won't be able to help us out here until tomorrow morning."

I put both my elbows on the table and started rubbing my forehead with my fingertips, thinking hard. "Okay. I'll call Nadine and tell her to go back over and feed Hans."

Poor Hans. What would his life be like if Goodie never returned? I didn't want to think about that right now, but I couldn't stop myself.

"Sylvia?" asked Sheriff D. "We're going to suspend our search when it gets dark. I'm having George's Tow come get the car right now, and it will be impounded until we figure this all out. Are you going to be okay?"

I nodded.

"Miss Sylvia," said Kanji, "I do not believe the sheriff can hear you when you nod."

"Hello Kanji," said Sheriff D. "I appreciate you telling me she nodded. Will Syl be able to stay there at the Clamshell with you and Jimmy tonight?"

The sheriff's question brought my voice right back. "Least you forget, I've stayed here with Jimmy many times," I said. "I get the bedroom, and he takes the couch, and don't you be going and telling Freddy that Kanji and I are—" I interrupted myself and abruptly changed direction. "I'm fine, Carter. And I'll be sleeping at home in my own bed tonight, thank you very much."

"I understand," said the sheriff. "I'll be in touch if or when I learn anything more here."

We disconnected, and I looked at Kanji, who looked rather like I'd slapped him across the face. "Kanji— I'm sorry— I didn't mean—"

"Do not worry, Miss Sylvia. We have already slept together twice this week, and I'm sure the sheriff just wants to be sure you are safe and well cared for."

Jimmy's eyes were about to pop out of his head. He turned to me. "You said you didn't sleep with Kanji!"

"I didn't!"

"But we did," insisted Kanji. "We most certainly did." He smiled from ear to ear, showing us every perfect tooth in his entirely too perfect, and looking quite kissable, mouth.

I wasn't sure if he were just teasing me to get me thinking about something else, or if he were truly unaware that in less time than it takes to say "Syl's been sleeping around," Jimmy would have informed the entire peninsula I was sleeping with more men than I knew what to do with.

Which, now that I thought about it, was probably true, and it struck me so funny that I started to laugh, and I laughed and laughed and laughed, until I suddenly began to cry, and my body started shaking with my sobs. At which point, Kanji took my hand and pulled me to my feet, and held me until I was all cried out. For now.

I must admit that his arms felt so good around me that I didn't want him to let go, now or ever. I just wanted to be safe and warm, and forget about everything else and—

And my cell phone rang again, right on cue, as if this were a Hallmark movie. This time the ringtone played "Bad boys, bad boys, whatcha gonna do? Whatcha gonna do when they come for you?"

I reluctantly left Kanji's embrace and picked up the phone. "Hi Freddy. What's new?"

"Are you still at the Clamshell?"

"I am, and you can tell the sheriff I've changed my mind. I'm going to spend the night here." I looked pointedly at Jimmy and shook my head in a warning to stay silent. "Jimmy wants double or nothing on the poker tab he owes me, and Kanji needs to learn the finer points of the game, so we'll all be playing cards later."

"Good," said Freddy. "I'll be there in 20 minutes." And he quickly hung up before I could say another word.

"Company's coming," I said to no one in particular. Then I looked at Kanji. "Is there any more of that chicken marsala left?"

"There most certainly is, dear Sylvia." Kanji bowed. "Would you like another serving?"

"It's not for me. It's highly unlikely that Freddy's had any dinner, and I'd bet Jimmy's poker tab that he'd like to try your cooking. He's already told me that he's looking to expand the casino restaurant's offerings, and that authentic Indian food is at the top of his list, since it's not available anywhere else on the peninsula."

Kanji had started to look disappointed when I mentioned Freddy, but soon his polite smile returned. "Yes, I have told Freddy about our traditional foods, and now is as good a time as any for him to try a small sample."

As gallant and well-mannered as a guy can be, Kanji had taken his rival's imminent arrival in stride. There was just so darn much to like about this guy. And I did like this guy. But I liked Freddy, too, and that's where things always got complicated. Why did I have to choose?

Freddy arrived, and I turned my cheek for his kiss as I continued to talk to Meredith on the phone. Thankfully,

Nadine had informed all the rainbow ladies that Goodie and Danny were both missing, so I didn't have to explain why I was checking in with my mother.

"I'm fine," Merri insisted. "Absolutely fine. Now I got to go, I've got a date."

"Whoa! Mom! Hold on!" I could feel my voice going up a couple notches in just a few syllables. "Is it with Les again?"

"Yes, of course it's with Les. He's coming over and we're watching a DVD together. And if I'm lucky…"

"TMI, Mother! TMI! But—" I wasn't sure how she was going to take what I said next, but plunged ahead. "You two got in touch with each other on Sole Mates, and the sheriff is interested in meeting all the guys The Veiled Rainbow has met through that dating site. Are you okay with that?"

Meredith was quiet for a moment. "Did you tell the sheriff I knew him years ago?"

"Yes. That's why I didn't ask you to take him to the police station for fingerprints before you went out with him again."

Meredith snorted. "That's a good one, Syl. Now just back off and let me enjoy my evening."

And all in all, it wasn't an unpleasant evening for any of us, with the sprinkles on the frosting of the poker cupcake being that I cleaned up, winning hand after hand. It also kept me from thinking too much about Goodie, and I was equally grateful for that.

I excused myself to go to bed a little after 1 a.m., and left the boys to fend for themselves. I really didn't care who slept where, as long as everyone was perfectly clear that no one was going to be sleeping with me tonight.

But for good measure, I locked the door.

CHAPTER 17

The sound of a helicopter awakened Goodie the next morning. She vaguely realized that it was Sunday, and that if she didn't hurry, she'd be late for church. Then she opened her eyes, and looked at all the sand covering her lower body. She had reburied herself for warmth, but was still cold, and shivering, and very, very, hungry. At least it had stopped raining.

Gathering her courage, Goodie butt-scooted a little ways away from where she'd been sleeping and relieved herself. She was sure she was getting plenty of sand inside her granny panties, as Nadine referred to them, but it couldn't be helped.

Then she managed to inch herself on up the sloping dune and peer over, looking to the south. Her car was gone! Danny must have taken it! When he left, or where he went, was of little concern at this moment, and Goodie was glad she'd already used this big sand box for her toilet or she might have wet herself in relief. Danny was blessedly gone! She was safe! Praise be!

Up the beach a little ways to the north, Goodie could see several police vehicles, a truck with a flatbed trailer attached to it, a nondescript white van, which was probably Medical Examiner John Stark's call car, and several private vehicles.

Out on the water in front of the vehicles were four wave runners, obviously brought in on the flatbed trailer. They were running a back and forth pattern, paralleling the beach, while overhead, the helicopter was running a similar pattern but farther offshore.

Goodie watched for several minutes before it dawned on her that they must be looking for her. Of course! The Veiled Rainbow gals all knew she'd gone clamming with Danny Friday night, and by now, on Sunday morning, they would all have tried to contact her. Her friends knew she was missing, and they had sent help, but the help was all looking in the wrong direction!

She took her green and yellow stocking cap off her head and waved it frantically back and forth in the air above her. "Yoo-hoo! Hey you guys! I'm over here!"

Naturally, since everyone was facing the water, and they were all at least a quarter mile away and working their way north, no one heard her. And even if they'd turned in her direction, she was just a spot on the dunes, barely discernable at this distance.

Goodie knew she must find a way to attract their attention. She wondered how long it would take her to scoot on her butt, or crawl, or roll far enough toward the water for them to see her. It would have to be done before they moved farther on up the beach.

Looking around, she spotted a piece of driftwood about 20 feet away. It wasn't much bigger around than her lower arm, but it still might work as a crutch. Unfortunately, it was in the wrong direction from the surf line. She'd have to spend some time working her way over there, then back to where she was, before making any forward progress.

For a few minutes, Goodie was frozen with indecision. Then she wiggle-walked on her hips toward the driftwood. It crossed her mind that this was a little like doing a hip-shimmy when she belly danced. Then it immediately occurred to her that she might be losing her mind to be thinking of belly dancing at a time like this.

Bolstered by sheer grit and determination, it didn't take as long as she'd feared to get to the driftwood she intended to use as a crutch. But when she tried to pick up the piece of wood, she discovered that not all of it was exposed on top of the sand, and that it was much longer than she'd first thought.

She clawed and scraped at the sand around the driftwood, and her fingernails broke and bled, but she finally uncovered the full length—it must have been 10 or 12 feet! It was much too long to use as a crutch, and now she'd just wasted valuable time.

Her disappointment was enough to make anyone cry, but when Goodie's lower lip started to tremble, she stuck out her chin in defiance.

"St. Christopher? St. Michael? Is anybody there? You're supposed to protect me. Are you on duty up there? Are you hearing me?" The sound of her own voice gave Goodie added courage. "What about Psalm 91, God? No harm shall befall me, no disaster will come near me, you will protect me and rescue me, because I acknowledge your name."

Goodie knew that wasn't *exactly* what Psalm 91 said, but she figured a decent paraphrase might still get her Higher Power's notice. "God! Listen up! I need help!" She almost giggled. Imagine talking to God like that! She tried again. "What I meant to say, God, was are you paying attention this morning? One of your flock needs you, good shepherd, so please send help!"

A little ray of sunshine chose that moment to shine down from the otherwise cloudy sky. "Is that a sign?" asked Goodie. "Or is that just to make me uncomfortably hot?" She reached up and pulled off her Oregon Ducks stocking cap and wiped her face with it. Then she unzipped the red hunter's vest and took it off, too. Impulsively, she hung the vest on the end of the driftwood pole, and a crazy idea suddenly entered her head.

She knew it was a long shot, but what did she have to lose? Goodie took her hands and started digging a hole in the sand between her thighs. When she got a hole about a foot deep, she made sure the vest would stay in place on the small end of the pole and pulled the driftwood up onto her shoulder.

Inch by inch, she advanced the driftwood farther past her shoulder, like a revolutionary soldier hoisting his rifle, bayonet attached. Fortunately, the weight of the larger end kept the pole from tipping downward, which would have turned Goodie's shoulder into something like the fulcrum on a teeter-totter.

Finally, she angled the bigger end into the hole in the sand, and pushed the rest of the pole upward with both hands. She got the pole standing, but the sand was soft, and her vest-turned-distress-flag started leaning heavily to one side.

Goodie grabbed it to steady it, but there wasn't much she could do to shore up the hole to keep the stick vertical. It leaned first one way, and then the other, and it took all her concentration to keep the pole from toppling over.

The effect of the vest waving back and forth did, in fact, draw some attention to her hiding place, but not in the way Goodie had planned, and not from the would-be rescuers on the shore.

The North Beach Peninsula is known for having a large number of eagles in residence, and it's not unusual for the eagles to hunt along the beach. As luck would have it, as Goodie was hoisting her distress signal, two eagles were flying back and forth along the high tide line right in front of her dune, looking for anything dead to snack on.

The vest had not been secured against an eagle attack, and when the first one swooped in to investigate, he lifted it right off the pole with his gigantic talons. The other eagle, wanting in on whatever it was the first one had, divebombed him, and tried to take it away. The result was a weird kind of back and forth ball game, with first one eagle stealing the vest, then losing it to the second one, and they screamed their displeasure as well as their joy.

Goodie watched the eagles whirl in the air above her in awe. "For those who hope in the Lord will renew their strength. They will soar on wings like eagles. They will run and not grow weary. They will walk and not be faint."

She abruptly abandoned the pole, now listing at an almost 45-degree angle, pulled her stocking cap back on, rolled over onto her knees, and began to crawl up the slope of the only dune between her and the water, over two hundred yards away. Goodie made it to the top of the rise, but exertion had taken everything out of her. She closed her eyes and allowed her knees to go out from under her, and her body collapsed on the top of the ridge that had both protected her from danger, and hidden her from help. She'd done all she could do. She was done.

Meanwhile, on the beach, the eagles had attracted the attention of Sheriff Donaldson. He'd been standing at the shoreline, watching the wave runners through binoculars, but the screeching birds invited him to look south.

Sheriff D turned his binoculars in the birds' direction and focused on something—or maybe someone—lying on the upper edge of the dune, directly beneath where the birds were wheeling and diving, apparently fighting over some treasure they'd found.

And in short order, an exhausted, dehydrated, unconscious, but otherwise appearing to be intact and alive Goodie Godwin was loaded into the M.E.'s call car. John Stark could transport her more quickly than waiting for an ambulance, to the hospital in Unity. And the sheriff didn't need to take her statement until later, after she'd been seen by a doctor, and probably admitted for at least a few days, depending on how advanced her hypothermia was.

Sheriff Donaldson and the rest of the recovery crew stayed on the beach, as their work was not yet done. Another hour passed, then two, and by now they were several miles farther up the beach. John Stark returned with the call car, telling everyone that Goodie was safely "at the hospital, but still unconscious."

Just minutes later, one of the four wave runners—the one working farthest to the north—signaled that they'd found a body, floating face down.

Three members of The Veiled Rainbow, plus Jimmy, Kanji, and I, converged on the North Beach Hospital at around the same time. We were told that Goodie had been given two IVs of fluids, and was now "resting," but that we could wait in the lobby if we wished.

We all wished. Not one of us was about to leave. We were too eager to find out what had happened on that ill-fated clamming trip, now nearly 48 hours ago.

The nurse couldn't estimate how long we'd have to wait to see her, possibly several hours. She told us that Goodie had been exhausted when she arrived and they wanted to allow her time to sleep. The best part was that they were optimistic for a full recovery, and Merri said that was probably due to the good shape Goodie maintained by belly dancing.

In the lobby, the six of us filled most of the available

chairs, and an odd display of party atmosphere prevailed. So much time had passed since any of us had seen Goodie that not one of us had expected such a happy outcome.

After a couple hours, Kanji, bless his heart, drove down to the Pier 103 tuna fish and chips boat and returned with dinner for us all. Yep, there was a lot to like about this man.

"Thank you, Kanji," I said when he handed me an order of just fish. Talk about thoughtful! He'd even remembered that I was trying to avoid French fries these days.

He bowed slightly before sitting down next to me. "It is my pleasure to remember how a lady I care for takes both her drinks and her food," he said. "I am not shy about telling you that it is my hope that someday we will be able to enjoy a meal in a nice restaurant, just the two of us, and with no distractions."

I smiled. "You mean like a real date."

"No," said Kanji, shaking his head. "I do not mean *like* a real date; I mean that the two of us should *have* a real date."

Meredith, who was sitting on the other side of me, leaned over and whispered, "I told you months ago that this guy was a keeper; what are you waiting for?"

Nadine and Orpha, sitting across from us, were busy eating, and thankfully didn't weigh in on the state of my love life, but Jimmy, sitting next to Orpha, pushed up his glasses with his middle finger, and raised an eyebrow at me, then used his head to motion in Kanji's direction, just as if he had heard what Merri had whispered.

I ignored the peanut gallery and dove headlong into my fish, determined not to look up until I was certain there'd be another subject on the table.

We were all just finishing our meal when Freddy appeared, in uniform, and walked directly over to where I was sitting. "Uh, Syl?" he said. He looked strange—almost apologetic. "Could I please talk with you outside?"

Something inside me went on high alert. "Why can't you talk to me here?"

Freddy looked around the lobby at the other five. Then he cleared his throat and leaned down so that only I could hear him. "Please, my Sylleegirl, don't make this any harder than it is, just come with me, and bring your purse and cell phone."

I wiped my hands on a paper napkin and stood up. "Fine. Whatever." Turning to the rest of the suddenly silent but very alert group, I added, "I'll be right back."

But I wasn't right back. As soon as I stepped outside, Freddy pulled a zip tie from his utility belt and started reading me my rights.

"Stop joking around," I said. I'd been thinking he'd lured me away from the others for a little private time and maybe a few quick kisses.

But Freddy pointedly finished reciting the entire Miranda warning. Then, in one motion, he swiftly turned me around, and fastened my wrists together with the zip tie.

"Freddy! This isn't funny! You're scaring me!"

Freddy opened the back door of his patrol car, put his hand on top of my head to keep me from banging it on the door frame, and firmly closed the door behind me, still without saying a word about what was going on.

Neither of us said a thing on the way to the police station. I was too angry to talk to Freddy, and apparently he wasn't inclined to get all chatty with me at the moment, either.

Freddy took me directly into the interrogation room, seated me at the table facing the two-way mirror, and left me there. After a few minutes alone, I looked up into the 8-foot wall mirror and stuck out my tongue.

"I don't know what's going on around here, but somebody better get their butts in here and clue me in. Have I done something wrong? Am I under arrest? How about some due process here?" I stopped myself just in time to keep from calling whoever was watching a numskull, dimwit, or moron. Calling names would probably do nothing to help my case—whatever my case turned out to be.

Sheriff D came in and shut the door behind him. He set his trusty recorder on the table before us, along with a manila file folder, his notepad, and a stubby pencil.

"Carter…" I began.

He held up his hand. "It's Sheriff Donaldson," he said. "And are you Sylvia Lee Avery?"

"You know my name."

"I need to verify who is talking on this recording," said Sheriff D. "We have to go by the book today, Ms. Avery."

Holy Criminitly! What in the world was going on? I swallowed hard, and could feel my hands, still bound behind me, start to grow clammy.

"Is the zip tie really necessary?" I asked, in the smallest voice I'd ever heard come out of my own mouth.

Without a word, Sheriff D got up and came around to my side of the table. He used his utility knife to cut my hands free.

I rubbed my wrists as he walked back around to his chair. "Car— Sheriff Donaldson—could you please tell me what's going on around here?"

"At the risk of sounding like too many TV crime shows," he said, "I'll be the one to ask the questions here, Ms. Avery."

"Am I being charged with something?" I asked, not heeding his directive in the least.

"At this time, you are here for questioning only," said the sheriff.

"Then why was I zip tied and not just asked to come in?"

"Because of the nature of the crime we're investigating," said Sheriff D. "It's standard procedure in the case of serious, violent offenses."

"Like what, for instance?" I knew I was on thin ice, but I pressed my luck anyway.

"Like murder, for instance."

Sheriff Donaldson had nearly spit the words at me, and I could see he was mad at himself for answering so many questions right after he'd said he'd be the one to ask the questions. He drew in a deep breath, leaned back in his chair, and used the thumb and index finger of his right hand to smooth his mustache from the center out.

For once, I kept quiet, although I was nearly bursting with more questions.

Sheriff D flipped open the file folder, lifted an 8 by 10 color photo out and turned it around to face me. "Do you know this man?"

I took a good hard look at the face in the photo. If I took away the beard, then added glasses and a little more than 30 years, then maybe… I posed my question aloud. "Sheriff?... I took a deep breath. "Sheriff? Is that Daniel Gardner? Is that my ex-husband?"

Sheriff D narrowed his eyes and considered his responses. "You tell me."

And from that I gathered that a positive ID on the body hadn't been made, and I went slightly on the offensive. "If you don't know who it is, then why did you drag me in here?"

He opened the file folder again, and handed me another photo, this one of the man's lower right arm, on which there was an intricate, calligraphed tattoo that simply read, "Sylvia."

I was on a first-name basis with that knot suddenly

clenching in my stomach, but I had to push past it. "What happened to him?"

"John Stark hasn't completed the autopsy yet, but it looks like it was either blunt force trauma or drowning."

I was surprised the sheriff gave me so much information, knowing his standard reply was "no comment" when asked about an open investigation.

"Sylvia?" Sheriff D held my gaze for several seconds. "Where were you Friday night?"

Every hair stood straight up on the back of my neck. "Damn it, Carter! You know perfectly well where I was Friday night! I called you Saturday morning and told you all about it!"

Sheriff D leaned back in his chair and stared at the ceiling. He sighed. "Do you have anyone who can corroborate your alibi?"

"Corroborate my alibi?!" It would have been almost funny if Sheriff Donaldson wasn't staring at me so intently, just like a hawk, turning his head slightly to the side and evaluating the prey's next move.

Patience was one of Sheriff D's strong suits, but not mine. I started babbling, filling in the silence, offering up more than I needed to say, but not immediately able to stop myself.

"Goodie left me at her house when she and Danny left for the beach, remember? I was there in case anyone came to break in. Her dog Hans and I fell asleep, then two guys picked the lock and started to come in, and my foot was asleep, and Hans's barking scared them off and..."

"So you allege that you were there alone for several hours," said the sheriff.

"But I called you Saturday morning—"

Sheriff D interrupted me. "Which was pretty smart for

someone who had no alibi."

"But Goodie can tell you! Ask her!"

"Unfortunately," said Sheriff D, "Goodie is still unconscious, and we can't ask her anything."

"But— But— The nurse said she was sedated and resting. She didn't say anything about Goodie being in a coma, or unconscious or…"

Sheriff D shook his head. "The nurse was instructed not to give out that information."

"Why not?" I felt my face turning red. "Why didn't she tell us the truth? It couldn't have been those stupid HIPPA rules. I'm designated as 'family' for the entire belly dancing troupe."

"I needed to know where to find you," said the sheriff. He shrugged. "I don't have enough manpower to send my deputies all over the county looking for you."

"So you had the nurse lie to keep all six of us handy?"

"Did she really lie?" asked Sheriff D. "Or did you just hear what you wanted to hear?"

"Semantics!" I glowered at him, and took a deep breath. "So… just because you saw my name tattooed on his arm, you decided I was a suspect?"

"Not exactly," said Sheriff D. He paused, considering his next words. "Remember when your house was broken into?"

"Oh for gosh and golly sakes, Carter! Of course I remember! That was only a week ago!"

"Well," said the sheriff, looking at me as if I were under a microscope, "when Freddy dusted your place for fingerprints, it turned out that quite a few of them were Daniel Gardner's."

CHAPTER 18

Motive and opportunity. Until—or unless—Goodie woke up, proving my innocence was not going to be so easy, and even then, I didn't have a rock-solid alibi, unless Hans, the German Shepherd who could confirm my whereabouts on Friday, suddenly started speaking English.

"But Sheriff," I argued, "they left the house together. They left just before sunset and went clam digging in Goodie's car."

"Yes," Sheriff D nodded. "And we found Goodie's car on the beach and impounded it. We're not sure how many people were originally in the car, and if or when anyone else might have arrived, and exactly who is directly involved. This is an ongoing investigation."

A light suddenly dawned, and in my excitement, I stood up. "Danny left his motorcycle in Goodie's driveway. We have to go check it out!"

Sheriff D had leapt to his feet the moment I did, and now he motioned with both hands for me to sit back down. "We've already been to Goodie's house. There was no motorcycle present."

I suddenly remembered Nadine telling me that on Saturday, and it took all the wind out of my sails. "So... what does all this mean?"

"It means, among other working theories, that you, yourself, could have followed Goodie and Danny to the beach on his motorcycle."

I had to laugh. "Sheriff, it was a Harley. There's no sneaking up on anybody on a Harley."

Sheriff Donaldson scowled. He knew I had a point. A very good point, I might add.

We sat in silence while the sheriff tipped back in his chair and ran his thumb and forefinger over his mustache several times, contemplating how the pieces of this puzzle fit together. Finally, he said, "You're free to go, Sylvia, but you are definitely a person of interest. Don't leave town."

"Don't leave town!" I stood up and glared down at him. "I was born in Fort George. I've lived and worked on the North Beach Peninsula my entire life. I have no place else to go!"

"Would you like Deputy Morgan to give you a ride back down to the hospital?" said Sheriff D without showing one lick of emotion.

I barely kept myself from shouting, "No! I want to walk!" but the hospital was over three miles away, and that would take me almost an hour, so I forced myself to sound civil when I answered him with a simple "Yes, please."

Deputy Morgan had obviously been watching and listening from behind the observation mirror. He now opened the interrogation room door and handed me back my purse.

"Your mother is worried about you; she's texted several times," said Freddy. "She said if you got this before midnight, to meet her over at Jimmy's."

I narrowed my eyes at him. "And what else did you learn while in possession of my cell phone? Did you go through all my contacts and recent calls?"

Freddy sighed. "Of course I did. It's standard protocol."

I froze in my tracks, halfway to the door, ready to fire all kinds of insults and swear words at him, but for once, my little voice of reason stopped me before I could make matters worse.

I held my tongue while Freddy politely escorted me to his cruiser, still parked behind the station. But this time, he opened the front passenger door for me.

"Oh, really?" I asked, a little snottier than I'd intended. "So now you're going to let me sit in the front seat without zip ties?"

"Don't press it, Syl," said Freddy, getting in and starting up the car. "Rules are rules, and no one gets special treatment." His eyes met mine, and I could see how truly, truly sorry he was. "No one, not even you, my precious Sylleegirl."

The party atmosphere in the hospital lobby had left the five remaining people shortly after I did. Jimmy was the first to say he needed to get back to the motel, and since he had ridden with Kanji, that meant they'd both left.

Meredith had picked up Nadine on the way down the peninsula, and Orpha had simply walked across the street from her senior living apartment. Now Orpha offered the two women a place to "freshen up" if they wanted to continue staying near Goodie until she woke up.

Merri got up and started for the nurses' station. "I should have done this hours ago," she said over her shoulder. "Sit tight." As a retired nurse, Meredith might be able to get a little more information, either from the nurses, or by sneaking a peek at Goodie's chart.

When Merri returned, the look on her face immediately alarmed Nadine. "What's going on?" she asked. The high-pitched tone of her voice gave away her panic.

"Goodie's not exactly resting—she's unconscious," said

Meredith. "They're not even sure if she'll ever wake up."

Nadine started to cry, but Orpha started defiantly down the hallway. "She just needs to hear our voices," she said. "I'll tell her a joke. I'll even read the Bible to her. We can't just sit here, we've got to *do* something!"

Meredith halted her progress. "No, Orpha, they won't let us in until they evaluate her in the morning. We all need to go home and get some rest."

"What aren't you telling us, Merri?" asked Nadine. "I know that look."

"I'm just wondering where Freddy took Sylvia, and why," answered Meredith. "I've been texting her ever since she left, but she hasn't answered any of my messages." Merri pursed her lips. "There's something else going on here that we're not privy to. Yet."

By the time Freddy and I arrived back at the hospital, my mustang was the only car I recognized in the parking lot. I went in to briefly check on Goodie's status, then made one quick phone call to Kanji before I drove myself to the Clamshell Motel. Even if Meredith had not texted me to meet her there, that's where I was going to go anyway. I needed Kanji's help.

"Honey!" Merri grabbed me and hugged me so tight I thought she'd break some of my ribs. "I'm so happy to see you!" she said. "Now tell us where you've been and why."

I extracted myself from Meredith's grip and retrieved a diet soda from Jimmy's fridge. I was pleased to see Kanji already sitting at the kitchen table, laptop open before him, and I smiled and nodded my gratitude.

The highly condensed and definitely edited account I decided to tell of my time in the interrogation room with Sheriff Donaldson was liberally punctuated by indignant interjections and questions from Merri and Jimmy, and it took a little longer to tell than I'd planned. Kanji, for his part, had sat quietly, never interrupting my story, and only nodded thoughtfully from time to time until I'd finished.

"My dear Sylvia," he said, "you have been through quite an ordeal. And I am only too honored to offer my assistance in helping you compile information and organize your thoughts."

Jimmy and Meredith both started to say something, but I held my hand up for silence. "Remember last spring, when Kanji made spread sheet magic and helped us clear all the merry widows of any wrongdoing in their husbands' deaths?"

Merri and Jimmy both nodded.

"Well, I asked Kanji to help me sort through the maze of so-called coincidences that may have had something to do with three houses being broken into, one attempted robbery, and the death of Daniel Gardner."

"That's smart," said Merri. She gave Kanji one of her brightest smiles. "When you need an expert, call an expert."

Kanji bowed his head. "You are only too kind, Miss Meredith," he said. "I will do what I can to assist in compiling basic factual data, along with potential theories, but it will take all of us to unravel the circumstances which have led us to this place in time."

"And I want to be proactive," I said. "I don't want to sit around just twiddling my thumbs, waiting for the sheriff to solve all of these crimes. Too many of us have a vested interest in figuring this out sooner rather than later."

Meredith looked at her watch. "Speaking of sooner rather than later," she said, it's already 9 o'clock," she said. "Jimmy? How about making us some coffee?"

Jimmy laughed as he went to the sink to fill the carafe.

"What's so funny, hotshot?" I asked.

"The image of you, Sylvia, just sitting around and twiddling your thumbs." He poured the water into the coffeemaker and turned to look at me. "Do you even know *how* to twiddle?"

"Oh yes," said Merri, "Sylvia learned to twiddle her thumbs while she waited for me to tie her shoes for her when she was four."

That garnered a welcome laugh from everyone, including me, and I was glad we'd had a convivial moment to break the tension I still felt in my stomach from the events of the day. We owed it to Goodie to figure out what had happened, whether she regained consciousness or not. Dang it all, just the thought of her not waking up tightened the grip in my gut again.

"Okay," I said, as soon as everyone but me had their coffee and was ready to go. "What do we know for sure?"

"We know that none of this happened until Felicity, Goodie, Nadine, and Meredith signed up with Sole Mates," said Jimmy.

"I don't want us jumping to any conclusions," I said, "but it is definitely another one of those coincidences of which we should take note." For some reason, I was proud of the fact that I'd worded that sentence so that it didn't end in "take note of." Boy, I must be more tired than I'd thought, but I knew we had to push through and get the facts down on paper. Or in this case, on the computer screen.

"Miss Sylvia," said Kanji, "I believe the most practical and efficient thing to do is to create a timeline for the burglaries that have been thus far committed to see if indeed, Sole Mates is the most common denominator."

"Agreed. So where do we start?" I looked at Merri.

"Of the three break-ins, we know mine was first," said

Merri.

"Yes," said Kanji, already typing. "It was the Saturday night before last, when Miss Orpha had her unfortunate cardiac incident at Spartina Point."

"I was with Earl," Merri continued, "and when we got home, well, you all know what I found. I'd been robbed."

"What did Earl say about the break-in?" I asked.

Meredith wrinkled her brow in thought. "He didn't come in," she finally said. "And come to think of it, he hasn't called—not even once." She paused then nonchalantly said, "But I think we both knew our relationship wasn't going anywhere, so I'm not sorry I haven't heard from him."

"EarltheSqwearl," said Jimmy, reflecting. "He really wasn't your type, Meredith. What made you choose him from out of all the men's profiles you read?"

"Actually, he chose me," said Merri. "I didn't know it at the time, but Goodie had already met Danny, who was my first choice, and when I logged back in to Sole Mates to take Danny off my Favorites list, there was a message from Earl."

I hadn't known that, and it probably didn't make any difference, but I had Kanji add that tidbit of information to what we knew about Earl. He had contacted her, right after Danny had contacted Goodie. Hhhmmm. In my own experience, the men rarely made the first move, but again, it could just be a coincidence—if I believed in such things.

"Anything else you remember from that night?" I asked Meredith.

"Well, sure," said Merri. "I'm not senile, you know." She started ticking them off on her fingers. "Sheriff D and Freddy made sure my house was safe for the night. The sheriff gave me a card from the security company to get an alarm installed, which is already done, by the way. Freddy asked Mrs. Carpenter if she'd seen anything, and she said a white van had turned around in her own driveway. And Kanji spent the night with me so I wouldn't be alone."

I glared at her, and she might have read my mind.

"Let me amend that," said Merri. "Kanji spent the night on my couch, to help me feel more secure staying in my own home."

Kanji nodded. "We watched several classic movies on television, but I do not think their titles need to be recorded here."

"No, but be sure to put down that Mrs. Carpenter had a turn-around visit by a white van," I said. I was wondering if the vehicle in Goodie's driveway Friday night might have also been a van, but it wasn't yet time to offer up that idea.

"My break-in was next after Meredith's," I said. "And Felicity and I discovered that the steamer clam harvesters had seen a motorcycle coming and going from my driveway several times on the two days we were all in Portland at the hospital.

"And now—" I paused, but decided to be as forthcoming as possible. "Well, Sheriff Donaldson said some of the fingerprints Freddy lifted from my house that night belonged to Daniel Gardner."

By the collective gasp in the room, and the way Merri's eyes almost popped out of her head, I could have considered withholding that particular bit of information a little while longer.

"Mr. X was in your house, and ate your food, and slept in your bed?!" exclaimed Meredith.

"And that gives you more of a motive to kill him," said Jimmy matter-of-factly.

"Mr. Daniel Gardner's death is not until later," said Kanji, "and at this moment, we are trying to formulate a robbery timeline."

"Thank you for keeping us on track, Kanji." I gave him a wan smile.

"We do know, however, that Earl was at my house the day of the break-in, Danny was at yours the next two days, and they both were on Sole Mates," said Merri.

I nodded. "And Nadine's house was next, robbed when she was out having an early supper with Paranormal Patrick." I couldn't help but grin when I said his screen name. "But here's another thing to consider. Nadine said he didn't come in when they got back to her place. She said he was anxious to get home, so he just hopped in his van and left before she'd gone inside."

"What color is Patrick's van?" asked Meredith.

"It's white," I said immediately. "Mercedes and I were parked right near it the first day Nadine met him at the beach, when they walked the boardwalk."

"To be truly objective," said Kanji, "there must be hundreds of white vans on the North Beach Peninsula, owned by both private parties and businesses. Electricians, plumbers, contractors, delivery services, morticians, locksmiths, telephone installation, cable repair—the list is quite extensive."

"And don't forget the ICE detention van," said Jimmy. "It's also a nondescript white van."

I couldn't help myself. Whether it was a classic case of jumping to conclusions or not, I softly said what I think we were all thinking. "But wouldn't it be ironic if the robbers had loaded Nadine's things into Patrick's van for him to drive away with the loot when he returned?"

Kanji chastised me. "Now Miss Sylvia, didn't we agree that we needed to adhere to the actual facts, and not products of our imaginations, until or unless we have definitive proof?"

"It's a theory, Kanji, just a theory," I replied.

"Well, let's wait a minute," said Meredith. "I want to follow this idea just a little further. When I was with Earl, Patrick and Danny could have broken in. And then when Sylvia wasn't home, it was all Danny's operation, but he didn't actually steal anything. Next is Nadine, and since she was with Patrick, Earl and Danny could have been doing the robbery."

"It makes sense," said Jimmy. "Two out of the three men were always free to be wherever, doing whatever. When Meredith brought Earl to the casino, Goodie said Danny wasn't able to be there, and Nadine said Patrick wasn't coming to the show either. And neither woman pressed the issue, because they both had dates set up for the following week."

Kanji stood up, stretched, put his coffee cup into the sink, and returned to his seat at the table. "I must sincerely request that we stay on some semblance of the task at hand. In 20 more minutes, I am retiring to my apartment to sleep."

He was blunt, but cute, and he had a point. We could guess ourselves blue in the face, and be no closer to solving these mysteries than the man in the moon—the same point Kanji had made without saying it directly.

"Now before you go freakin' out, *Mother*," I said pointedly, "I'm here, and I'm fine."

"Whatever are you talking about dear?" asked Merri.

I took a breath, and all in a rush I said, "Friday night, when Goodie and Danny went clam digging, I was hiding at Goodie's house, protecting it in case her home was going to be robbed while she was out, too."

"You what?" said Merri, incredulously. "Are you serious? You could have been killed!"

"Ah, so this explains why Deputy Morgan transported

you to the police station for your chat with Sheriff Donaldson," said Kanji, nodding. "You have no discernible alibi."

"But won't Goodie alibi you when she wakes up?" asked Jimmy.

I sighed. "Even if she wakes up, Goodie leaving me at her house doesn't mean I stayed there," I explained. "Goodie will need to remember exactly what happened to Danny, and that I wasn't involved, for me to be officially cleared of any wrongdoing."

While they each contemplated my somber statement, I sighed heavily a second time. "Danny arrived at Goodie's on a motorcycle. But when the sheriff went to check it out, there was no motorcycle to be found."

"Do you think someone had stolen it?" asked Merri.

"It is far more likely that Mr. Gardner's accomplices retrieved it when Danny did not return that night," said Kanji. "If the motorcycle was registered and licensed properly in Oregon, that would have given Sheriff Donaldson a clear paper trail, perhaps to all of the men involved."

"Curiouser and curiouser," said Jimmy. He got up and poured a few cat kibbles in Priscilla's bowl. The sound apparently awakened both Priscilla and Elvis, who had been sleeping compatibly together on Jimmy's couch in the living room. Now Priscilla came to check out the food dish, and Elvis came and put his head on Kanji's knee.

"I agree, Elvis," said Kanji. "It is time now for us to go home and go to bed." He stood and closed his laptop. "We shall reconvene to add whatever else we believe to be pertinent to the investigation at another time," he said. "It will do us all good to sleep now. It will help us think of other things."

We all agreed, and went our separate ways.

I had doubted I'd sleep much, considering it was the first time I'd ever been accused of murder. But I was more tired than I'd thought, and as soon as my head hit the pillow, I was out like a light, completely forgetting my vow to turn off my cell phone at night.

And, as luck would have it, it was the ringing of my cell phone that awakened me the next morning. Well, maybe "ringing" was the wrong word, as it was the sheriff's personalized ringtone that yanked me from my deep slumber. And the sound of a police siren suddenly wailing on my dresser, just inches from my ear, was plenty to jar a few years off my lifespan.

"Hello, Carter." I tried to sound both awake and not annoyed.

"Goodie has regained consciousness," he said, foregoing all pleasantries before jumping right to the point.

"That's wonderful!" I replied. "And she said I was nowhere near the beach the night Danny died, right?"

"Wrong," said Sheriff D. "She's refusing to talk to anyone about anything. She just lies there and shakes her head back and forth on the pillow, all wild-eyed."

"Oh dear," I said. "And you called to tell me this, because…?"

"Because maybe she'll talk to you, Sylvia. I can't let you be in there alone with her, of course, but I've sent Freddy to come pick you up."

It was déjà vu all over again. "You sent Freddy? And you won't let me talk to Goodie alone?"

"I can't have you two corroborating your stories," said the sheriff. "And Freddy's picking you up on his way down from Spartina Point because I need you here as fast as possible. The doctor isn't sure how long Goodie is going to remain conscious. Maybe forever, or maybe this is what they call a surge prior to death."

"Oh my gosh!" The thought of Goodie regaining consciousness and then dying anyway was almost too much for me to handle.

"And," continued Sheriff D, "it's also possible that a traumatic memory could send her back into shock. So you'll have to be gentle with her."

But before I could say anything, I heard Freddy tap one "whoop" out of the siren as he pulled into my driveway. That gave me about two minutes to get some clothes on and get out there before he came to the door to drag me to the hospital, dressed or not dressed.

"Radio Freddy and tell him I'll be out there in three minutes," I told Sheriff D. "And tell Goodie to hang on, I'm on my way!"

CHAPTER 19

The ride to the hospital was down the same road that Freddy and I had taken together just a few months before when Nova's husband Mateo had been lost at sea. But this time, even though Freddy wasn't in uniform, he took full advantage of both the lights and the siren.

Goodie was a tiny little waif anyway, but there in that bed, she looked like a doll tucked in under the white sheets. All was covered except her face, almost as pale as the bed covers, and her ankle, which was air-casted and in traction. I could tell by the look in her eyes that she was grateful to see me, and I hoped that was a sign that her memory of Friday night was intact.

"Hello, honey," I said, taking her hand in mine. "How are you feeling?"

Goodie's grip was strong, but her eyes shifted from mine to the two men standing between me and the door, and she shook her head, just once.

I turned to face them. "Would you mind?" I said, already knowing that the sheriff had no intention of leaving us alone in the room.

But Sheriff Donaldson surprised me. "I'll be right outside," he said. "But don't you want Freddy here for moral support?"

That cagey old fox! I turned to Goodie. "Is it alright if Freddy stays?"

Goodie's eyes darted back and forth a few times, and I knew she was trying to think clear through the ramifications of what I'd asked.

"I'd like him to stay, Goodie," I added, even though my heart wasn't in it.

She nodded hesitantly, and the sheriff went out and closed the door behind him. Freddy, bless his heart, took a couple steps back so he wasn't directly in Goodie's line of sight.

"Goodie! Sweetie! What happened?" I asked. "Can you tell me what happened?"

A sob broke through her sealed lips. "Where's Danny?"

"Why do you ask?" I knew better than to drop a bombshell that size on her; it could potentially send her back into shock—or worse.

"I had to hide in the dunes, Syl." She sniffled. "Danny was trying to kill me!"

I shot a look over at Freddy. His eyebrows were up somewhere near his hairline, but he didn't say anything.

"Why do you think Danny wanted to hurt you, Goodie?"

"He turned off the lantern. I couldn't see. And he put his hands around my neck and started squeezing, and—" She broke off in a sob that racked her whole fragile little body.

"How did you get away, honey?" I asked softly.

"I hit him with my clam gun and when he fell, I ran away from the water." Another big, gut-wrenching sob. "But he had my car keys, Syl. And I fell and twisted my ankle." She looked at the support on her leg. "Well, I guess we know now that I actually broke my ankle."

She looked so sad, lying there, but I waited while she gathered her thoughts.

"I had to hide, Sylvia. I almost died out there even

without any help from him." Unbridled fear came into her eyes. "Do you know where Danny is, Sylvia? I don't know why he tried to kill me, but I don't want him coming back and finishing the job."

I cleared my throat, and looked to Freddy, but he was no help. "As a matter of fact, I know exactly where he is, Goodie, and he won't be able to hurt you ever again."

"Then he's in jail?" Her expression turned from fear to relief to confusion. "That's good." She gripped my hand tighter and looked directly into my eyes. "Was my house broken into while you were there?"

"No, honey. Two men tried to break in, but Hans scared them away."

"Hans? My Hans? You mean my little scaredy-cat of a love German Shepherd actually protected my home?"

I smiled. "You should change Hans's name to Adolph."

"Adolph? Why?"

"I know a little German, Goodie, and while Hans means 'God is gracious,' Adolph means 'noble wolf.' You should have seen him, Goodie. He had those guys on the run so fast, they almost tripped over each other getting to their—" I paused briefly. "—to their van." I looked at Freddy again, and saw that he was taking notes.

"I couldn't see their faces, but now I remember seeing a vehicle behind them as they stood in the doorway. I'm sure they were driving a light-colored van. I remember your porchlight reflecting off the vehicle as it tore out of the driveway."

Goodie squeezed my hand even tighter, if that were possible. "I'm so glad you weren't hurt." She looked sadly at her leg. "I guess The Veiled Rainbow is going to have to look for a violet *and* a yellow—at least until I'm ready to dance again."

Seriously? That's what she was worried about? I gave her a kiss on the cheek. "You rest, now, honey. I'll tell everyone you're going to be just fine."

I rode with Freddy, and Sheriff D followed us to the Sandy Bottom Coffee Cup. I had plenty to share, but adamantly refused to talk to either one of them at the police station. I'd had enough of that place in the last 24 hours to last me quite some time.

Our regular octagon table back by the roaster was vacant, and Bim had our usual order of coffees and biscotti ready for us almost before we sat down. Sheriff D took off his Stetson and placed it on the table, and then asked me, not unkindly, why I'd called this meeting.

As best as I could remember, I went over the spreadsheet that Kanji, Meredith, Jimmy and I had put together, then added in the additional information Goodie had provided from her hospital bed. I was pleased that both the sheriff and Freddy seemed to listen intently, leaning forward, and making eye contact, and neither one of them interrupted, not even once.

When I finally stopped talking, Sheriff D politely asked me if I were finished. When I said I was, he looked at Freddy, winked, and said, "Well, what do you know?"

Freddy grinned from ear to ear. He reached over and squeezed my hand. "You'd make a fine detective, my Sylleegirl," he said.

I jerked my hand away and looked from man to man. It annoyed me no end to be on the outside of an apparent inside joke. "Would either of you mind telling me what's going on?"

"What do you think we do all day?" asked Sheriff Donaldson. "You think we just sit around drinking coffee and eating donuts?"

I looked pointedly at the coffee cup before him and our empty biscotti plate, but said nothing. I looked to Bim for backup, but she'd been swamped making coffee orders from the moment we'd arrived, and she hadn't even had time to eavesdrop on our conversation.

"What the sheriff is trying to tell you, Syl, is that we pretty much came to nearly the same theory you did, but we're now busy collecting some real evidence to back it up." Freddy drained his coffee cup and stood up. He bent down to give me a quick kiss on the cheek.

"I need a favor, Sylvia," said Sheriff D, putting his hat back on. "Could you, and all your friends, possibly just hold your horses for awhile and allow us to finish this investigation before any of you go and get yourself into some real trouble?"

Bristling, I was about to object when the sheriff extended his hand in front of me to stop me from saying anything. "I'm just asking for 48 hours."

Freddy opened the coffee shop door, and we all hollered our good-byes back to Bim as we stepped outside.

"Forty-eight hours," Sheriff D repeated. "Just lay low, and I promise I'll explain everything."

It's amazing how much can happen in 48 hours.

The best thing was that Goodie had a very successful ankle surgery, and the doctor said she'd be able to be up and dancing lightly in six to eight weeks, and that belly dancing would be an excellent activity to complement her physical therapy.

The worst thing was that it turned out that Danny still had me listed as next of kin, and it would be up to me to collect his ashes after cremation and find a proper place to disseminate them. When the time came, The Veiled

Rainbow, along with Felicity, Jimmy, and whoever else wanted to attend, vowed to come with me when I said a few words, then scattered the ashes into the ocean, out where he'd ultimately met his end. It seemed like the perfect way to say goodbye.

So when the sheriff's time was up, it was almost anticlimactic. Almost.

We all gathered at Jimmy's once again, and when I entered the motel office, I could smell the delightful aroma of Indian food wafting deliciously through the air. Kanji was at the stove, of course, and Jimmy, Nadine, Orpha, Freddy, and Sheriff D were in various states of "hovering about" when I arrived.

Jimmy handed me a diet soda as I came through the door. "Nova coming?" I asked. I hadn't seen her car out in the lot, but she could still be on her way. "And what about Felicity?"

"Nope, they won't be joining us," said Orpha. "Nova and Rich are out on the ocean, and Felicity and Mark went to a teaching conference in Spokane this week."

"And how do you know so much about everyone's comings and goings?" I teased her.

"Unity's my town, and I do get around!" recited Orpha. She laughed. "Not too much happens down there without me knowing about it. I'm like the unofficial mayor of that place, if you know what I mean."

Well, no, I didn't know what she meant, but I sure wasn't going to argue with her. "So where's Meredith?" I asked of no one in particular.

"She's en route," said Nadine, "but she's running a little late. She said to go ahead and start without her." She grinned. "But if you're going to be driving, or you're on duty or something," she looked pointedly at Freddy and the Sheriff,

"I'm warning you not to eat the spinach dip I brought for an appetizer." She grinned and winked exaggeratedly.

Good grief and gravy! Nadine had brought pot dip to a gathering that included the local cops! What in the world had gotten into her?! "Uh, Nadine?"

"Chill out, Nervous Nelly!" said Nadine, anticipating my objection. "They both said it was okay in a private residence, but they've both decided to stick with plain chips."

Jimmy brought two folding chairs and squeezed them in at the table usually set for six. "We're all friends here, right?" he asked, looking around hopefully.

I shot a glance warily at the sheriff. I wasn't ready to commit to being his friend just yet, but again, I chose not to argue.

"What's for dinner?" I asked, going over to Kanji, who had all four burners going at once, along with several casserole dishes showing through the oven window.

"Murg Makhani, otherwise known as butter chicken," said Kanji. "Rogan Josh, which is red lamb. Then Malai Kofta, or vegetarian meatballs, and Chole, also known as chickpea curry." He pointed to each one as he said their names. "The rice is over on the counter in the rice cooker, of course."

"Of course."

"Freddy wanted me to make an assortment of entrees," explained Kanji, "so he may decide which ones he will include on the new Spartina Point restaurant menu."

I know my face showed disappointment. "No Chicken Tikki Marsala? No Naan?"

Kanji laughed. It was a full-bodied, beautiful laugh, and one I very much enjoyed hearing. "Of course, my Sylleegirl!" he said. "I made those entrees especially for you, and they are now keeping a constant temperature in the oven."

The room had gone unusually quiet when Kanji had called me his 'Sylleegirl,' and I knew without turning around what the expression would be on Freddy's face. That was a pet name that until now, only he had ever used.

Fortunately, Sheriff D chose that moment to ask us all to take our seats at the table. He wanted to fill us in before we ate on what had transpired during the past two days of their investigations. Everyone but Kanji, who continued manning the stove, immediately sat down.

"As you probably all know," Sheriff D began, "Goodie struck Daniel Gardner on the head with her clam gun in self-defense, and no charges will be pressed."

We'd all heard that, alright, but nevertheless, a collective sigh of relief went around the table.

"John Stark has officially ruled Mr. Gardner's cause of death as accidental drowning."

We murmured our acknowledgement to that information, too.

"And, as some of you had suspected, there was a three-man burglary ring using Sole Mates to find vulnerable, mature women on which to prey."

I was proud of the sheriff for not using the words "aging," "old," or "naïve." Maybe I could call him my friend again after all.

"Two of these men met in the Oregon State Penitentiary. One of them was brought on board later. They looked for women in small towns. Women who might have some good jewelry that could be quickly fenced, or perhaps have a quantity of cash on hand."

"You mean like a cache of cash from a life insurance policy?" chirped Orpha.

"Yes, I'm sure that was one criteria," said Sheriff D.

Orpha laughed. "Good thing they didn't break into my

house. All I have in my fireproof lock box is the report from my last mammogram."

Dead silence. Silence born of shock, no doubt, but someone evidently had to ask, and so I asked, "Why are your mammogram results in your security box, Orpha?"

"Because my boobs are free of cancerous masses, and I don't want to lose the proof! Those blasted doctors would make me go through all that squishy pain again next year if I didn't keep the test results safe with me," Orpha declared.

Her thinking might be a little flawed, but Orpha had what she thought was a good reason for doing what she did, and since her answer seemed to satisfy everyone's curiosity, Sheriff Donaldson continued.

"In Mr. Gardner's apartment in Portland, there were a number of clippings taken from the North Beach Tribune. One was about the 'Merry Belly-Dancing Widows,' written by Raven Coldwater."

"So they were being targeted even before they signed up on Sole Mates?" I asked.

The sheriff nodded. "Yes, Sylvia. These men had read about the life insurance windfalls and targeted The Veiled Rainbow months before you helped them sign up online. You can stop feeling guilty now."

It was a huge relief to know that, and I was grateful my assistance was not what initially put them in harm's way. I hadn't exactly felt guilty, but I hadn't felt like I'd done all I could to protect them, either.

"It was impossible for us to run immediate background checks, as Danny Smith and Earl Jones were obviously not using their real names," said Sheriff D. "The first break came when we followed up on Earl's confession to Meredith that he was no longer allowed to work in investment counseling because of his prior conviction, and the second break came from fingerprints Freddy lifted from the glass Earl used at the casino.

"So we knew who Earl was, but it was the license plate number Sylvia got from Danny's motorcycle, which was registered in Oregon in his real name, and the fingerprints he'd left in her house when he stayed there a couple nights that definitively identified him.

"Earl Jones, a.k.a. EarltheSqwearl, is Earl Hudson. And Earl Hudson was a cellmate of Daniel Gardner. So they used Smith and Jones as aliases. Not all that original, but I guess somebody has to be named Smith and Jones, since those surnames are so popular."

"I guess so!" said Orpha. "Not everyone can be a Starr, like me!"

It was at that moment I began to suspect how much Orpha had been generously enjoying Nadine's chip dip, and I removed the bowl from the table and set it on the kitchen counter.

"I'm sorry Meredith is not here at the moment," continued the sheriff. "The reason Earl was directed to contact Merri was because Danny was sure Meredith would recognize him, even with a beard and the fact that he now wore contact lenses. He had to lay low and not let their paths cross while they were all on the peninsula. And as I already explained, this was an in and out operation. Danny figured he could avoid Meredith, even in such a small town, for the week it took them to rob Merri, Nadine, and Goodie."

The sheriff chuckled. "As for Patrick O'Leary, his real name was Patrick Paulsen, but he had it legally changed because he didn't want people to think he was related to the comedian on the Smothers Brothers show who ran for President back in 1968."

"I knew all about that," Nadine piped up. "He was totally

honest and above board, and he shared that info with me right away."

"May I finish?" asked Sheriff D. And without waiting for an answer, he continued. "As some of you had already put together, when one of the theft ring was wining and dining the target, the other two were busy robbing her place."

"So get to the point," said Orpha. "Did you catch them? Are they all locked up? Did you throw away the keys?"

"There are two suspects now in custody," said Sheriff D. "Mr. Gardner, of course, is deceased, and the other two are busy trying to finger him as the brains of the operation. And perhaps he was, now that I've had a chance to talk with each of them." He sighed.

"These were the modern-day smash and grabs. The burglaries in each town always took place inside a week, and the guys were gone. Poof! No real way to trace them, always leaving several broken-hearted women in their wake, but never taking anything too big to carry or too unique to trace.

I looked at Nadine. Either the pot dip was helping her feel no pain, or she hadn't put two and two together yet. I knew she'd really liked old Paranormal Patrick, and I felt kind of sorry for her.

"Dinner is served," said Kanji, and he and Jimmy started bringing the serving dishes to the table. I wasn't sure the sheriff had finished talking yet, but I was sure the rest would wait until after we ate. My stomach had been growling from the moment I'd come into the room.

Over dinner, Jimmy mentioned that crimes committed on dating sites were on the upswing all over the world. He had just read about one senior citizen man who'd spent 11 months in prison in Spain when he'd thought he was just delivering real estate papers. Turns out he was used as a drug mule by a hot, young woman who was just as bad as any man for luring people looking for love into being the fall guy for their nefarious plots.

A lively discussion followed, and it made it easier for me to sit between Kanji and Freddy and not totally lose my appetite. Talk about pressure!

Dinner was more than fabulous, and we were still relaxing around the kitchen table when I saw Merri's car pull into the parking lot.

Jimmy got up and went to the door. "We've got company," he said unnecessarily. "Is there enough food left for two?"

Two? I couldn't fathom who was accompanying my mother, but when they came through the door, I vaguely recognized him as the man she'd pointed out online. Each of them were carrying a bottle of champagne, and for about a heartbeat and a half, I was afraid they were going to announce they'd eloped. I quickly checked Meredith's left ring finger, which was blessedly bare, not that that ever meant anything.

Nevertheless, I wanted nothing to do with any more men from Sole Mates, not now, and probably not ever. But I quickly made a silent promise to myself that I'd play nice, for Mom's sake, at least for this evening.

"Everyone!" exclaimed a beaming Meredith. "I'd like you to meet my friend—"

"Lester the molester!" shouted Nadine, jumping up, running over, and throwing her arms around the man. "Oh my gosh! Aren't you a sight for sore eyes! How the hell are you?"

"Deenie-Bo-Beanie," replied the man, hugging her back. "Save any whales lately?"

The light suddenly dawned, and I realized that yes, indeed, Nadine and Les had apparently worked at

Greenpeace together in a past life. Well, that certainly answered my question as to whether Les was a bad guy or a good guy, and I was pleased for Meredith that she'd reconnected with someone I wouldn't have to have arrested.

Her thunder somewhat stolen, Meredith composed herself and tried again. "Everyone *except* Nadine, I'd like to introduce you to my friend Les."

We all laughed, and nodded to him as Merri pointed us out and offered our names as she worked her way around the table. When she got to me, she smiled, and said, "Actually, Sylvia, Les has been using the name Les Woods for his online dating adventures. His first name is actually Sylvester, but back when we first met, I always called him 'Woody.'"

Woody? I kind of choked on his nickname, and wondered if Meredith meant it to elicit sexual connotations, or if that was just my own dirty mind at work.

Merri turned to Les/Sylvester, tipped her head to the side, smiled fondly, and continued. "So now, Woody," she said with what sounded like genuine affection in her voice, "I'd like you to meet Sylvia—our daughter."

CHAPTER 20

Obviously, Les/Sylvester/Woody had already known what was coming, so that made exactly one of us in this introduction who wasn't caught completely off guard. "It's true, Sylvia Lee," he said, grinning from ear to ear. "I am your father."

"Wow! Oh wow!" exclaimed Jimmy. He was hopping up and down without leaving his chair. Perhaps he'd also had too much of Nadine's dip. "It's just like in Star Wars, when Darth Vader tells Luke—" He abruptly clamped his hand over his mouth, most likely because he saw at least eight other people in the room who desperately wanted to do that for him.

As for me, I opened and closed my mouth several times, just like a guppy caught in the headlights. On some level, I knew that guppy in the headlights thing was a horribly mangled mixed metaphor, but I didn't even care to correct my own disconnected thought.

Every eye was on me, and I knew they all expected me to say *something*, but at the moment, I had no idea what that something might be. I couldn't very well heartily embrace this 75-year-old man I'd never met before and call him "Daddy," could I?

"It's... uh... It's very nice to meet you," I stammered, extending my hand. "I'm sorry I never came looking for you, Mr. Woods, since you're my birth father and all. I guess I just thought you might be dead or something."

My real fear had been that I was afraid my birth father would turn out to be the long-lost brother of Charles Manson or Jack the Ripper, or someone equally awful, perhaps in the field of politics, and if that were so, I could live my entire life quite happily without knowing the specifics of the man I privately referred to as "my sperm donor."

"You can call me Les," said Les/Sylvester/Woody. "I'd be really happy if you did."

Meredith and Les exchanged a knowing glance. Then Merri grinned. "Sylvia, didn't you ever once wonder why I didn't have a cat named Sylvester?"

"Uh, no." I couldn't begin to process what Merri was trying to tell me. The thought had never occurred to me—until now—that if Sylvester, the man I'd been told all along was my father, had been deceased, that Merri would have named a cat after him the same as she had for Harlan, Charles, and Robert.

I just stood there, still at a loss, wrestling for something to say—anything sounding like I might have at least a few of my wits still about me. Fortunately for me, Orpha, who was obviously quite high on pot dip, came to my rescue.

"Ain't it a pip?!" she exclaimed clapping her hands excitedly in front of her like a trained seal. "It's like a big old family reunion around here, or the story of the prodigal son, or something you might see on reality TV but never believe it wasn't staged for extra drama in the script. Imagine it, Sylvia! Your ex-husband and your father both returned like bad pennies to the North Beach Peninsula in the very same week!"

It was something, alright, but I wasn't all that eager to call it a "pip." Calling it a nightmare might be a little closer to the truth, but since she'd gotten the attention off me with her rather astute, and certainly pot-induced observations, I wasn't going to rain on Orpha's parade.

"I think we should have a toast," said Merri, "to new beginnings." She and Les handed the bottles of champagne over to Jimmy to open, and Meredith checked to see if anyone besides the two of them needed a glass or cup in which to put a little of the bubbly.

I was surprised Jimmy didn't make some sarcastic remark about not being the head waiter at this fine restaurant, but perhaps he was also still grappling with Meredith's bombshell. I didn't want to stare at Les, but I couldn't help it. My birth father was here, standing in Jimmy's kitchen with my mother, acting like 55 years hadn't passed since the two of them conceived me.

The sheriff, Freddy, and I all chose to toast without alcohol, but we dutifully raised our cups along with everyone else as Merri began to speak again.

"As I said," said Meredith, after all the glasses and cups had one or another beverage in them, "here's to new beginnings with old friends." She and Les exchanged endearing smiles, and I would swear Merri's eyes were all misty.

"Hey," said Les, sliding his free arm around Merri's waist and pulling her to him, "just who you callin' old?"

"You're the one with all the gray hair," said Merri, as if everyone in the room didn't know she constantly touched up her own roots with red hair dye.

Les laughed, and returned to the toast at hand. "And here's to Sole Mates, which somehow managed to bring us back together after more than half a century!"

Merri shrugged. "What can I say? Fifty-five years ago, I fell head over heels for you, Les—hook, line and sinker." She kissed him smack on the lips, right in front of everybody. "We're definitely soul mates, Les, no doubt about it."

"And if I may," said the sheriff, after we'd all taken a sip of our preferred beverage, "I'd like to add to our celebrational toasting the fact that both Sylvia and Goodie have been officially cleared of any wrongdoing in Daniel Gardner's demise."

A rousing cheer went up in the room, even though we all considered the sheriff's announcement just a rubberstamping of a foregone conclusion.

"I'd kind of like to drink to that, myself," said Freddy, smiling at me, "but unfortunately, I'm on duty."

"And I think," I said, looking fondly at our eldest friend, "that we should also toast to Orpha's continued good heart health."

"Hear, hear!" said Meredith.

"And let's toast for me meeting Grandpa Beebops at the hospital," said Orpha. "He hasn't been down to see me yet, but we Skype a lot." She bobbed her head a few too many times, got a bit dizzy, grabbed her head to stop the bobbing, and sighed deeply. "At least this way I won't be tempted to kill him."

Jimmy, who knew all about Orpha's prior beijiu-powered confession to killing her husband Bill, immediately jumped in and said, "And here's to Goodie's ankle healing as fast as possible!"

"Absolutely!" said Nadine, quickly getting into the spirit of things. "And let's drink to my beloved Paranormal Patrick, for not turning out to be one of the bad guys."

Say what? Everyone except Sheriff D and Freddy looked startled by Nadine's pronouncement, and several of them choked on whatever they were drinking.

"Uh, Nadine, honey?" I softly asked. I looked at the

sheriff for confirmation. "Wasn't Patrick arrested for his involvement in the home burglaries?"

Sheriff D laughed. "I'm happy to say that our investigation proved Patrick had nothing to do with the break-ins, Detective Avery."

"Then who, besides Danny and Earl—"

"The third man in the theft ring was Orville Anderson," said Freddy.

The collective gasps were enough to suck the air right out of the room, and I think it was fair to say that none of us had seen *that* coming.

"You mean Felicity's Orville?" I asked incredulously. "You mean the guy who's profile name was O-fer? You mean *HE* was the third bad guy?"

"I believe Freddy made that perfectly clear already," said the sheriff. He paused briefly while we all settled back down, then continued.

"I guess I need to fill in a few more gaps after all," said Sheriff D. "I so enjoyed the ethnic feast that Kanji prepared, I forgot that I hadn't finished explaining our findings."

The sheriff paused, as if waiting for someone to urge him to continue, but speaking strictly for myself, I was too shocked to say anything at all, so after a short pause, he finally went on.

"Orville was their inside man. He constantly monitored the police scanner. That's how he knew who was where, and at what time, all over the peninsula. That's how Danny knew it was safe for him to hide out at Sylvia's house. Orville had heard the call for the medivac chopper, and the dispatcher had said an elderly belly dancer needed transport to Portland. So Orville told Danny that Sylvia and the other gals would no-doubt be with Orpha at the hospital.

"Orville drove the white mortuary van for work, and he

often took it home with him. He used it not only at the break-ins, but also to retrieve Danny's motorcycle from Goodie's driveway. Had Hans not foiled Orville's and Earl's attempt to rob Goodie's house, they would have taken the bike with them right then. As it was, they had to leave Danny's backpack of clothes behind, because they didn't want to risk being bitten by the German Shepherd, but they knew it contained only clothes, and there was nothing to identify any of them.

"What you missed, Detective Avery, was that Goodie's neighbor saw the motorcycle being loaded into a white van just after daylight on Saturday, well before Nadine came over to do a wellness check on Goodie. The plan all along was for Danny to return from the beach alone, driving Goodie's car, that they planned on painting right away. Orville went back and picked up the bike before Danny was supposed to rendezvous with them, thinking he needed to keep Danny's cover even if he and Earl hadn't completed the heist."

Wow! That was almost too much to wrap my mind around. No wonder Nadine hadn't seemed at all upset. She was free to continue dating Patrick, if she wanted to, and it certainly seemed like she wanted to.

There was a short silence in which the majority of us were trying to mentally follow this unexpected chain of events. I thought of the high school principal, Margaret Anderson, Orville's mother, and figured this would probably push her right into retirement. She wasn't such a bad gal to work with, as I had many times, but I knew the shame would devastate her.

Then Kanji cleared his throat for attention, and I was grateful for the distraction. "If I may offer another addition to our already lengthy delineation of things worthy of toasting," he began, "I would like to say that I have at long last purchased a beautiful home, perfectly suited for Elvis and me, right here in Tinkerstown."

Kanji looked questioningly at Nadine, who said, "It's okay, Kanji. Goodie said it was fine for you to tell them."

Kanji beamed. "Then I will formally announce that I have purchased Miss Goodie's very well-cared for and pet-friendly home."

"But I thought Goodie was going to be fine," said Orpha.

"She is," said Nadine, patting Orpha's hand. "She'll be absolutely right as rain in no time. But Goodie wants to keep an eye on me to be sure I don't feed the bears any more, and I want to keep an eye on her and her ankle for at least the next six months, so we've decided it would be prudent for us to just move in together."

I couldn't help myself, I had to say what I was pretty sure several of us were thinking. "So what happens if you two can't get along?"

Nadine laughed. "Goodie said you'd be the one to ask that. But we've been friends for so long now, we'll just find a way to figure it out as we go. Our biggest concern was whether Hans and Stella would be compatible, and they are, so we're all set.

"But what about Patrick?"

"Patrick's cool with it," said Nadine. "He's decided to cut back on doing seances, and he's going to start a lawn mowing business right here on the peninsula. He's agreed that as long as Goodie doesn't mind us walking around the house without clothes on, he's happy to have another female friend—but without the same benefits, of course!"

All of this was just too much information, and I suspected—or hoped—that Nadine was just messing with us. I was pretty sure our little Goodie-two-shoes would never consent to coed nudity in *her* home!

Orpha, however, was not so sure, so she put her hands over her ears and started trilling a high-pitched zaghareet.

Elvis, who had been napping with Priscilla on the couch, set to howling, and to top it all off, Sheriff Donaldson's collar radio started crackling.

"*SILENCE!*" bellowed Sheriff D, and we all immediately complied. Even Elvis.

"We have a report of a 10-89 at the Spartina Point Oyster Farm," said the dispatcher. "I repeat, a definite 10-89, with possible shots fired."

"A 10-89?" asked Les.

"Bomb threat!" yelled Jimmy, Freddy, and the sheriff, all at once.

Freddy jumped up, gave me a kiss on the forehead, and admonished me to "Stay put!"

And before anyone else could say anything, Sheriff D and Freddy both bolted for the parking lot, started their vehicles, and with lights flashing and sirens screaming, threw gravel in their wake as they took off for the north end of the peninsula.

"A bomb threat at an oyster farm?" asked Les.

"Welcome back to the peninsula, honey," said Merri, sliding into the chair Sheriff D had just vacated. She patted the empty seat next to hers and looked at all the food left on the table. "I'm so sorry that we've already had dinner, Kanji. This looks wonderful."

Kanji dipped his head in a small bow. "Mr. Freddy is going to be having a variety of ethnic food nights at the casino, and if Indian foods catch on, he will add them to the permanent offerings at the start of the new year. Perhaps that will give you a reason to visit us more often."

"You two are not eating?" asked Jimmy. "You sure?"

"We're sure," said Merri, answering for both of them.